A Sweet, Nerdy Romantic Comedy

LOVE $^{IN}_{THE}$ LAB

JULIE MILO

www.juliemilo.com

For Ana

Like Molly, you will amaze the whole world one day. Until then, you amaze me every day.

AUTHOR'S NOTE

Molly and Jonathan, the main characters in this book, are scientists. I am not. Though I've done my best to ensure the details are correct, my more scientifically-minded readers may find inaccuracies. In some cases, I deliberately used details that I knew were not quite right for their convenience to the plot.

This novel is light, sweet, and funny–it's a rom com after all–but the characters deal with tough things in their lives just like real people. Here are some topics that are a part of this book:

- Divorce of parents (in the past)

- Estrangement from a parent

- A main character's struggle with self-worth related to neurodiversity

- Descriptions of a Category 1 hurricane

- Implication of intimacy between a married couple (but no sex on the page)

The book contains very limited swearing and no deaths (animal or human).

Chapter One

Molly

I hate Jonathan Stanch's stupidly handsome face, with his smug smile, dark sexy curls, and mischievous hazel eyes. I glare at him from over my computer screen as he walks into the office, disrupting my focus. It's Sunday evening, for crying out loud. Why is he here? Why is he *always* here?

When Jonathan passes my cubicle, I bob my head at him icily. "Dr. Stanch," I say.

His eyes twinkle, and I hate that it always feels like he's making fun of me, but I never quite get the joke. "Dr. Delaney," he responds, and he bows. BOWS. The audacity.

This guy is my archnemesis. Okay, I'm being dramatic. I don't have an archnemesis, but Jonathan gets on my nerves. It's like his entire existence rubs me the wrong way, though I'm not sure I can articulate exactly why.

He always seems to be around, bothering me and distracting me from my work. It doesn't even make sense because he's primarily in charge of fieldwork, so why is he in my lab instead of out by the shore or on a boat where he belongs?

Jonathan and I work on the same coastal environmental science research team at New Orleans State University. We both came up through the ranks at NOSU together as graduate students and lab assistants, then full-fledged members of the team once we finished our PhDs in coastal and marine science. Like I said, he always seems to be around, always my competition for grades, positions, and grants. We traded off being ranked first and second in the class all through grad school. He won some scholarships I applied for. I won some scholarships he applied for.

Fortunately, in this lab Jonathan focuses on fieldwork and collecting samples out on the water, while I have a more be-hind-the-scenes lab and office role, so we don't often have to work together directly.

I check my watch and my eyes widen. I've been analyzing the data on my computer screen longer than I thought. When did it get so late? As I'm stretching in my chair, my stomach gurgles, and I realize I worked right through dinner.

I stand and put my hands on my hips, rotating to stretch out my back. Our lab takes up the entire second floor of an environmen-tal sciences building on the outskirts of NOSU's downtown New Orleans campus. Entering in from the elevator or stairs is our office area with cubicles, a few enclosed offices, and a decently sized break-room with a refrigerator, microwave, and tables and chairs. Through the office area, the lab area is a separate section with workbenches, equipment, and a couple of large storage closets.

As I head to the refrigerator in the breakroom to get my lunchbox, I hear my phone ping from somewhere inside the pocket of my sweater. I frown, patting my sides and feeling nothing. *Maybe it's in the pocket of my pants? Ah, yep. Here it is.*

I have a text from one of my sisters in our group thread. I smile, anticipating news from my favorite people.

Nicole:

> Classes start in one week and I'm nowhere near ready

Nicole is a librarian at a small college in Florida. At twenty-six, she's a little more than three years younger than me. She's usually totally on top of her work, which she's passionate about, so her text is surprising. Well, sort of surprising. Nicole also started dating her boyfriend, Adam, earlier this year, and it seems to have done wonders for her work-life balance. Not something I can particularly relate to, either the dating or the balance part.

My phone pings again.

Olivia:

> well stop sucking face and do your job

I laugh out loud. Only Olivia would be so blunt.

She's our baby sister, seven years younger than me and almost four years younger than Nicole. She graduated from college this past spring and lives with our parents in Austin, Texas, until she figures out her next step.

I start typing a response to my sisters when I'm startled by a voice directly in front of me.

"What's funny?"

I look up to see Jonathan standing a smidge too close for comfort. I take a step back and scowl at him. "None of your business."

Jonathan continues standing in front of me, arms crossed and that pompous smile on his face.

I narrow my eyes. "Did you need something?"

His smile widens as he gestures behind me. "Just to get into the breakroom."

With his words, I realize with surprise that I'm blocking the doorway. I'm a little concerned that I can't remember if I was already standing here when the group chat started pinging, or if I mindlessly walked over while staring at my phone.

I jump out of the way, and Jonathan makes a beeline for the refrigerator. He opens it, pulling out a bottle of root beer and my lunchbox, which he hands to me. I take it reluctantly, watching him with narrowed eyes.

"Having a late dinner?" he asks. "How long have you been here today?"

My normal routine is to get to the lab at ten on Saturday and Sunday mornings and work until I'm done. I'm here during the week, too, but so is everyone else, and I have a hard time concentrating. A whole day passes, and I have no idea how I actually spent those hours. The lab's deserted on the weekends, so I use the time to get caught up. Well, usually deserted, until recently when Jonathan started showing up in the evenings.

He and I actually worked together for several years on a different research team at NOSU, one focusing on coastal erosion, before I heard about the team Dr. Phyllis Gantt was putting together to study harmful algal blooms in the Gulf. It's my dream project. The mixture of chemistry, biology, and the ocean blends all my favorite research topics.

Working with Dr. Gantt is a huge honor; she's one of the world's leading experts on algal blooms, and has the journal citations to prove it. She's the principal investigator, or PI, of the project, which means she oversees the entire research process. She hired me to her lab in January, and then Jonathan moved over a couple of months later, much to my chagrin. I didn't even know he was interested in algal blooms. I can't seem to shake the guy.

"Dr. Delaney?" he prompts now, and I remember he asked me something. "How long have you been here?"

"Oh, um, I don't know." *None of your business.*

He grins like we're in on a secret together. "All day then, huh? Were you about to eat?"

You know what? No. I'm at a pretty good stopping point for the night. There's no need to stay and force small talk with my archnemesis.

"Actually, I'm on my way out," I answer archly.

His eyebrows rise slightly, but he maintains a smile. "Alright. I'll see you tomorrow."

"I'm sure you will," I mutter.

"What was that?"

"Have a good night, Dr. Stanch."

"You too."

I wake up groggy the next morning, too early. I had trouble falling asleep and even once I finally did, I didn't sleep well. My cat, Beaker, decided it was a great night to run around the apartment yowling.

I shower and get dressed in my usual yoga pants and T-shirt combo. As long as my clothes are comfortable and have lots of pockets, they work for me. I probably use something like 0.5 percent of my brain power on clothing. I don't even mean 0.5 percent of my total potential brain power. I mean 0.5 percent of my day-to-day brain function.

It's like in cartoons how the characters will open their closets, and the joke is that it's just a row of all the same shirts and pants they always wear. Honestly, that sounds like a dream. When I find a piece of clothing that fits me comfortably, I buy five more, in various colors if they have them.

I head to the kitchen for breakfast. My apartment is a studio, cozy and small. Other than the front door, the only other door in the place is for the bathroom.

On my way to the kitchen, I notice the pile of photographs and empty picture frames on the coffee table in the living room, which I left there last Friday after my Target run. My apartment walls are too bare. I didn't think about the walls at all for the three years I'd been living here. Then I noticed them a couple of weeks ago, and now it's all I can think about. My plan is to choose a few photos of my family to hang up.

I check my watch. I have a few extra minutes this morning. I sit on the couch, avoiding Beaker, who has finally decided to sleep now that I have to be awake, and sort through the photos, trying to narrow them down to the four I want to display. There's one of my sisters and me before I left for college. Olivia was still so little. One of all five of us, parents included, last Christmas. My sisters and I were wearing matching Christmas pajamas as a surprise for my mom. Then, one of me with Nicole when she visited New Orleans earlier this year.

I pick through the photos until I've made my final decisions. I seal the deal by putting my choices into frames. Now I'm looking at the walls, trying to determine where to hang each frame.

A blaring noise from my phone brings me back to the coffee table. Wait! That can't be the alarm I set to remind me when I need to leave the house to get to work on time. But it is. *How have thirty minutes passed?*

I skip breakfast, gather my things, and head out the door. My apartment is only a few blocks from the lab so unless the weather's bad, I typically walk.

When I get to street level, the humidity slams me in the chest. August in New Orleans is unbearable—hot and sticky, and no matter where I go, it smells like I'm standing inside a dumpster.

Mostly, I like New Orleans, though it's very different from where I grew up in Texas. I like the food, by which I mean beignets. I like being near the water. I like my lab.

I arrive at the lab, and I've hardly had time to set my water bottle on my desk before my boss, Dr. Gantt, approaches.

"Good morning, Dr. Delaney." She smiles. "Can I speak with you in my office for a few moments, please?"

Um. Okay.

Hands sweating, I follow her across the room to her office, where she ushers me in and shuts the door. I feel like I've been called to the principal's office, though I'm not sure what I might have done wrong.

She gestures for me to sit in the empty chair in front of her desk while she settles behind it. Dr. Gantt is young for her position—somewhere in her forties, I'd guess. Her tight box braids are pulled into a high ponytail on top of her head, and the strands bounce as she rolls her chair closer to the desk.

She folds her hands and places them on her lap. "Dr. Delaney, I want to discuss the work you've been doing this year."

My pulse quickens. "Is there a problem?"

"No. No, not exactly. Before I invited you to join this research team, I talked to Dr. Shepherd." He's my former boss. "He told me about some of the creative connections you made in his research, how those connections produced breakthroughs."

I nod. "Yes, he included me as an author on three different publications because of my contributions."

"And that's wonderful. It was your creative problem solving that helped me to know I needed you on this research team. But I just haven't seen it here, yet."

My face heats. This lab is bigger and more bustling than my previous one, and I've had a hard time concentrating. I make sure to get my work done, hence my weekend hours, and I know it's all accurate, but she's right. I haven't had any of those *aha* moments that seem to pop into my head out of nowhere.

"I'm sorry, Dr. Gantt," I start, but she interrupts me.

"No, no. This is not an apology moment; this is a growth moment. Molly, we need you on this team. I want to try something to help stir up your creativity. A change in scenery."

A change in scenery? What does that mean?

"I'm going to have you partner with Dr. Stanch for a while. Get out in the field in the fresh air and sea spray. See if we can't kick-start that amazing brain of yours."

My stomach drops, and I fight to keep my expression neutral. Work with Dr. Stanch? In the field? Hard pass. I can barely stand being in the same lab as him for a couple of hours.

I start to protest, but Dr. Gantt holds up her hand to stop me. "This is not negotiable, Molly. I think you need this. Sometimes we can get in a rut because of a rigid schedule or too much routine. Creativity *is* possible in those circumstances, but if what you're doing isn't working, it stands to reason that you have to try something else. We've got to get you out of your comfort zone and into your growth zone."

Out of my comfort zone? The problem for me is that my comfort zone isn't about being comfortable; it's about functioning. It's about being able to do life with any modicum of control. I've carefully honed my routine for years to make sure I can focus on what matters most to me other than my family: my work. Disrupting the system now is risky.

I wipe my palms on my thighs and take a breath to try to calm my racing pulse.

Resigned, I ask, "When is this happening?"

"I'll talk to Dr. Stanch today. Don't worry. I won't share details. I'll simply let him know that I've asked you to learn the fieldwork side of our research, too. You two can start tomorrow."

Tomorrow is soon. Dr. Gantt stands, so I follow suit. Before I leave, she walks around her desk and places her hand on my arm.

"Molly, I know you're not excited about working in the field. I promise you it's not any kind of punishment. I see so much potential for your future in this discipline. It feels like you're boxing yourself in when outside of the box is where we'll find the solutions we need. Get out of the box, Molly."

I tip my head once in acquiescence, but internally I'm fuming as I leave her office.

Get out of the box? Outside of the box is just chaos and failure. The box keeps me on track.

Without the box, I'm honestly afraid of what will happen.

Just outside Dr. Gantt's office door is Jonathan. Maybe when she said she'd talk to him today, she meant right now. He leans his back against a wall, one foot on the ground, the other leg bent at the knee with his foot propped on the wall. His arms are crossed in a casual pose. Of course, he's smiling.

I level a withering stare his way before stomping toward my cubicle.

Chapter Two

Jonathan

Today part one of my plan to win over Molly Delaney starts. When Dr. Gantt told me yesterday that Molly would be joining me in the field for the foreseeable future, I knew I had to find a way to get her to at least tolerate me.

Why is winning her over so important to me as to warrant a plan? Yeah, I'm not really sure. I mean she's gorgeous: petite with brown hair the color of caramel, usually tied up or back in a practical ponytail, and deep blue eyes framed behind round glasses and long, fluttery eyelashes. She'd be attractive even if I wasn't already predisposed to think women in science are hot.

I hope I'm not so shallow that her looks are the reason she intrigues me. Molly Delaney is a puzzle. I've known her for about six years now—we're the only two scientists in Dr. Gantt's lab that came up through the grad program together—but I don't really know much about her. Her brilliance, and peculiarity, are widely known around the department, not just in our lab. Peculiar in that she's quiet, even aloof, and serious to a fault.

And she doesn't like me. I have a reputation for being a likable guy, so honestly the fact that she doesn't like me kind of makes me not like her, because what the heck? Not even sure what I did. I like when people like me, so it also makes me want to change her mind.

So yeah, Molly's a puzzle, but one I'm willing to put in the time to solve, at least for the harmony of my work life for the next couple of months.

Of course, Dr. Gantt forcing Molly to work with me in the field makes the whole winning-her-over thing more difficult. I know she wouldn't be working with me willingly, and the daggers she shot at me as she came out of Dr. Gantt's office yesterday made it clear this is against her will. Molly gravitates toward the lab-based work of testing samples, studying data, and writing up reports. The understanding around the lab is that she has a fear of the ocean and doesn't like boats. Doesn't make sense to me considering our line of work, but what do I know?

The field is where the real action happens.

Which is why I'm excited for my assignment today. I'll ease her into my work by collecting water samples from a nearby swamp. No boats required, just wading boots.

I get to the office and find Molly at her computer, swiveling her chair back and forth as her eyes remain focused on the screen.

"You ready?" I pair the question with my most charming smile.

Molly lifts her gaze from the computer screen and stares at me blankly. "For?"

"Fieldwork. We've got some water samples to collect."

Her jaw clenches, and she narrows her eyes. "We're doing that today?"

"Yeah. Didn't anyone tell you?"

She appraises what I'm wearing—lightweight fishing pants and a long-sleeve UV shirt. "I'm not dressed for fieldwork today. I'll come with you another time."

From what I can tell, she's wearing yoga pants and a T-shirt. "Your clothes are fine. I have waders you can borrow."

She looks appalled. "I'll just go with you another time. I didn't plan to do fieldwork today. I mean, I ... put makeup on and everything this morning," she finishes lamely.

I know she supposedly has this fear of the ocean, but I never pegged her for prissy. And *is* she wearing makeup? I study her face. She looks the same as always— beautiful, natural, fresh.

"Look, I don't want to play the boss card, but Dr. Gantt told me that you should come with me for field research whenever I go until she says it's enough." I widen my eyes in a pleading look. "Don't make me let our PI down, Dr. Delaney."

She huffs. "Fine. Just ... fine. Can you at least give me about twenty minutes to finish what I'm doing?"

"Absolutely. I'll check my email and meet you back here at," I check my watch, "nine thirty."

She grumbles something under her breath, so I whistle as I walk away. Why does it give me so much pleasure to annoy her? Is it because I know she hates me? Or does she hate me because I tend to annoy her? It's a chicken-egg situation, for sure. I'm not sure which came first.

The thing is, my behaviors that seem to annoy her the most are the ones that charm other women. The smiling. The winking. Paying extra attention to her. I usually get good results with these tactics. Not that that's what I'm doing here, of course. I'm not trying to get any results from Molly except annoyance. Well, I guess now I'm trying to get her to tolerate me well enough that we won't kill each other as we work together. Which means I should probably stop intentionally aggravating her.

Because I'm feeling generous, I give Molly an extra ten minutes before I'm back at her desk. "Ready now?"

"No, but let's get this over with."

I grin. "That's the spirit!"

Down in the parking lot, I point Molly toward my blue pickup truck. "I've got all the gear loaded into my truck, so I'll drive."

She doesn't answer but follows me across the lot. I try to decide if opening her car door falls into the "intentionally annoying her" category. Erring on the side of caution, I leave it alone and get myself situated in the driver's seat.

Cranking the engine, I set my phone in the center compartment. "Do you mind music?"

She shakes her head, looking miserable.

I pull up my Avett Brothers playlist on Spotify and "Kick Drum Heart" starts playing over the truck speakers. I love this song. I turn the volume up.

"Come on, perk up." I grin. "How can anyone be sulky with this song on?" I drum my fingers on the steering wheel as I back out of the parking space and start down the road.

"I don't know what this is," Molly grumbles. "But it's too loud."

"Sorry." I turn the volume back to a normal level.

"Thank you, Dr. Stanch."

I chuckle. Man, she kills me. "We don't need to be so formal, you know," I say. "Just call me Jonathan."

"Fine."

"And I should call you...?" I know her first name, of course, but she's just too easy to irritate.

"Molly."

"Can I call you Mol?"

She pinches her lips together. "No."

"How about Mollywog?"

She glowers. "Absolutely not."

Molly turns her head toward the window, so I take the hint and stop talking to her. The song changes over to "I and Love and You," and I have to stop myself from singing along.

When we stop at a red light, I glance over at the passenger seat. Molly's searching around like she lost something.

"What's wrong?" I ask.

"My phone. I think I probably left it on my desk." She pats her pockets one more time.

"Do you need it? We can turn back."

"No. I'll be fine." She folds her arms across her chest.

"Are you sure? It wouldn't be a problem to—"

"I said it's fine," she snaps.

"Okay. Jeez. We're almost there anyway." Even though I know I'm pushing her too much, the words still sting.

Molly sighs. "I'm sorry. This is all a little—"

A trilling ringtone interrupts her, followed by a robotic voice repeating, "Incoming call from ... Dad" over the speakers in the cab.

Inwardly, I groan. I'm not dealing with this today. I let it ring.

Molly stares at me. "Do you need to get that?"

"Nope."

After another few seconds, the phone stops ringing and the speakers switch back to music.

I try to shake off the irritation my dad's call brought up by focusing my attention back on Molly.

I grin at her. "We're almost to the first site. We need to collect samples from four sites today. We can probably get two of them done before lunch and two after."

"This is an all-day thing?"

"Yep."

I pull off the road near what used to be the Bayou Bienvenue Wetland Platform. The Wetland Triangle is our first stop. Without waiting for Molly, I get out of the truck to pull supplies out of the bed.

I pause to admire the scenery. Looking out over the water, I'm reminded once again how much I love my job. Here it is, a weekday, and I get to be outside in the sunshine playing in the water. Bay-ou Bienvenue is approximately four hundred acres of open water stretching out in front of me, though some remnants of the cypress swamp it used to be are evident in the handful of limbless trunks poking out from under the surface.

They call it a ghost swamp because it's now a sad echo of the thriving ecosystem it once was. Still, the water sparkles and the grass surrounding it is green and lush. Sure beats sitting in front of a computer.

Behind me, I hear Molly's door slam closed. She walks around the back of the truck and stops next to me. I hand her my extra set of chest waders.

"Aren't we going on a boat?" Molly asks.

"Not today."

I see a flicker of emotion cross her face, but it's not relief. It's ... disappointment? Weird. Not that I know her expressions, so maybe I'm reading it wrong.

She stares at the rubber clothing. "I can't wear this."

"It'll be big on you, but it'll work."

She shakes her head, her cheeks turning pink.

"Oh." I set a wide-brimmed fishing hat on top of the pile in her arms. "You'll need that, too."

The pink on her cheeks turns to red and spreads up to her hairline. I brace myself for a tongue lashing, but instead she sets her jaw and moves to the back of the truck. When she starts shoving her shoes into the waders, I look away and refocus on putting on my own gear.

I've just gotten the suspenders on my waders fastened when she appears in front of me again, hands on her hips. As soon as I realize what I'm seeing, I crack up. I can't help it.

I've never noticed how *tiny* Molly is. The spare waders swallow her whole. I'm six feet tall, and she's got to be a good nine inches shorter than me. The extra material bunches around her ankles, and even though she adjusted the suspenders to the smallest setting, the bib still sits under her um ... let's just say chestal region. The built-in boots are clown shoes on her.

Between the oversized clothes and the furious expression she's wearing behind her big round glasses, she looks freaking adorable. I can't stop laughing.

Molly scowls at me, her dark eyebrows pulled down just above the bright blue of her eyes, and her lips pursed into an attractive cupid's bow. Suddenly lightheaded, my laughter dries up. I suck in a breath. I really shouldn't find a scowl so enticing. What is wrong with me?

I take a beat to refocus my thoughts. *Water samples. Right.*

"Follow me." I tip my head in the direction of the water, carting the cooler containing the sample bottle with me.

Molly clomps behind me, trying to walk in the huge boots. I bite back a smile. When I turn to check on her, she's gritting her teeth, a stoic and determined edge to her movements. If this is going to be a long-term arrangement, I'm going to tell Dr. Gantt that Molly needs her own set of waders, ones that fit her properly.

When we get to the water's edge, I drop the cooler after taking out the sample bottle we'll be using. I've already filled out the label on the sample bag, marking the sample as being from this location, with the date, and what to test for.

Because our lab focuses on harmful algal blooms, we're looking at the nutrients in the water, along with the presence of pesticides or hydrocarbons. We track the levels over time from strategic sites around the area. If the nutrient level drops or the pesticides and hydrocarbons increase, harmful algal blooms are more likely to develop.

Molly follows me as I wade out until the water hits just below my knees. I sneak a glance and, again, have to smother a smile. Because she's so much shorter than me, the water reaches halfway up her thighs.

It's too good not to document. Sliding the bottle under my arm, I reach into the front of my waders and fish my phone out from a pocket in my shirt.

Holding it up, I call, "Say cheese!" Before she can protest, I snap a picture. When I review it on my phone screen, I grin. The look she's giving the camera—giving me—is murderous. It's perfect.

I've given some thought to how I want to handle working with Molly out here in the field. She's thoroughly knowledgeable about the theory behind all the processes we're doing, likely she's even done them before, even if it's been a while. I don't need to patronize her with explanations of the why of things she can put together herself. It will be better to have her watch me go through the process, and I can answer any questions she has.

Tucking my phone away again, I instruct, "Okay, Molly, stand downstream from me and watch."

I dunk the bottle, with the cap still on, into the water upstream from us. When the bottle is about halfway down, with plenty of space beneath the microlayer on top, I unscrew the cap underwater and let the bottle fill all the way up. Air from the bottle bubbles to the surface. I screw the cap back on and pull the bottle out of the water. Unscrewing the cap again, I dump the water downstream. Then, I repeat the process three more times, except on the fourth time, I don't dump the water. The first three fill-ups are to rinse the bottle with the sample water, and the fourth is to actually get the sample.

I turn back to Molly and raise my eyebrows. "Any questions?" She shakes her head. "Do you want to try one?"

I hold out the bottle to her, and she takes it. She moves upstream of me and then waits a few minutes for the sediment from her steps to settle. She uncaps the bottle and dumps it behind her. After the cap is back on, she runs through the whole process—even filling and dumping three times, though I've already done that, so we know the bottle has already been rinsed.

"I went through the process as if you hadn't already," she explains. "To practice."

I meet her eyes. "I figured. So, the last step is—"

"Put it in the sample bag and put the sample bag in the cooler?"

"You got it." I smile and to my surprise, she smiles back at me. As much as her scowl affected me earlier, this rare smile throws me more. Her blue eyes shine brighter and crinkle at the corners. We're standing only a couple feet from each other in the water, so I'm close enough to notice that when she smiles, one eye stays open slightly more than the other. I stare a little too long.

She steps away and holds up the bottle. "I better get this in the cooler."

I have to swallow before I can brilliantly respond, "Yeah."

But when I start to follow her out of the water, I've forgotten how to move my legs. I slosh ungracefully to shore, where we remove the boots and waders and pack everything back in the truck.

It's a quick drive to the next site, farther east. Again, we park on the side of the road, suit up, and wade into the water.

As Molly collects the sample, I can't help but tease her. "Hey, Mol Madness!" I call.

When I'm certain she's looking at me, I stretch my hand to the side and dip it in the water as if I'm going to splash her.

She glares at me, face as hard as stone. "No."

"Aw, come on! Water fight?"

"No. I'm working."

I exaggerate a sigh. "Don't you think work should be fun?"

"No," she answers. "I think work should be work."

Molly finishes filling the sample bottle the final time. She looks like she wants to chuck it at my face. "I need to focus, Jonathan."

My pulse races when she says my name. I think it's the first time she's ever called me Jonathan, or at least the first time in a long time, and I like it a little too much.

"We'll see." I smirk.

With a withering look, she shoves the sample bottle into my chest and stomps away. Or at least she tries to. Instead, the next thing I know, she's tripping forward. I try to grab her, but she's already out of arm's reach.

I'm too late, and Molly tumbles face-first into the water.

Chapter Three

Molly

I'm soaked to the skin. Worse, these waders are filling up with heavy water, which makes it impossible for me to move. At least my glasses stayed put, though the lenses are dotted with water droplets.

"Are you okay?" Jonathan asks as he pulls me back to my feet, his expression alarmed.

No. I am *not* okay. I haven't been okay this whole freaking day. My clothes are sticking to my skin. The suspenders on the waders are rubbing across my shoulder blades and have been driving me crazy. My hair feels too heavy on my head, especially with this terrible hat on. Plus, the water dripping off me smells like rotten eggs mixed with decaying vegetables, *and I think some went into my mouth!*

But this is Jonathan asking, my archnemesis, so I answer with, "Yes, fine."

Jonathan helps pull me to shore, and I shuck off the waders, holding them upside down to drain the water out. When I look up again, Jonathan's frozen in place, staring at me with a dumbfounded expression.

"What?" I demand, removing my glasses and fruitlessly trying to dry them on the hem of my shirt.

He clears his throat. "You're soaked."

I roll my eyes. *No kidding.*

"What happened?" he asks.

"What happened was I tripped in your giant clown boots because apparently you have feet the size of tugboats."

Jonathan's eyes twinkle. "I have towels in the truck." He hesitates. "Do you have a change of clothes?"

Oh, heck no. I *told* him I wasn't prepared, but he bullied me into coming anyway. Is it my fault I forgot that Dr. Gantt told me I'd be starting fieldwork today? Well, yes. But still, he has the nerve to ask this? "Do I have a change of clothes? *Do I have a change of clothes?*"

"Right. Stupid question. Sorry."

He assesses me, and it suddenly dawns on me that *my clothes are sticking to me.* I quickly move the waders in front of my chest. I swear I see Jonathan blush before he ducks his head.

"I have extra clothes in the truck you can change into."

Great. More oversized clothes made for giants.

At the truck, Jonathan pulls a thick towel from the back seat and hands it to me. I wrap it around my shoulders and snuggle into it. It's warm from sitting in the truck and smells subtly of laundry detergent.

As I run the towel across my arms and legs, Jonathan rummages through a duffel bag and produces gray joggers and a red T-shirt.

I look around. We're on the side of the road, no buildings in any direction as far as I can see. "Where am I going to change?"

He nods toward the backseat of the truck.

My mouth drops open. "I don't think so."

"There's nowhere else. I'll wait out here."

"Facing away from the truck." I glare at him.

"Yes, ma'am. Of course."

After much wiggling and contorting in the humid truck cab, I manage to peel off my wet clothes and don Jonathan's dry ones. They have the same fresh laundry smell as the towel, but stale, like they've been sitting in his gym bag for a while. Maybe because they have been, they feel warm against my skin.

I keep peeking out the window, and true to his word, Jonathan is turned away from the truck each time I look. I pull the drawstring on the joggers as tight as it will go and tie the ends in a double knot, just in case. I wrap the towel around my wet hair to squeeze it dry.

My shoes are soaked, so I leave them off and climb into the front passenger seat.

"Okay!" I call out the window to Jonathan.

He turns around and, without a glance in my direction, finishes putting the gear away. When he gets everything stowed, he joins me in the truck. He meets my eyes. "We should call it a day. What do you think?"

"I never wanted to come in the first place."

"Right. Of course."

My damp hair is starting to irritate me. It clings to my neck and ears, sticky in the humidity. I pull it off my neck with my hand, gathering it together, and then groan in frustration.

"What's wrong?" Jonathan asks.

"I don't have a hair tie."

He looks around the truck. "Would a rubber band work?"

I scowl. "Only if I want knots in my hair."

Jonathan holds his hands up in apology. He clears his throat. "How about lunch before we go back to the lab?"

"My lunch is in the refrigerator at the lab."

"We could stop somewhere."

I pointedly look down at my clothes, which are his clothes, and my bare feet.

He beams. "I know a drive-in place near here. Come on, I'm starving. Aren't you hungry?"

"No," I say, and my stomach gurgles loudly.

He chuckles. "I think you are. Come on, please?"

Instead of answering, I turn my head toward the window.

"I'll take that as a reluctant yes. You'll love this place. Their hot wings are incredible." He starts the engine, so I buckle my seat belt.

He'll do what he wants whether I agree or not. I just hope this restaurant has something on the menu I can eat.

The truck is quiet as Jonathan drives us to the restaurant. Now that I'm mostly dry except for my hair, which still feels uncomfortable against my neck, and I'm wearing reasonably cozy clothes, I feel more regulated. I've been overstimulated all day.

I have ADHD, and one of the ways that shows up for me is with sensory processing issues. The simplest explanation is that my brain gets overloaded, my nervous system thinks there's a threat, and my body goes into fight, flight, or freeze mode. Today, I've been choosing *fight* an awful lot.

My ADHD also looks like losing focus easily, interspersed with long bouts of hyperfocus. Forgetting things, like my phone at the lab or the fact that Dr. Gantt said fieldwork would start today. Disorganization, if I'm not super proactive. And pickiness about food, which is also tied to my sensory challenges.

Years ago, I developed a set of rules designed to minimize the effects of my ADHD and help me appear totally normal.

First, stay in the lab. It's a predictable, fairly low-distraction environment where I can, usually, control the variables.

Second, keep a rigid schedule. If each day has the same cadence, it's easier for me to keep track of what comes next.

Third, focus on work. No dating, friends, or other distractions. My sisters are my best friends, and they're all I need.

These rules have worked well for me. I got into my first choice masters and doctorate programs, where I was top of my class (well, I tied with Jonathan). I had my pick of postdoc research teams to join and contributed meaningfully once I got there. Aside from publications related to my PhD research, I've been a third or fourth author on five publications and have presented at six conferences.

Not bad for a scientist who hasn't yet turned thirty, especially a woman in a male-dominated field.

At least, everything's been fine until recently. Until the principal investigator of my lab, a woman I deeply admire, decided I'm not being creative enough in my work. It's a blow to my confidence, for sure. I know I do good work. I also recognize that Dr. Gantt, our PI, understands better than I do what it takes to find success in this field because it's something she's fought for herself despite the challenges. I only wish she had designed a way to stimulate me that didn't involve fieldwork. Or Jonathan.

It's not Jonathan's fault. Not really. He's actually been pretty great today, which I can't believe I'm thinking. I've been the difficult one.

My stomach growls, and I pat my midsection. Hopefully that growl was an internal sound and not something Jonathan could hear. I glance over at him, but he's focused on the road. I often don't notice my body's signals until they're extreme—I don't realize I need to pee until I'm bursting; I don't pay attention to how tired I am until I crash. Likewise, I usually don't notice I'm hungry until I'm past hungry, until I'm *hangry*.

Fortunately, we pull into the parking lot of a local dive restaurant called The Saucy Wing. Jonathan parks the truck in front of a large menu board posted on a wall near the order and pickup windows.

He turns to me. "Let me know what you want, and I'll go place the order and bring it back when it's ready. You won't have to get out of the truck."

I study the menu. It's limited; this place is mostly a wing joint. I can't stand eating anything that has bones in it. I don't like foods that are creamy. Most dairy makes me gag. I can't get near any foods that have strong smells like seafood or garlic. Fruits and vegetables are hit or miss. I can eat one grape and it's amazing, crisp and juicy, and then I eat another grape from the very same bunch and it's squishy and sour.

"I'll have the boneless barbecue wings," I tell Jonathan. "With fries. And just water to drink."

Jonathan opens the truck door to go place the order.

"Wait!" I call. "I don't have my wallet with me."

He turns his face back toward me and smiles. "My treat. It's the least I can do after everything I've put you through today."

I start to protest, but my stomach growls again, and I can tell by Jonathan's smug expression that it definitely wasn't just an internal noise this time.

"Fine. Thank you. I'll pay you back."

I watch through the windshield as Jonathan talks to the guy at the order window. I can't hear what they're saying, but they're both smiling and laughing. I may need to come to terms with the fact that if everyone likes Jonathan except for me—and it really seems that way—maybe it's not him that's the problem.

Or, I think as he tosses his curly hair out of his eyes and slides his hands into the pockets of his pants, making the muscles in his forearms pop, *he masks his evilness with looks and charm, and I'm the only one who sees past the ruse.* Yep, that's it.

When Jonathan climbs back into the truck with two white paper sacks dotted with grease, a bottle of water, and a large paper cup, he's still smiling. He hands one of the bags to me, and I practically rip it open.

I eat the fries first because once they get cold, they're disgusting. After I polish off the fries, I reach back into the sack for the chicken wings. I hazard a glance toward my dining companion. He's watching me, the ever-present smirk on his face. He hasn't started eating yet.

"What?" I challenge.

His smirk gets ... smirkier. "Nothing. I just like a woman who can eat."

I scowl at him. "I don't care what kind of woman you like."

His eyes twinkle. "Noted." He opens his bag and pulls out a cardboard container of hot wings. "I love this place. I used to go to that chain restaurant for wings, but then I found Saucy, and it's so much better. The wings at the other place are consistently undersauced."

As the fries settle into my stomach, and the gut-brain connection signals to my brain that we're not starving anymore, I'm less crabby.

I even allow a slight smile when I tease Jonathan. "Consistently undersauced, huh? Sounds like a real problem."

Jonathan barks out a laugh. "Yes. Consistently undersauced. I stand by the phrase."

We both return to our food, and the truck is quiet for a few minutes. Even if Jonathan deserves it, I feel guilty about my behavior today; I've definitely been at my worst. I've been uncomfortable and overstimulated and took it out on him.

Finally, I take a fortifying breath and blurt, "I'm sorry."

Jonathan stills. I'm looking at the food in my lap, but I feel his gaze turn to me. "For what?"

"Being such a crank today. How rude I've been."

He shrugs. "You're fine. I know this isn't your ideal assignment, and I'm not your ideal lab partner. I'd probably be cranky, too."

The thing is, I'm not sure he would be.

"But listen," he continues, rubbing his sauce-smeared fingers on a napkin. "Were you serious earlier when you said work shouldn't be fun? Don't you love being a scientist?"

I nod. "I do love being a scientist, but that doesn't mean I need to goof around all the time or, I don't know, start a prank war or something. I take my work seriously."

"I think work should be fun. You know,"—he rubs his chin—"back in high school, they called me the Prank King of Ohio."

"Did you have buttons made?" I ask dryly.

He grins. "I didn't, but what a good idea."

I stare at him. "You think pranks are fun?"

"I do. Have you ever played a prank on anyone?"

"No." But my pulse ticks up at the thought. My brain craves novelty, and I often have to talk it down from trying something new. Novelty may sound fun, but it's untested. Unsafe.

"Hmm," he muses. "Could be a way to have more fun at work."

"Are you suggesting we have a prank war?"

He winks. "Of course not. That would be unprofessional. But, if *someone* played a prank on me at work, I would enjoy it. And retaliate, of course."

For a second, I actually consider it. A prank war could be a way for me to act on my feelings of rivalry for Jonathan while still being able to work cooperatively with him when I need to. But introducing that much unpredictability into my life is a recipe for disaster.

Instead of entertaining his suggestion any further, I turn to face forward. "I'm ready to go home now."

The drive back to the lab is quiet. Because I don't have shoes, Jonathan offers to run in and get my bag from my desk for me. When he realizes I walked to work, he offers to drive me home.

He pulls the truck up to the curb outside my apartment building.

"What's your number?" he asks.

I stare at him. "Excuse me?"

What about anything that happened today would make him think I'd give him my phone number?

He smirks. "So I can text you about our future fieldwork excursions. No funny business."

Oh. That makes sense. I rattle off my number.

Jumping out of the truck, I collect my bag and soggy shoes before I walk up the stairs to the entrance of my apartment building. I type in my entry code, and the door unlocks. I turn back and give Jonathan a little wave.

Upstairs in my apartment, I strip and shower. Afterward, I put on my coziest comfort clothes and settle on the couch to binge *Anne with an E*, one of my emotional support shows.

I check my phone and see a text from an unknown number. I open it to find a picture of myself from today, standing in the water in ridiculously large waders and glaring at the camera. I cringe. The message says, "Thought you might want this to help you remember our eventful day together."

I shake my head and forward the photo to my sisters in our group chat.

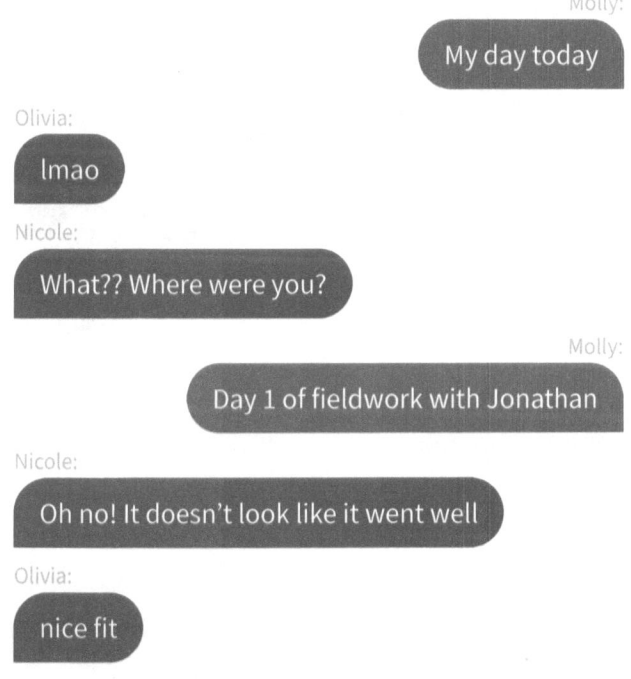

Molly:
My day today

Olivia:
lmao

Nicole:
What?? Where were you?

Molly:
Day 1 of fieldwork with Jonathan

Nicole:
Oh no! It doesn't look like it went well

Olivia:
nice fit

Nicole:

Ha! Olivia that's funny because it could mean fit like outfit or fit like how it's way too big on her

Olivia:

I know

Molly:

Anyway, hope your day is going better than mine

Olivia:

oh yeah livin the dream. maybe if I get a fourth part time coaching job I can afford to move out of my childhood bedroom

Molly:

You'll get there

Molly:

Nicole?

Nicole:

My day is fine

Olivia:

Nicole

Nicole:

Okay... remember you asked for it

Nicole:

> Adam is taking me on the sweetest date tonight! It's a tour of a candy factory where we can create our own chocolate bars at the end! [heart eye emoji]

I groan. I'm so happy for my sister, really. She's dated some real duds, and I'm glad she and Adam found each other. He's a super nice, super good guy.

But also I'm just a smidge ... jealous? Which is stupid, I know. No sense wanting something I can't have. I'm not sure any man would want to put up with all my ... eccentricities once he got to know them. If I loved that man, I'm not sure I'd want to put him through that anyway.

I set my phone on the coffee table and turn on the show. Oh well. I'll just lose myself in the romance of Avonlea instead. While this newer adaptation strays quite a bit from the original, it's well done and easy to watch. The movie series from the eighties is hard to find without buying the DVDs or paying for a special streaming service. I do love it, though.

Beaker jumps up next to me and settles on my lap. I stroke her back absently as the opening credits come up on the TV.

I sit back and relax. And that's when the itching starts.

Chapter Four

Jonathan

After I dropped Molly off at home yesterday afternoon, I went to the last two sites by myself and got the samples we needed. The cab of my truck smelled like lavender the rest of the day. The fragrance seemed to radiate from Molly the minute she was drenched. Her shampoo, maybe? Either way, it lingered in my nose long after it faded in the truck.

Now we've got a few days for Molly to recover in the lab before we need to venture out again.

As I walk into the lab, I feel uncharacteristically nervous. My palms are sweaty, and my muscles feel twitchy. What am I nervous about? Seeing Molly?

I saw *a lot* of Molly yesterday. Her drenched clothes didn't leave much to the imagination. They clung to every curve, though I tried my hardest not to notice. Strangely, I think seeing her in my sweatpants and T-shirt, baggy as they were, caused an even more intense reaction in me. I liked it. A lot. I found myself fighting these primal urges to protect and defend her. In evolutionary terms, men are biologically predisposed to protect their mate and offspring to ensure the survival of their genes. But Molly isn't my mate. I don't want Molly to be my mate. Molly would never want to be my mate.

I'm pulled from these ludicrous thoughts when my boss approaches me.

"What exactly happened yesterday?" Dr. Gantt asks.

"What do you mean?" I ask quickly, my mind still on Molly in my clothes. Molly changing into my clothes in the back seat of my truck. Her stunning blue eyes narrowed at me as she scarfed french fries while wearing my clothes and sitting in my truck—

"Molly called in sick today."

A flash of adrenaline makes my stomach tighten. "What? She was fine when I dropped her off yesterday."

Dr. Gantt puts a hand on her hip. "She said she had an allergic reaction to mosquito bites. Didn't y'all wear insect repellent?"

I did. Plus, I had on long sleeves. The mosquitoes didn't bother me. But ... Molly had on short sleeves, and did I ever give her the spray to put on? I'm guessing no.

Good thing Molly isn't my mate. I'd do a sucky job protecting her. *Great.* Another reason for her to dislike me.

"Do you mind if I go check on her?" Dr. Gantt narrows her eyes as if trying to analyze pieces of a problem. "I feel responsible," I explain. "I forgot to make sure she had insect repellent on."

"Go ahead then. Tell her we're all thinking about her, and that I hope she feels better soon."

"Thanks." I turn around and head back out the door. Of course I can't show up empty-handed, but I'm also not sure what she likes, other than boneless barbeque wings, which don't seem appropriate at nine in the morning.

I do know a New Orleans treat that everyone loves, though. I can stop on the way.

💕 💕 💕

I grab the paper sack from the passenger seat and walk toward the entrance to Molly's apartment building. It has an intercom system with labels for each of the residents. I find the code for "Delaney – 2B" and punch it in.

The speaker crackles to life. "Hello?"

"Hey, Molly ... it's Jonathan."

"Go away."

I rub my chin. "I just wanted to check on you. Dr. Gantt said you had an allergic reaction to mosquitoes?"

"I'm fine. Go away."

"I brought beignets." Even though she can't see me, I shake the bag in front of me.

The intercom goes silent. Then the door buzzes and makes a loud clanking sound. I grin as I pull it open. After it closes securely behind me, I find the stairs and make my way up to 2B.

I knock. "Molly?" I call.

I hear rustling behind the door. "Can you just leave the beignets on the doorstep?"

I chuckle. "I'd really like to come in and check on you."

"And if I say no?"

"More beignets for me."

She sighs so loudly I hear it through the door. A lock clicks and those blue eyes peer out at me from a tiny crack.

I flash a smile. "Hi."

She sighs again and opens the door wider. Her face and arms are covered in gloppy white cream mixed with what looks like aloe vera gel. Her hair is tied in a messy bun on top of her head and the lenses of her glasses are smudged.

Adorable.

I quickly school my expression.

"Come in, I suppose," she invites.

As I walk through the door, I take in the apartment. I can't tell how big it is, but it looks like a studio. The living room is crammed with bookshelves full of messy stacks of books and papers. The love seat sized couch is a nest of blankets and pillows. A small television across from the couch is paused on an image of a young Anne Hathaway in a peasant blouse and long blue skirt, a cape wrapped around her shoulders. A light blinks on a DVD player on the shelf under the TV. I do a double take. Who still has a DVD player?

I move a blanket to the side to sit, placing the bag of beignets on the coffee table next to tubes of antihistamine creams, a large pump bottle of aloe vera, and a bottle of Benadryl. She opens the bag and pulls out a beignet, immediately taking a bite.

"Mmm," she says. "They're still warm."

My heart rate ticks up, and I take a breath to calm my reaction. "So, what happened, Mol of America?" I ask.

Donut squarely in front of her face, she narrows her eyes. "Are these inane nicknames off the cuff, or do you have a list somewhere that you work on in your free time?"

I consider a minute. "Mostly off the cuff, but a list isn't a bad idea." I scratch my chin thoughtfully.

"Anyway, what *happened* is that some jerk made me go in a swamp yesterday. I got bitten up by mosquitoes, and apparently, I'm allergic to certain types of mosquito bites. My whole face swelled up, and I had to DoorDash medicine through the tiny slits of my swollen eyelids. Also, I got sunburned, so that's painful."

The attitude is on point, but there's no fire in her tone.

"And if the jerk is really sorry and promises to give you insect repellent next time?" I ask, hoping she feels more forgiving now that I've plied her with sugar.

She lowers the donut. "Ugh. Next time."

The powdered sugar from the beignet is stuck to the cream on her face. I smother a smile. "But can you forgive the jerk?" I wheedle.

She glares at me out of the side of her eyes. "Only if he brings beignets."

I grin. "Perfect." I knew bringing beignets was the right move.

She pops the last bit of donut in her mouth and chews thoughtfully. Then, she sits up and levels me with a stern gaze. "I get there has to be a next time for fieldwork. Dr. Gantt says. But, please, next time, can you give me a heads up? Let me know what to expect so I can be prepared? I'll be easier to work with if I know what's going to happen."

Does not like surprises. Got it.

"Understood. I'm sorry. I'll communicate better next time."

She takes a deep breath. "Thank you."

Then, she smiles—a real smile with her teeth showing and her eyes crinkling in the corners. Just like yesterday when she smiled at me in the bayou, I'm breathless. I'm desperate for more of her smiles. *What I wouldn't give to be the one to make her smile like that every day.*

That's a weird thought. This is Molly Delaney. Yes, I've always been attracted to her, but she hates me.

I run a hand through my hair and stand, suddenly eager to leave. "I'll get out of your hair now. There's more beignets in the bag. All yours. I hope you feel better soon."

"Thank you for the beignets." She stands and walks with me toward the door.

I step into the hallway. I'm halfway to the stairwell when she calls, "Jonathan!" I turn around and from the open doorway, Molly tips her head in a teasing expression. "I still don't like you."

She makes me work for every inch of progress, that's for sure.

I grin. "I didn't expect you would."

My phone rings on my way back to the lab. It's my sister, Tamara, so I answer.

"Hey, sis! How are the girls?" My sister is mother to my three delightful nieces, aged somewhere between two and ... nine, I want to say?

"Hi, Jonny. The girls are great. They miss you. We all do."

Tamara and her family live in Ohio, just a couple of streets over from our dad, who still lives in the house I grew up in. When she says, "we all do," I know she's including Dad. It's her subtle way of saying I should call him more.

"Did you miss a call from Dad yesterday?" And that's her not-so-subtle way of saying it, I guess.

"Oh, um, not sure. I was busy yesterday."

"Jonny," she scolds.

Even though she can't see me, I roll my eyes. "Okay, yes. He called when I was out with a colleague." I realize how that sounds and backtrack. "Well, you know, not 'out' with a colleague like a date or anything. She was ... we were ... visiting our sample sites and ... collecting samples," I finish lamely.

Tamara is quiet for a second. "Okay, there's a lot to unpack there, but I just don't have the time today, baby brother. Dad's going to call you again tonight. You should answer."

"Maybe I have plans."

"Do you?"

"No. But I often do have plans, you know." I could have plans if I wanted to have plans. I just haven't wanted to lately.

"I'm sure you do, Casanova. Tonight, your plans are to talk to Dad when he calls you. Okay?"

"Why?"

"He has news he wants to tell you."

I consider this for a minute, dread already starting to turn my stomach sour. "Good news or bad news?"

"*I* think it's wonderful news. You may not agree."

I groan. "He's marrying Sharon, isn't he?"

"Talk to Dad. And be nice."

"I'm always nice," I grumble.

She laughs. "You're usually nice. Less so when you talk to Dad." I hear a crash in the background. "Ugh, gotta go. Mia's getting into something. Love you, Jonny!"

"Love you, Tams."

The call ends just as I'm pulling into a parking spot at the lab. I switch off the engine and groan as I lay my head back against the headrest.

My parents have been divorced since I was twelve, and Dad's been dating Sharon for two years now. She's a nice lady. I don't have anything against her, except that she's the total opposite of my mother in almost every way. Mom has black hair and Sharon's blonde. Mom is outgoing, the life of every party, and Sharon is quiet and reserved. Mom has strong opinions about most things, and Sharon goes along with what everyone else wants.

It's as if, by now choosing Sharon, Dad is admitting how wrong he was to choose my mother the first time around. It's like he's saying their marriage was a mistake; my mother was a mistake.

Tamara loves Sharon. Tamara's husband, Mike, loves Sharon. The girls love Sharon. My dad, obviously, loves Sharon. And I guess he's going to marry her.

Chapter Five

Molly

I 'm not sure if it's the antihistamine cream or if I took too much Benadryl, but I haven't been able to stop thinking about pranks since Jonathan came to my apartment this morning.

Juvenile pranks. Stupid pranks. *Funny* pranks.

No. I need to redirect my brain. Think about work instead.

I hate missing work today. Before I had to step out with Jonathan for our little fieldwork adventure, I was working on a model that would collate all the data we've collected from our sample sites over the last two years and find patterns that could help us better predict harmful algal blooms.

Standard stuff, right? *Except* my model also incorporates weather data, specifically hurricanes and other tropical storms.

Harmful algal blooms, more commonly called red tide, are absolutely devastating to beach tourism and the seafood industry on the Gulf coast. Red tide tends to get particularly bad during or following an active hurricane season. Though it's widely believed that this is because of chemical runoff from pesticides and the like from the land as flood waters recede, I have a half-baked hypothesis that it may also be partly caused by how the water temperature and pH levels change during the storms themselves. I'm not sure yet how to test that, but my data model will at least set the foundation.

Did you know that in Hitchcock's *The Birds*, the birds' crazed behavior was likely due to them ingesting toxins from fish poisoned by harmful algal blooms in Monterey Bay?

Ooh, maybe it would be a funny prank to have Jonathan unknowingly eat fish with toxins from algal bloom in it and then record his erratic behavior.

Wait, what? *No, Molly, that would not be funny. It would be dangerous and potentially result in assault and battery charges. Calm down, Prank Sinatra.*

The character Winston in the show *New Girl* called himself Prank Sinatra even though all the pranks he came up with were either way too big, like releasing a badger into the air ducts at a friend's wedding, or way too small, like putting a feather in someone's shoe.

Ugh, my arms are itching again. Okay, mind over matter. I'll help my brain stop focusing on the itching by instead brainstorming what pranks *would* be appropriate to play on Jonathan. Not that I'm actually going to. Just brainstorming here.

Let's see. I could put a taxidermy seagull in his locker at the lab. It would scare him to death when he opened the door. I could put tape over the sensor on the bottom of his computer mouse, so it doesn't work. I could cover his cubicle in sticky notes. I could switch out his shoes to much larger ones, so he has to flop around the lab. That's dumb. When does he ever take his shoes off at the lab?

Wait. Instead of shoes, what if I switch out his lab coat? And instead of larger, I go smaller. It's simple, easy to pull off, and effective. The perfect inaugural prank of the prank war. If I were participating in a prank war, which I'm absolutely not.

But I can't get it out of my head. I'm fixated now on this idea for pranking Jonathan.

For the next week, whenever I see Jonathan take off his lab coat and hang it on the back of his desk chair, which he does often, my fingers twitch, begging for permission to grab it and make the switch.

Somehow, I end up with a medium-sized lab coat tucked into the bottom drawer of my desk. It was in the lost and found. Almost unintentionally, I took it home, washed it, and folded it neatly into the drawer.

I'm not sure what I'm doing. I hate pranks. I hate myself for even thinking about playing a prank, especially at work. But I can't stop.

The day I hit my breaking point is an otherwise normal Tuesday at the lab. After coming out of the lab, Jonathan hangs his coat on the back of his desk chair, badge included, and then leaves to have lunch off-site. I watch him walk out the door. I spring to the window and watch for him to appear on the sidewalk downstairs. I watch him get in his truck. I watch him drive away.

I can't fight the impulse anymore. It's too strong. I slip the medium lab coat out of my desk drawer and slink toward Jonathan's cubicle. I shift my eyes around the room. Most people are at lunch or on the other side of the lab working with water samples. No one's paying attention to me.

Quickly, I unclip Jonathan's badge from his lab coat and reclip it in the exact same spot on the smaller coat. I take his coat off the chair and replace it with the prank coat. Then, I scurry back to my own cubicle and shove Jonathan's coat into my desk drawer.

Now, I wait.

I can't focus on my work; instead I keep running to the window to check if he's back yet. Finally, I see his truck in the lot and watch as he walks through the front door. I estimate how long it will take him to come up the elevator—or stairs, he seems like a stairs guy—and enter the office, based on how long I observed it took him to exit before lunch.

My calculations are only thirty seconds off. He's quicker than I expected.

I lean back in my desk chair just enough to see Jonathan approach his cubicle. He lifts the lab coat from the back of his chair and starts putting an arm through one of the sleeves. He stops and frowns. Pulls his arm back out. Looks at the lab coat. Checks the badge on the pocket. And tries again to slide his arm into the sleeve.

The look of raw confusion on his face is thrilling. I feel a surge of adrenaline, mixed with giddiness and pride. I know I'm smiling like an idiot, but I can't help it. I keep watching Jonathan and can tell the very moment when understanding dawns. He lifts his head, a half-smile on his lips, and looks directly at me.

I quickly snap my chair upright and focus my attention on my computer screen, clicking around like I'm in the middle of something important.

A beat or two later, I hear a throat clearing behind me. I swivel in my seat to see a smirking Jonathan, stuffed into the too-small coat. It hangs open in the front; he couldn't button it if he tried. The cuffs are halfway up his forearms, the fabric pulled so tight around his biceps that it reminds me of sausages. Sexy sausages. *Wait, what?*

"Good afternoon, Dr. Delaney." Jonathan bobs his head. He lifts his elbow and tries to lean it against the cubicle wall but can't get his arm high enough.

I hold back a laugh, but I know he can hear it in my voice when I respond, "Dr. Stanch."

His eyes twinkle as he asks, "Is this how it's going to be?"

I shrug and shake my head but don't say anything.

"Okay, then." The twinkle in his eyes turns to a glint of challenge. "Good," he says with a nod, then turns and walks away.

He wears the damn coat the rest of the day.

Jonathan's retribution is swift, and though not unexpected, it still catches me by surprise. Two days later I'm at my desk when Lila, one of the grad students, hands me a napkin with a jelly-filled donut perched on top.

"There's donuts in the breakroom," she says with a smile. "I brought you one."

My stomach growls, and I realize all I've had so far this morning is coffee. I accept the donut from her with a grateful sigh.

I take a large bite and realize my mistake instantly. It's not jelly inside this donut. It's toothpaste. The sharp mint flavor mixes jarringly with the saccharine frosting and flaky pastry. Without thinking, I spit it onto my desk, dropping the rest of the donut onto my lap, and use the napkin to scrub the taste from my tongue.

"Lila," I say through a gag. "Where did you get this donut?"

Her eyes are wide. "Um, I was in the breakroom and saw the box of donuts, and Dr. Stanch handed me this one and said it was your favorite."

Of course he did. I stand up and whirl around looking for Jonathan, oblivious to the donut tumbling onto the floor. I find him leaning smugly against the wall outside the breakroom, arms crossed over his chest, dark curls flopped across his forehead.

"I'm sorry, Dr. Delaney," Lila trills, her tone panicked. "I don't know what happened."

The nerve of this guy! Using a poor, unsuspecting grad student as a pawn in his nefarious scheme!

I pat Lila's arm reassuringly. "Don't worry, Lila. *You're* not the one in trouble here."

I use the napkin to clean up the mess of donut on my desk and floor. I walk past Jonathan on my way to the garbage can.

"Good morning, Dr. Stanch," I say primly.

He nods, hazel eyes glittering. "Dr. Delaney."

When I get back to my desk, I grab my phone and open the text chain with my sisters. Desperate times call for desperate measures.

Molly:

Code Red, ladies. I need prank ideas.

Chapter Six

Jonathan

A week has passed since the jelly donut prank. As I come up the stairwell at the lab, I peek around every corner. When I get to my desk, I test my chair before sitting and carefully slide open the desk drawers, just in case. At lunch, I pull apart the layers of the sandwich I brought from home and stored in the breakroom refrigerator, making sure only the turkey and Swiss I put in there remain. As Willy Wonka said, "The suspense is terrible! I hope it'll last."

It's a silent prank war. We don't discuss it, don't acknowledge it. Our unspoken rules are to never interfere with the specimens and samples, and don't let Dr. Gantt find out. We're sticking with unobtrusive tricks. The parameters make thinking of ideas all the more exhilarating.

I'm still shocked Molly decided to prank me in the first place. I could tell the idea made her uneasy. She's been clear that she doesn't tolerate nonsense at work. That day, as I tried to put on what I thought was *my* lab coat and quickly realized what was happening, an emotion bubbled up inside of me that I can only describe as giddiness. Excitement was mixed in there, too. Was straitlaced Molly Delaney loosening up for *me*?

Post-lunch, I feel confident that today is not the day for Molly's next prank, which is why I don't think twice when Molly calls me over to her workbench as soon as I walk into the lab, before I even have a chance to finish putting on my safety goggles.

"Can you please check this specimen?" She gestures at the microscope. "I need a second opinion. Does this look like residue from pesticides?"

She's asking me for help! I must be making progress if she's willing to ask my opinion.

Feeling smug, I sit on a nearby stool and peer into the microscope at the specimen.

I straighten and look at Molly. "No, it looks clean to me."

Molly smiles ... or actually, she looks like she's trying to hold back a smile. "Ah, cool. Thanks."

Wait a minute. Molly's being too nice to me. She hasn't insulted me once since I walked over here.

Her lips clamp together as her face turns red.

I narrow my eyes. "What did you do?"

She shrugs and turns away, her shoulders shaking. She's laughing. Something is definitely going on.

I bend close to the microscope again and study it. I run a fingertip along the eyepiece, and it comes away smudged with some sort of dark, creamy substance. I groan. I pull out my phone and open the camera, flipping it into selfie mode to use like a mirror. Yep. There are black rings around my eyes.

Molly turns back around, her fist pressed against her mouth. "You've got ... you've got some gunk on your face, there, Dr. Stanch."

"What *is* this stuff?" It's gloopy and soft and smells vaguely of ... coconut?

"I'm sure *I* don't know. Looking at it for the first time, which is what I'm doing now, it looks like it could be lip balm mixed with charcoal powder."

No longer bothering to hide her mirth, Molly is outright beaming now. It's a glorious sight. So much so that I'm mesmerized and not remotely prepared when she lifts a paper towel to my face. I hadn't noticed it sitting on the lab table.

"I'm sure it will come right off. Let's see..."

Molly places one hand on my shoulder to stabilize herself, then gently dabs around my eyes with the damp towel. She leans close as she focuses on her work—so close that she's standing between my knees where my legs extend off the stool, so close I can feel her breath on my nose. It smells like spearmint. The tip of her pink tongue peeks out from between her lips as she concentrates on cleaning my face.

With every delicate swipe, the tightness in my throat grows. She puts more pressure on my shoulder with her fingers, and the hair on the back of my neck rises, my skin heating despite the layers of clothing that separate it from her touch.

I want to raise my arms from where they're currently immobilized on my lap and grip her hips. I want to bring my knees together, containing her against me. I want to tilt my head and slant my lips closer to hers. I want to kiss her.

I don't do it.

Primarily because she's given no indication she'd welcome that kind of contact, but also because it would complicate things. We have to keep working together as long as Dr. Gantt says, and my goal is to work harmoniously with Molly, not make things awkward.

When she finishes and steps away, I shiver in the absence of her body heat. I swallow hard and search her face. She looks calm, collected. Seemingly unaffected by our proximity five seconds ago.

"I think I got it all. Good thing whatever that substance is cleans off so easily. Should be easy to remove from the microscope, too."

"Thanks," I croak.

She smirks. "Be more careful next time."

I've got no smart-aleck retort, not even a charming line. I've got nothing. My mind is mush. "Yep," I stutter, standing from the stool so quickly it crashes to the vinyl floor with a thud.

"Sorry," I mumble. I set the chair back upright and back away, needing to create distance.

My attraction to Molly is evolving into a full-fledged crush faster than I care to admit. I need to nip this in the bud, which is a challenge considering the amount of time Dr. Gantt is forcing us together.

I lay low for a while. No pranks. No excuses to tease Molly or spend time with her.

Instead, I busy myself with pick-up basketball games with a few guys down at the rec center and mastering the All-American level in my *NCAA Football* video game.

My dad calls one night while I'm relaxing at home playing *NCAA*. I'm tempted to let it go to voicemail or even answer while I continue my team's run to the national title game. Instead, I pause the game. Ever since he officially broke the news to me that he and Sharon are getting married, I've been trying to be more supportive.

"Are you coming home for Christmas this year?" he asks.

"I'm not sure yet. Maybe." I have no plans to go to Ohio for Christmas. As much as I'd like to see Tamara and the girls, I don't know that I can keep up the veneer of support in such close quarters with my dad and Sharon for so many days.

"We'd really love for you to try. Sharon and I thought it would be a good time for the wedding, small of course, if everyone is around for Christmas already anyway."

Grateful not to be on a video call, I drop my head back against the couch cushion and squeeze my eyes shut. They're planning the wedding already?

I sigh. "I don't know, Dad. I'll see what I can do. I might have to work."

The line is quiet. "Jonny…"

"I'll try, Dad. Okay?"

I hear a heavy sigh on the other end of the call. "Okay. Thanks, Jonny."

"Talk to you later, Dad."

"Bye, kid. I love you."

"Yep," I say and end the call.

I groan, hot pokers of guilt piercing my chest. I'm thirty years old. When am I going to stop feeling and acting like a sulky teenager whenever I talk to my dad? The divorce was almost twenty years ago, but I still can't help reliving those painful days after Mom left. Can't help the grudge that grew and festered after I realized our family breaking apart was his fault; he wasn't supportive enough of his wife's career. Now he wants a new wife, when he already failed to be the husband my mother needed.

It was an indelible lesson for me. Someday when I meet the right woman and become part of her life, I'll become part of her *whole* life. Her career will be as important to me as my own, maybe even more important. I recognize how much women have had to sacrifice historically to get ahead in their work. I watched it play out with my own mother.

My mind drifts to Molly. Like my mother, Molly is a woman who knows what she wants out of her career. I admire that about her. I appreciate her intelligence, her ambition. Her quick wit. Her eyes the color of the Mediterranean Sea...

I shake my head to dislodge the thoughts. *You're supposed to stymie your crush, not feed into it*, I scold myself. Either way, I can't lay low much longer. We have to go out again and collect samples at the various sites we're tracking.

Two days later, Molly and I are back in the field. As promised, I give her ample warning and suggestions for what to wear and bring. She has her own waders now that fit properly. The day goes smoothly, but I hold back. I'm not sure how to act around her. My normal behavior with anyone is sunny and flirty, but I can't flirt with Molly because I actually mean it, which is concerning given how often she scowls at me.

As the day goes on, her frowns transition into worried looks. In the truck on the way to our final sample site of the day, she turns to me abruptly and asks, "Are you okay?"

I shift my eyes to her briefly before focusing back on the road. Her hair isn't wet today, yet somehow the lavender scent is back, permeating the cab of my truck again. Though I'm not looking at her, I can't forget she's here, and it makes me feel fidgety in a way I can't explain. "Yeah, I'm fine."

She wrings her hands. "You've just been so ... serious today. Businesslike."

"Whereas normally I'm flippant and unprofessional?"

"Well ... yes."

That's fair. In actively trying not to act weird around Molly, I'm apparently acting even weirder than if I just acted normal. Or something like that.

"And the ... issue ... you had with the microscope was more than a week ago," she continues.

My lips curve into a smile. Seems Molly is as invested in this prank war now as I am. She *is* the one who started it. "You feeling a little tense, Molly Rancher? A little on edge, perhaps?"

Her mouth drops open. "Is *that* your plan? Drive me crazy with anticipation?"

I pull up to a stop sign and use the pause as an excuse to study her face. My eyes linger on her lips, pink and glossy from her SPF 30 lip balm. I wonder if it's flavored. As if she can read my mind, Molly's tongue darts out of her mouth, licking her upper lip. I suppress a groan. Who's driving who crazy with anticipation, exactly?

I turn my head back to the road in front of us, flipping on the blinker and turning the wheel to the right.

"You'll just have to wait and see," I rumble.

I get to the office early the next day. I want to be there before Molly. She told me yesterday that the deadline's looming for the third-quarter report she has to write about the team's research findings. I'm counting on her working on it today, so I make a small adjustment to her word processor.

Then, I wait. I stay at my cubicle, so I make sure I see when Molly arrives. When she does, I watch as she puts her lunch away in the breakroom refrigerator and settles in at her desk. From where I sit, I can't see her computer screen, so I'm not sure if she's working on the report yet.

She must sense my eyes on her because she lifts her head and catches me. She glares and I duck my head. Okay, clearly, I can't sit here staring at Molly all day to see her reaction to my prank, or for ... other reasons.

Instead, I head into the lab and busy myself testing the water samples we collected yesterday. I find a quiet workbench in the corner, but there aren't many people in the lab today anyway.

It's not long before Molly finds me, a single piece of paper pinched between her fingers. Her other hand rests on her hip, her head is tilted, and she has an amused scowl on her face.

"Hey," I greet her.

She holds up the paper and points to the title in bold at the top. "Do you have any idea why I'm writing a report called 'Determinants of Harmful Orlando Bloom in the Waterways of Southern Louisiana'?"

I grin. "No, but that sounds fascinating. How does one even test for determinants of 'harmful Orlando Bloom' in the waterways?"

"Yeah. Funny thing. Whenever I type 'algal bloom', which I do at least ten times per page, the computer automatically changes it to 'Orlando Bloom.' Why do you think that is?"

I hold a hand to my chest. "I'm sure I have no idea. There's probably an autocorrect setting in your word processor."

She raises her eyebrows. "I wonder how that could have happened?"

"Computer goblins, maybe."

A hint of a smile creeps across her face. "I heard there's been an increase in computer goblin attacks this year."

I nod seriously. "Yeah. It's becoming a real problem."

Her lips twitch. *Come on*, I think, *just a little more and it'll be a real smile*. "Do you know how to fix it, or should I call IT?" she asks.

I smirk. "You need my help, huh?"

She frowns. Oof. I guess that was the wrong thing for me to say. "No. I don't *need* your help," she responds airily.

"Come on, Molly Parton," I urge. "Let me help."

"I can figure it out on my own."

"I have no doubt. But if you let me help, you won't have to."

She grimaces but seems to be considering it. I can't help but wonder if she's hesitant because it's help from me, specifically, or because she's used to doing things on her own. Does she have anyone in her life that helps keep the weight off her shoulders? Is she open to applicants?

Before I think better of it, I reach out my hand and tuck a lock of her caramel brown hair behind her ear. My fingers linger, brushing over her jawline. "Please, Molly," I murmur. "Let me help you."

She's anchored in place, her eyes fixed on mine. She leans slightly into my hand, as if she doesn't realize she's doing it.

"Okay," she whispers, quickly turning away and breaking contact. But not before I see the shy, pleased smile on her lips.

There it is.

Chapter Seven

Jonathan

Molly and I have been working together for about a month now, and it's time to ramp up the fieldwork. Today, we're going out on the boat. We'll pull some water samples from the Gulf and pick up one of our gliders that has finished its mission. Ocean gliders are autonomous underwater vehicles about six feet long that look like torpedoes from old war movies. They collect and transmit ocean data like temperature, salinity, pressure, and pH.

The dry dock where the university stores our boats and other equipment is in Slidell, close to the Rigolets, which is a strait connecting Lake Pontchartrain to the Gulf. It's about a forty-five-minute drive from the lab. I expect Molly to be nervous—again, the word is that she's afraid of boats—but she looks relaxed in the passenger seat of my truck as we roll up US-90. If anyone's acting nervous, it's me.

We'll be out on the boat all day, just me and Molly. The sea air, the salt spray, the warm early-September sunshine—and the gorgeous coworker who *still* seems to hate me. And because I'm an idiot and apparently a masochist, I suggested she wear a bathing suit under her board shorts and long-sleeve UPF shirt. Yes, it's the practical thing to do. We're going to be on a boat, and we're going to get at least a little wet. But seeing Molly in a bathing suit is the last thing I need when I'm still trying to tamp out this crush before it gets out of hand.

Fortunately, I'm all business on the boat, especially with a newbie onboard with me. When we get to the marina, I focus on introducing Molly to our research vessel. *The Ocean Pulse*, as she's been dubbed, is not a sleek and comfortable leisure boat. She's a dull gray aluminum, practical and fully equipped with the research tools we need. And expensive—forty feet of Class 3 research operations that we are responsible for bringing back to shore safely.

If Molly is afraid of boats, I don't want to freak her out more, but she does need to be aware of the basics of boat safety. As soon as we're on the *Pulse*, I point out where the life jackets, throw ropes, and flares are kept and walk her through emergency procedures.

Again, though, Molly isn't acting like she's worried about being out on the boat at all. In fact, she's in the best mood I've ever seen from her. She's smiling and teasing, asking questions about the *Pulse* and the instruments aboard.

"Remind me," she says, "which is port, and which is starboard? And isn't there an aft, too? Which way is that?"

"Starboard is right. Port is left. Aft is the back of the boat, and forward is the front of the boat."

Her eyes twinkle. They actually freaking twinkle. I didn't know Molly Delaney's eyes *could* twinkle, but I'm seeing it for myself right now. It's captivating.

"Will I get to drive?" she asks.

I frown. "It's 'pilot,' not 'drive,' but yeah, I could teach you." I run my hands through my hair and tilt my head to study Molly's face. She doesn't look scared at all.

"Are you always this serious on the boat? I thought you said work should be fun." And she giggles. Freaking giggles. If Molly with twinkling eyes caught me off guard, Molly giggling blows me completely away. It magnifies her cuteness factor by about one thousand. Not enough to knock me off course, though.

I narrow my eyes, suspicious of where she's going with this. "Hey," I say in my most austere voice, "No pranks on the boat, Molly. It's too dangerous."

Molly stares at me with wide, innocent eyes. "Pranks?" she asks. "I'm not sure what you mean."

I stoop until our eyes are level. "No. Pranks. On. The. Boat. Clear?"

Her pupils dilate, her eyes a dark island ringed with pools of cool blue.

"Clear," she says, her voice husky. She clears her throat and takes a step back.

I blink. What just happened? If I didn't know better, I would think Molly felt attracted to me just then. What a weird, exhilarating day. Her eyes are twinkling, she's giggling, and she's acting like she's attracted to me. Plus, she doesn't seem at all worried about being out on the boat today.

I scratch the scruff along my jawline. "Molly, are you okay? Everyone says ... I mean, I think ... Look, the talk around the lab is that you're afraid of boats. That's why you never want to do fieldwork."

Molly's eyes widen, and her cheeks turn red as she ducks her head. When she looks at me again, her apathetic mask is back in place.

"Don't worry about it," she snaps. "Mind your own business."

Ohh-kay. I guess I'm minding my own business, then.

I walk her through the rest of the launch checklist. We have plenty of fuel, the anchor looks good, the radio is working. The weather is supposed to be clear and dry today, so we don't need to worry about that.

I plug the coordinates of the glider into the navigation system, do a final check, and then we're off. We motor slowly through the Rigolets and under the railroad bridge into Lake Borgne.

I slow the boat and anchor. We need to collect a water sample from the lake before we venture out to the Gulf. The process of collecting the sample works differently out here than when we were wading in the bayous because we need to get water samples from several different water depths.

I call Molly over and demonstrate how to use the equipment that will help us do that without cross contamination. Then, I let her take the lead on pulling samples from the other depths we need. Of course, she's a natural. She even reminds me we need a surface sample, too. That's one we can just scoop out of the water with a sample bottle without using the specialized equipment. The freeboard—or distance between the waterline and deck—for the *Pulse* is about four feet, except in the back where the swim platform sits right on top of the waves for easy access to the water from the boat and vice versa.

As we work, the boat bobs on the waves, and though I'm sure Molly isn't used to it, the motion doesn't faze her. *Why?* Everyone believes she's afraid of being out on the boat for fieldwork. She hasn't seemed afraid or even hesitant at all so far. She seems to be loving it, actually. But when I asked her about it, she lashed out.

I watch her as she zips the sample bags closed. My curiosity is building. I must be missing some of the puzzle pieces here because the ones I have are *not* fitting together to create any kind of whole.

"All set," Molly says, her head still down as she cleans up the equipment. When she lifts her gaze, she's smiling, at least until she catches me staring. The smile turns into a scowl.

I blink and refocus on the task at hand. Piloting the boat. Right. That's what I'm supposed to be doing. I take my place at the helm and resume our trek toward the glider's coordinates.

Molly inches closer to me at the wheel. The cockpit is enclosed but the slide windows are open. It's noisy with the engine roaring and the wind whooshing past us, so I can't quite hear her when she shouts.

"What?" I gesture to my ears and shake my head.

She leans closer, the hair on the top of her head tickling my jawline until she tilts her chin up so that her mouth is just below my ear. My body tenses at her nearness, yet I lean closer.

"How do we know where to go to get the glider?" she asks.

I'm still stuck on her proximity; it takes my brain longer than normal to process the question and shout out an intelligible answer. "When it finishes its mission, it surfaces automatically and sends its coordinates." I point to the GPS screen embedded in the console. "I enter the coordinates, and the GPS creates a waypoint."

She nods thoughtfully at the screen. The wind whips her hair so it's flowing behind her, dancing along with the peaks and valleys of the moving air. I guess she didn't bring a hair tie on this expedition either. When a strand blows across her face, she flicks it away impatiently.

"How long will it take to get there?"

I study the GPS screen. "About another hour, maybe. We've got to go past Grand Island and through the Chandeleur Sound. The glider's out in the Gulf."

With this information, I think she'll go sit on the bench seat or even below deck. There's nothing fancy down there, but it would be an ideal place to hide away for someone uncomfortable on boats. Instead, she pushes up on her tiptoes to sit in the captain's chair directly behind where I'm standing at the wheel. She's not touching any part of me, but I feel her behind me, and it's extremely distracting.

I slow the *Pulse*, and the noise from the engine and wind slow with her. I turn my head. "Do you want to learn to pilot the boat?"

Molly's instantly back on her feet. "Can I?" she asks.

I shrug. The water is calm today; our navigation is set. Piloting at this point is really just a matter of steering to keep us aligned with the GPS waypoint. "Sure. It's not hard." Molly frowns at my words, so I rush to add, "And even if it was, you'd catch on in no time."

"That's right; I would," she mutters.

I bite my lip to keep from smiling. I lift one hand off the steering wheel and use it to nudge Molly in front of me. Her back is aligned with my chest, not touching, but close enough that my heart rate jumps up, and I'm sure she can hear it pounding in my chest. I grasp her hand and, ignoring the tingling on my skin as my nervous system goes haywire, guide it to the throttle.

"This is called the throttle," I explain, my hand covering hers. "You push it forward to go faster and pull it toward you to slow down. If you like your speed, you don't have to touch it." I move her hand to the steering wheel, and she lifts her other hand to the wheel, too. "This is the steering wheel. If you know how to steer a car, you've already got this down, except the wheel is bigger. No tricks to it; you turn the wheel right to go right and left to go left." I bracket my hands on either side of hers. "You just want to keep us following the course marked out on the GPS screen. See?" I point to the route laid out in front of us.

Molly tips her head back to look at me, her hair once again tickling my chin. "That's it?" she asks.

I nod. "You have to watch for currents. They can make it harder to steer."

She chews her bottom lip and stares up at me through her eyelashes. "Maybe you better keep your hands on the wheel, too, for now. In case we run into a current."

She turns forward again, and as she does, she leans her shoulders back into my chest. I stop breathing, stop moving, stop anything that could disrupt the status quo. I grip the steering wheel as Molly pushes the throttle forward bit by bit to increase our speed. The wind picks up again and her hair goes wild, strands flittering into my mouth, sticking to my lips.

Can't breathe. Erratic heartbeat. I could collapse right here on this deck and die a happy man.

Molly reaches up to smooth her hair. When her fingers hit my chin, her head snaps back. "Oh my gosh, I'm so sorry!" Her cheeks turn pink. "You can take the wheel."

She lets go of the steering wheel and quickly ducks under my arm to stand to the side. She combs her fingers through her hair and holds it against the back of her head in a fist. "I forgot to bring a hair tie," she explains. "I didn't realize it was hitting you in the face."

I find my voice. "It's no problem." Highlight of my week, actually.

Her face is still flushed, so I shift my focus to the water in front of us and the route highlighted on the GPS screen. In my peripheral vision, I see her hesitate in front of the door leading below deck. Then she disappears down the stairs.

Guess piloting lessons are over.

Chapter Eight

Molly

This is bliss, I think as I sit near the front of the boat. The wind blowing through my hair, the sea spray hitting my face, the sun warming my skin. We've slowed down as we get closer to our destination. I've felt so settled today out here on the boat. Everything about this trip has been appealing and stimulating to my senses and my mind, sometimes perhaps a little too much.

The proximity to Jonathan feels both intoxicating and dangerous. I'm leaning into the weighted, charged moments between us instead of shutting them down like I normally would. Being attracted to my archnemesis is an inconvenient problem to have, especially when he's really not a bad guy. Especially when I have no room in my life or routine for relationships of any kind other than my family. Hating him is safer.

I close my eyes and focus on the sensations of being out on the water. My breathing slows and a content, closed-mouth smile creeps across my face.

"See," Jonathan shouts from the steering wheel, "it's not so bad."

I quickly school my features. "No, it's fine," I say as Jonathan kills the engine.

He grins. "We're here. The glider's just off the starboard side."

I stand, trying to remember which side is starboard. The right? I cross the deck and peer over the right edge of the boat. Bright yellow, the glider is easy to spot in the water. Because I haven't done fieldwork since starting on Dr. Gantt's team, I haven't seen a glider up close. I work with the data they collect all the time—it's a primary part of my job in the office.

The technology fascinates me. These self-contained vessels use an internal pump to change buoyancy, allowing them to move up and down in the water. They have propellers and an internal compass that help them move slowly on a pre-set course, and all the while, they collect data about the water and transmit the data back to shore in real time.

"How long has this one been out?" I ask, tossing a glance over my shoulder at Jonathan.

"Two months."

"What was its mission?"

"Recording pH levels, water temperatures, and oxygen levels, among other things, at varying depths out here in the Gulf."

I frown, thinking back over the datasets I've been working with in the office. "This is glider four?" Jonathan nods his confirmation.

"The pH has increased slightly over the last few weeks, especially closer to the surface, but not anywhere near dangerous levels."

Jonathan rubs his chin. "That makes sense. Pesticide runoff from the Mississippi would be higher right now as the growing season comes to an end."

I pause. I consider telling him my hypothesis about the effect of storms on the water temperature and pH levels, but it's been a slow hurricane season, thankfully, and we haven't had much impact. A couple of storms in the Gulf skirted up the coast of Florida, but none have come close enough to New Orleans that our data would be affected.

Besides, I'm not sure I can really trust him. I've had so many male colleagues over the years who belittle my ideas or even try to take credit for them. It's best to keep my data model close to the vest until I know more about the findings.

"Water temperatures have stayed about the same since summer even though the water should have started cooling off already," I add instead. My eyes are drawn back to the glider bobbing in the water. It's as long as Jonathan is tall. I turn to face him. "How do we get it in the boat?"

Jonathan smiles. "It weighs about 140 pounds, but between the two of us, it won't be hard to pull it in."

I watch as he reaches a long pole with a hook on the end into the water and secures it through a handle on one end of the glider. Using the pole, he guides the glider through the water to the platform at the back of the boat.

He snaps open the gate and motions me over. "We can pull it in here, so we don't have to lift it as high."

One thing I reluctantly appreciate about working with Jonathan is that he doesn't overexplain. He demonstrates the processes we need to follow, gives some commentary, but assumes I'm competent enough to connect the dots. I've worked with a lot of men in this field, and I'm sorry to say that most of them get a little too much pleasure from mansplaining concepts that I understand better than they do.

But not Jonathan. Like now, he positions himself on the edge of the platform to get behind the glider, and without conversation, I take my place near the front to pull. We don't need to spell it out or belabor the process. We understand each other.

With just a little lifting, we easily slide the glider aboard. Jonathan is still kneeling at the edge of the platform, so I mimic his position to get a better look at the autonomous vehicle. The outside is sleek for better hydrodynamics, with the moving parts and scientific instruments safely stored inside the fiberglass hull.

"What happens to a glider when there's bad weather?" I ask.

Jonathan keeps his eyes on the glider as he inspects it for damage. "During some of the summer storms we had gliders that went dark for an hour or two. When the storm passed, they surfaced and were able to transmit the missing data, along with their location; they were off course. They adjusted though and were able to course correct on their own." He looks up at me, his eyes bright. "If the water's rough enough or if it's in shallow water with rocks or other obstacles, a glider could get damaged, but we haven't had that happen to any in our fleet."

I absorb this information, adding it to what I already know about the gliders and the rows of data they transmit that end up on my computer. Jonathan finishes his inspection and stands, his board shorts and long-sleeve sun-protection shirt splotched with dark spots where water splashed onto him while we were hauling in the glider. Fat droplets roll down his legs and drip onto his bare feet.

I smirk. "Looks like you got a little wet there, Dr. Stanch."

He looks down at his clothes and grins. "You call this wet? Nah, this isn't wet at all."

He grabs the hem of his shirt with one hand, and before I know what's happening, his shirt hits the deck as he plunges into the water behind him.

My mouth drops open as I wait for him to resurface. He bursts back up in a fountain of white spume and sparkling water, his bare chest shimmering in the sunlight before it dips back below the surface. Not before I ogle the firm ridges and planes of said chest and suddenly find my mouth dry and my brain incoherent.

You know he's attractive, I remind myself. *You've always known that. That's why you keep your distance.*

The logical part of my brain must be on break, though, because I can't tear my eyes away from Jonathan bobbing in the water, his dark curls plastered to his forehead, his broad shoulders glistening, and the green in his hazel eyes electrified against the aquamarine waves.

He turns in the water and starts swimming farther from the boat, tossing me a carefree smile over his shoulder. "Come on, Molly Pop, don't let me have all the fun by myself," he goads.

I feel my lips stretch out in a smile of my own. I try to fight my desire to jump in, but it's a gorgeous sunny day. I'm on a boat surrounded by nothing but sparkling water, and a handsome man just invited me to swim with him. My impulse control is nonexistent in these circumstances. Who could blame me?

I feel Jonathan's eyes on me as I shimmy off my outer layer of clothes and step onto the platform in my black one-piece bathing suit. I don't feel self-conscious, and even less so when I meet his gaze and bask in the raw admiration I see there. How long has it been since I've felt seen like this? How long since I've felt like a desirable woman? Too long, I realize as I remove my glasses and toss them onto my pile of clothes.

I step off the platform, and the ocean rises up around me. I'm suspended, floating weightless underwater. The ocean is cool against my skin—the buoyancy compressing my body and soothing my senses. Gone are the stressors and distractions that constantly overwhelm my system, gone are my regimented schedule and rules, gone is my anxiety over confining myself in the carefully controlled box that allows me to fit in a world not designed for me.

I surface on a laugh, joy bubbling out of me, crowding out any lingering insistence that Jonathan is my archnemesis, at least for now. Out here, I'm free.

I spin around until I'm facing him. He's floating a few feet away, his wide eyes unabashedly fixed on me. He drifts closer. Fighting a grin, I flick my hand across the surface and send a wall of water toward his face. I stick around long enough to see him splutter and laugh before I swim in the opposite direction. My limbs feel light, but my muscles are inefficient and out of practice.

Jonathan catches me easily, hooking an arm around my waist. Smirking, he plants his hands on top of my head and dunks me under. I flap my arms to push the water up and myself down, sinking lower. I grab Jonathan's ankle and pull him under with me. He twists, his hand finding my arm and tugging it toward the surface. We both come up laughing, sucking air into our oxygen-deprived lungs.

I wipe the saltwater from my eyes. We're face-to-face, and I still, my breath slowing. Up close, his eyes are mesmerizing, a ring of brown around his pupils melding seamlessly into the deep green in the outside ring. My hands float up, settling against his chest. I kick my legs in a circle pattern to stay afloat. He moves his hands to my waist, his fingers slipping over the slick Lycra of my bathing suit. My heart is pounding so loud I'm sure he can hear it.

"Molly," he whispers, leaning toward me.

My lips tingle, and I dart my tongue out to lick them. The taste of salt filling my mouth is enough to jolt my logical brain back into place. Before Jonathan can reach me, I duck under the water, flip around, and start swimming toward the boat.

I don't dare look back until I'm sitting safely on the platform. When I do, I catch the last glimmer of disappointment on Jonathan's face before he flicks his head back and forth, spraying droplets from his hair into the water around him and starts toward the boat.

My body's heavy, a combination of my own chagrin and the need to readjust to the effects of gravity after floating weightlessly for so long.

Kissing Jonathan would have been disastrous.

Kissing Jonathan would have been perfection.

I push myself up to stand, walking to the back of the boat to get my towel and spare clothes from my bag. As I towel off, I see Jonathan climb aboard from the corner of my eye. Still shirtless, he pulls the glider farther onto the deck and latches the gate to block off the platform. When he starts heading my way, I quickly climb below deck to change.

Chapter Nine

Molly

When I come back up on deck, Jonathan has his shirt on and is pulling up the anchor. I settle on the bench seat near the helm of the boat to wait.

It takes only a few minutes for Jonathan to finish prepping the boat. When he's done, he comes to the helm.

"We've got a few more samples to collect on our way in," he says, eyes directed at my forehead.

I nod and clear my throat. "Okay."

He fiddles with some switches on the console and presses a red button. I hear a clicking noise.

Jonathan scratches his chin. "Huh." He presses the red button again, and this time, nothing happens at all.

"What's wrong?" I ask.

"Okay, don't freak out—"

I stiffen. "Always a reassuring way to start a sentence—"

"—but the boat won't start."

I stand up, peering at the console as if I can offer a second opinion. "Why not?"

Jonathan shrugs. "I'm not sure. I'd guess a dead battery."

"Like in a car?" I'm not an expert, but my parents made sure my sisters and I know the basics of car maintenance. If my car's battery dies, I have jumper cables in the trunk, and I know how to hook them up to another battery to start mine.

"Sort of."

"Can you jump a boat battery like you do a car?" I look around at the wide expanse of water around us—no other boats in sight.

"Yes, but we'd need a working battery, or at least a portable jump-start kit." Jonathan also looks around us, but all is quiet.

"And we don't have that." He shakes his head. "So, what do we do? Is there such a thing as waterside assistance? Like roadside assistance for boats?"

"There is. I'll call a commercial tow service. If they can't jump-start the battery, they'll pull us in."

He uses the radio on the boat to make the call and then leans against the railing across from me. They said it would take at least thirty minutes to get a boat to our location.

I hold my body still, feeling awkward and tense about our almost-kiss in the water. Jonathan, always assessing, always watching, must notice my body language because he tries to reassure me. "Hey, we'll be fine. The towboat will be out to us soon enough. We're perfectly safe out here until then."

So, he noticed my unease but misunderstood its cause. I'm not overly concerned about the boat not starting. It's still early afternoon, the sky is cloudless, and we have plenty of food and water on board. I *am* anxious about the fact that I got so distracted by the fun of being out on the water I lost focus on the work we're here to do and almost kissed my coworker slash archnemesis. Very typical of how my brain wants to work and exactly the kind of circumstance I try to avoid by sticking to my regimented schedule and rules.

Jonathan continues. "I don't know why someone afraid of the water would become a coastal environmental scientist," he grumbles. It isn't a question, more like a wondering into the void. For once, he's not even looking at me. It may be that apparent lack of attention that makes me feel safe enough to tell the truth.

"I'm not afraid," I murmur.

"What?" Jonathan, flustered, steps closer.

I clear my throat to speak louder, stronger. "I love boats. I love the water. I'm not afraid."

I watch as emotions register and then disappear across his face—surprise, a little bit of annoyance, settling on confusion.

"Then why—," he starts. He's standing above me now, looking down with the same glint in his eye that I see in the lab when he's determined to figure out a puzzling compound. "Why do you avoid fieldwork?"

I sigh. "The lab is a controlled environment. It's predictable. Out here," I motion to the expanse of water surrounding us, "anything can happen."

He drops into the seat next to me. "That's what's so incredible about it."

"Yes," I agree. "Incredible, but dangerous. Distracting."

His lips pinch together. "I don't understand."

I puff out a breath. "Actually, I suppose it is fear that keeps me in the lab," I admit. "But not fear of the water. Fear of failing."

I'm not sure what he sees on my face, but he says nothing, waiting for me to continue. I sit taller, shoring myself up.

"I have ADHD," I say. Jonathan peers at me, his intense expression unreadable, so I shift my gaze out to the sea before I continue. "When I was in high school, my parents did a lot to help me manage it. But when I started college, I wanted to do it on my own."

But I didn't manage it well. I was excited to be away at school; I was meeting new people and experiencing new things. My attention was divided into a million different directions and my schoolwork suffered. "I was lucky to get a C average that first semester, even with my accommodations. You have to understand that I'd always been a straight-A student, always told how smart I was." It was a huge blow and an even bigger wake up call. "I knew I had to find a way to stay focused on my top priority: school."

To make matters worse, when I buckled down the next semester, my new "friends" didn't understand. When I stopped participating in their version of fun, they told me I was "too much" and cut me out of their social group. It was a difficult time for me, and I didn't really have anyone to talk to about it. I was too ashamed to tell my parents. My sisters were young—Nicole was in high school, but she was dealing with her own stuff.

"I realized that to have the kind of success I wanted, I needed to cut out distractions. I became all about my classes, and later, my work," I finish.

I close my eyes and take a breath before turning toward Jonathan again. His eyebrows are furrowed, his lips pinched. His eyes don't hold the condescension, or even pity, I expect to see, instead they shine with something softer, and it caresses my heart.

"Thank you for sharing that with me," he starts, and I can tell he's choosing his words carefully. "I can't imagine what that was like for you." He hesitates for just a moment before rushing on. "But it's okay to focus on something besides work sometimes. It's okay to have more balance in your life. I mean," he chuckles, "you're brilliant. Anyone can see that. No one would think less of you if you took weekends for yourself once in a while."

I bristle. I know there were compliments in there somewhere, but all I hear are the attacks: obsessive, workaholic. He doesn't understand.

I defend myself coldly. "You're one to talk. I see you at the lab more Saturday nights than not."

He opens his mouth as if to retort but then snaps it shut again. We sit silently, the boat bobbing up and down with the rhythm of the waves.

"I didn't mean to upset you," he finally says. "I just don't want you to deprive yourself of living a full life, of being authentic to yourself, because of fear. Or deprive others of getting to know you, the real you."

I study his face. "Why do you care?"

His ears turn red. "I ... care ..." He trails off, his discomfort assaulting my own nervous system like strong cologne.

I tilt my head. "Why?" I ask again, my voice hardly audible over the sea breeze.

Jonathan leans closer, his mouth opening to say the words I can see, but can't discern, spinning in his eyes. His gaze shifts to something over my shoulder and when his words finally come out, all they say is, "The towboat is here."

Chapter Ten

Jonathan

To sum up my day of fieldwork yesterday on the boat with Molly:

One: I almost kissed her.

Two: She almost let me kiss her but didn't.

Three: She told me something personal and vulnerable, which is actually better than a kiss.

Four: She got kind of mad about my response to her personal sharing, which isn't great. I have an idea to make it up to her. Technically it's her turn to play a prank on me, but what I have planned isn't *really* a prank.

I arrive at the lab early, well before anyone else will be there. I need a couple of trips out to my truck to bring everything in. I'm pleased to find that my estimations were correct that the surface of Molly's cubicle desk can fit five large vases. I fill each vase about half full with water and add little packets of flower food. Then come the lilies. I bought dozens of them—close to a hundred. Lilies are supposed to symbolize humility, sincerity, and adoration, a perfect choice to say *I'm sorry*, and also kind of hint that I'd like to be more than coworkers and more than friends.

I'm embracing my crush now. The biggest obstacle before was that Molly seemed to hate me. After yesterday on the boat and in the water, I no longer believe that to be true. The attraction is there, for sure. I'm pretty sure she feels the same pull that I do. Given what she shared about needing to be laser-focused on her work, I'd guess that dating falls into the "distraction" category. Ergo, she's fighting her attraction to me because she thinks I'll be a distraction.

I fully intend to be a distraction to Molly Delaney. I also intend to show her that she can do well at work *and* have a life outside it. Not because I think I know what she needs better than she does, but because she's too afraid to even try.

I arrange the lilies in the vases myself. When I finish, Molly's desk is covered in vases filled with beautiful pink-and-white stargazer lilies. It's quite a spectacle. As a finishing touch, I add a note to the vase closest to her desk chair. I write simply, *From your secret admirer*.

When I finish arranging everything, I leave. I head to the parking lot, get in my truck, and buy myself some breakfast down the street. I don't come back until I know most of our coworkers will be there.

When I arrive at work for the second time today, a current of excitement reverberates through the lab.

I hide a grin as I walk to my cubicle. "What's going on?" I ask one of the grad assistants.

"Dr. Delaney got a flower delivery! Huge vases covering her desk."

I play dumb. "Oh? Who from? Does she have a boyfriend?"

The grad assistant claps her hands with glee. "I don't think so. The card says they're from a secret admirer!"

I raise my eyebrows. "Wow. Lucky her. What a mystery."

She sighs dreamily. "Yeah, it's so romantic!"

I barely contain my laughter as I hazard a glance toward Molly's cubicle. A small crowd of women surround her desk, Molly standing in the middle. I can't see her face, so I don't know yet if my plan is a massive success or a dismal failure.

One woman shifts to the right, revealing Molly's face. She's smiling. She's clasping her hands in front of her, and the corners of her eyes look pinched, but she's smiling. She lifts her head and catches sight of me. She shakes her head slowly as if to say, *I can't believe you did this*. I wink in response, and she blushes. Her smile turns shy, and she bites her lip.

My body feels so weightless I'm almost floating. As much as Molly's scowls lure me in, her smiles will keep me hooked. No question.

Dr. Gantt comes out of her office and claps her hands while walking toward Molly. "Okay, everyone. Exciting morning, but let's get to work."

The crowd disperses, some to cubicles and others to the lab. I'm still rooted next to my cubicle, so when Dr. Gantt finishes admiring the flowers and turns her head, her perceptive eyes are aimed directly at me.

She purses her lips and raises her eyebrows. I suddenly feel like I'm five years old and just got caught with frosting-smudged lips after the last cupcake went missing at my sister's birthday party. I swipe at my mouth and duck into my desk chair.

The morning is busy. I process the water samples we took out in the Gulf yesterday and make plans for Glider Four's next mission. Molly's working on her own stuff, so we don't interact.

At lunch, I step outside for some fresh air. Because I'm so often in the field, the days I'm in the lab can feel stifling. Getting outside during my breaks helps refresh my brain. Around the back of the building is a small grassy alcove with a bench right in the shade. It's my respite on lab days, and it's where I'm heading now.

I sit on the bench just as Molly comes around the corner of the building.

"Hey!" I call, my surprise evident in the lilt of my voice.

Molly does a half wave. "I didn't know this was back here."

A grin takes over my face. "Did you follow me?"

Instead of answering, Molly says, "I have an embarrassingly obnoxious display of flowers on my desk."

My smile widens as I scoot over and gesture for her to join me on the bench. "Do you now?"

"Yep." She sits, farther away from me than I would prefer, but closer than I would have expected. She tilts her face toward me, and I study her expression. She's not mad. She's holding back a smile—I see it dancing in her eyes. A feeling of triumph moves into my chest. She likes the flowers! I did something right!

"Huh. How about that."

She shakes her head. "Nothing else to say?"

Emboldened, I stretch my arm across the back of the bench. It doesn't quite touch her shoulders until she leans back. The contact creates a buzz that travels up my arm and right out of my mouth.

"I have three things to say, actually. First, I'm sorry. Second, you're welcome. And third..." I pause here, making sure her eyes are on mine. "I had a really great time with you yesterday."

"Working? You had a great time working with me?"

"And playing." I shrug. "We did both, right?"

She nods thoughtfully. "We did. What are you sorry for?"

My smile falls, and my shoulders tense. "I don't like the way I reacted to you sharing about your ADHD. It's none of my business how you manage your life. I shouldn't have acted like I know better than you how your own brain works. I'm sorry."

Molly looks stunned. "Apology accepted."

My shoulders relax. "Thanks. I can be a little ... relentless once I've made up my mind about something." I laugh. "Just ask my sister."

Molly smiles. "What did you do to your sister?"

"Well, it's not so much what I did to her as what she's witnessed over the years. When I was a kid, I watched the movie *Twister* and became obsessed. I knew then and there that I wanted to be a scientist, but, like, a cool scientist like Bill and Jo. I like water more than weather, though, so that set my course. You can see how it worked out. I still consider *Twister* my favorite movie."

"My favorite movie is from my childhood, too. *Anne of Green Gables*. The Canadian version from the eighties."

I shake my head. "I haven't heard of that one."

Molly puffs out a breath. "Really? It's so good."

"I'll have to watch it sometime."

"Yeah, right." She nudges me with her elbow. "Probably not your thing."

We'll see about that. "You don't know anything about what might or might not be my thing."

"Except action movies, hot wings, playing pranks, boats, swimming, root beer, folk rock, and…" She gives me a knowing look. "…avoiding phone calls from your father."

Something in my chest loosens, warmth radiating through me. She noticed all those things about me? My body craves more points of contact with hers. I reach my arm forward and tug gently on a strand of hair that has escaped from her ponytail. "Show-off."

Suddenly, Molly gasps. "I know who you remind me of! Gilbert Blythe."

"Gilbert…?" I repeat blankly.

"Gilbert Blythe," she reiterates, "from *Anne of Green Gables*. Ooh, I bet if I had red hair, you would call me Carrots, too."

I have absolutely no idea what she's talking about, but her half-scowl, half-smile is everything. I shrug. "Okay."

She shakes her head. "Anyway, I need to get back to work." She stands, and I immediately mourn the loss of her body heat on my arm. She hesitates before turning to walk away. "Jonathan?" she says, her voice soft.

I meet her eyes. "Yeah?"

"Thank you for the flowers. They're beautiful."

Her expression is serene—her eyelids languid, her cheeks the same pink as her lips. *Not as beautiful as you*, I think. What I say is, "You're welcome."

I google Gilbert Blythe later, and yeah, I see the resemblance. I also see that this Gilbert character has quite a few fandoms dedicated to him and his good looks, so I'll take it. That's a win in my book.

That night I'm cleaning up after dinner when my phone rings. It's Tamara.

"Can't you just text me like a normal person?" I ask when I accept the call.

"No. You can hide too much in texts. I need to hear the tone of your voice, so I know what you're thinking."

I grimace. "Creepy, Tams."

"Are you coming home for Christmas?" My sister is not one to beat around the bush.

"I don't know yet." I'm still trying to figure out how to get out of the whole thing. I flop onto the couch with a soft grunt and close my eyes.

I hear her frustrated sigh clearly over the phone. "Dad doesn't want to get married without you."

"Then he shouldn't get married," I mutter.

"Well, he might not if you can't stop being a brat. This isn't about you. This isn't about Mom. Dad and Sharon love each other and want to get married."

I don't say anything. I know Tamara is making sense, and I know I'm acting childish. I'm not sure how to turn it off.

"Jonny," she continues in a gentler tone. "You are sweet and charming and thoughtful and way too personable. You're good at your job and responsible and smart. You are a good man. But you have this emotional block when it comes to Dad. Frankly, you're a jerk to him. He notices, and it breaks his heart."

Guilt constricts my chest like a vise around a tomato. She's right. I know she's right. My sister is always right. "I hear you. Is scolding me the only reason you called?"

"No. Tell me about this woman."

I freeze. "What woman?"

"The coworker you got so flustered about the last time we talked. What's going on with her?"

"Nothing," I answer truthfully, because as much as I wish there was something going on with Molly, she's not there yet.

"Ah ha! So you know exactly who I'm talking about. What's her name? What's your plan?"

"I don't have a plan. It's ... complicated. Molly's my coworker, and she kind of hates me." Actually, I'm not sure how true that last part is anymore.

"But you like Molly?"

Like is probably an understatement. I'm almost obsessed with her, desperate for any chance she might give me. "Yeah, I like her."

Tamara squeals. "Ooh, this is so exciting! It's about time you found someone. You're like one of those creepy old bachelors at this point."

I hold the phone away in front of me and stare at it, shaking my head. Bringing the phone back to my ear, I say, "I'm only thirty, and I've dated plenty, including at least two serious relationships."

"I didn't like either of them."

"You don't know if you like Molly, either. You don't know anything about her."

She hums. "I know she's giving you a hard time, so I like her already."

"Even so, it doesn't bode well for me actually dating her, does it?"

"She'll come around. Like I said, you're a good man." Tamara sounds a lot more confident than I feel, though I appreciate her words. My interaction with Molly today was encouraging, so we'll see.

"Thanks."

"Do you want to tell me about her?"

I clear my throat. "Actually, I do." I grin. "Do you have five hours?"

Chapter Eleven

Molly

It's my turn to prank Jonathan, and my sister Olivia gave me the fun, time-consuming idea to cover his cubicle in sticky notes. Getting up early to stick the notes was not a realistic plan for me—I do recognize my own limitations—so I'm here at the lab late. I wish my ADHD had a control panel because now would be a fantastic time to hyperfocus. Unfortunately, the task is not nearly interesting enough to flip that switch in my brain. Despite the seven different colors of notes I'm using, this is drudgery.

I chuckle as I put up another row in perfect rainbow order. It wasn't easy, but I bought sticky notes in red, orange, yellow, green, blue, indigo, and violet. Finding indigo—a blue-violet hybrid that most resembles a darker blue—was especially challenging. I did it, though, and now I'm ROY G BIVing the heck out of Jonathan's cubicle.

Technically, I should get two pranks in a row now because he did, if you count the flowers as a prank. The fuss everyone in the lab made about them was embarrassing, which makes it more prankish. But they made me feel really ... happy, which makes it more a sweet gesture than anything else. I've never gotten flowers before. I suppose that's a strange admission for a twenty-nine-year-old woman to make, but it's the truth.

I haven't dated much. In high school, I was focused on my schoolwork and was also kind of the weird girl, so I didn't exactly have guys knocking down my door to ask me to the homecoming dance. After my first semester of college—and I wouldn't call what I did in that first semester of college "dating"—I was all about focusing on my classes. I've been that way ever since.

I've also been focused on blending in, masking my ADHD so my classmates and coworkers won't think twice about me or my behavior, won't think I'm too much. *Who, me? Just a typical, normal person like everyone else.*

Jonathan's flowers made everyone see me. I felt special, *not* like everyone else. And it felt good. All of this—the pranks, the goofing off at work, the time out of the lab, the almost kissing a handsome man—feels very much unlike me, at least the me I've curated over the last ten years, and feels very *good*.

Maybe too good? Maybe the kind of good that is self-indulgent and will distract me from my goals. My brain wants instant gratification, new and shiny, constant stimulation, and messy, emotional reactions. I fight against those inclinations every day. Until recently with Jonathan, when I've been giving in, a little here, a little there, convincing myself it doesn't matter. It's a dangerous game.

I shake my head, realizing I've been lost in thought and have stopped putting up sticky notes. I refocus my attention, filling in the last row on the cubicle walls before I move on to the desktop and computer monitor.

Good thing Jonathan's desk is clean and uncluttered, unlike mine. My desk has so many piles of paper and notebooks crammed on top of it that placing sticky notes would be a challenge.

When I finish, I stand in the doorway and admire my work. I grin. It looks amazing. I dig a pen out of my bag and add one last detail. On the backside of a sticky note in the corner, I draw a small heart. Jonathan will probably never even see it, and I don't want him to. I'm not even sure why I'm drawing it. Just another example of giving in to my impulses where Jonathan is concerned.

I'm late for work the next morning, rushing in while balancing my lunchbox, computer bag, and water bottle. I overslept, stumbled through getting ready, and then couldn't remember if I had fed Beaker or not. Considering the way she was yowling at me all morning, I wondered if I had even fed her last night. That's the nice thing about having a cat—they don't let you forget to take care of them. Plus, my mom called as I was driving in to let me know that she and my dad were planning to visit this weekend. I told her I'd have to call her back after work to hear more.

I stop short when I see Jonathan's cubicle. I didn't forget I plastered it with the colors of the rainbow, of course. I just hadn't thought about it this morning, and it is an unmissable blast of color. I instantly perk up, discreetly peering through the doorway to see if Jonathan is here.

He's sitting in his chair, crushing the sticky notes covering the seat, with his laptop—which was not in his cubicle last night—set on top of his sticky-noted desk. He hasn't connected the laptop to the external keyboard or monitor—both covered in sticky notes—but he's busy typing away as if nothing is amiss.

He casually glances up and sees me standing in the doorway of his cubicle. He grins. "Oh, hey, Molly."

"Hey." I look around pointedly. "What happened to your space?"

He scans the cubicle and frowns. "What do you mean?"

Now, I frown. "Jonathan," I warn.

He's trying to keep his expression serious, but I notice the way his eyes are dancing, and the corners of his mouth are twitching. "Molly."

I'm startled by a voice behind me. "Dr. Stanch, what is all this?" asks Dr. Gantt.

Jonathan rubs the back of his neck. "I redecorated," he says, putting an upturned hand out to the side in a *ta-da* gesture.

Dr. Gantt's forehead pinches. "Take it down, please. Let's keep things professional at the lab, shall we?"

"Yes, ma'am," Jonathan responds.

As she turns to leave, Dr. Gantt says over her shoulder, "It's been awfully exciting around here this week, hasn't it?" She levels a look at Jonathan, her eyebrows raised, before walking off in the direction of the lab area.

"Oof," Jonathan says, and I cringe.

"Sorry," I say softly. This prank war is getting out of control. Neither of us were supposed to get in trouble over it.

Jonathan shrugs. "Don't be. This is amazing. And all for me, huh? ROY G BIV and all." He stands and steps closer to me.

Warmth creeps into my cheeks and across my chest. He noticed and recognized the pattern. "Want help cleaning it up?"

He inches closer so we're standing toe to toe. "Nah, but thanks. Go get some work done, Mollapalooza." He smirks, looking down into my face. I tip my head back to see him, my heart pounding. "I've got you."

Despite the time I've spent recently on fieldwork and pranks at work, I finally finished my data model. As I hoped, it shows a correlation between harmful algal blooms and tropical weather systems. That is to say, years with higher tropical activity were also years with water conditions suited for harmful algal blooms to prosper. Of course, as any even mediocre data scientist will tell you, correlation is not causation. The data don't prove that tropical storms and hurricanes contributed to outbreaks of harmful algal blooms. I wish I had real-time data of water conditions *during* a tropical storm or hurricane.

I'm focused on the finer points of my research when my phone rings. It's my mom. I forgot I told her I'd talk to her later today about her and Dad visiting this weekend. I check the time. Somehow, it's already seven in the evening, and I'm still at the lab.

Stretching my back and shoulders from my desk chair, I answer the phone. "Hi, Mom. Sorry I didn't call you back. I got caught up with something at work."

"Hi, honey. No worries. I figured it was something like that." I can hear the smile in her voice even over the phone.

Now that I'm not wrapped up in my work, I realize I'm famished. I didn't plan on being at work late tonight, so I only packed a lunch, which I ate at lunchtime, of course.

"So, you and Dad are coming to New Orleans?" I put my phone on speaker and set it on my desk while I rummage through my bag for a granola bar or *anything* edible.

"Yes! Your father and I both took some time off work, and we're going on a road trip! We'll leave Austin on Thursday and see you in New Orleans this weekend, and then we'll leave New Orleans Monday morning and see your sister in Florida next week."

I chuckle, pulling a pile of receipts from my bag. "Is this because you want to meet Adam, and I just happen to be on the way?"

"Not *only* because we want to meet your sister's boyfriend. They do seem serious, though, and even though Nicole promised she'd bring him home for Thanksgiving this year, we just don't want to wait that long."

I shake my head. Thanksgiving is only a couple of months away, and when my mom says *we*, I'm pretty sure it's mostly her that's impatient to meet Adam. My dad wants to meet him but is probably fine waiting until Thanksgiving.

"But," my mom continues, "we also want to see *you*. You haven't been home since Christmas, Molly, and we miss you."

"I'm coming to Texas for Thanksgiving this year, too, you know."

My mom has started responding when a hand comes down heavy on my shoulder. I yelp and startle halfway out of the chair. I spin to find Jonathan standing behind me, a sheepish look on his face.

"Sorry!" he mouths, taking a step back.

I glare and wave him away while Mom worries on the other end of the phone. "Molly, honey, are you okay? It sounded like you yelled. Where are you? Are you safe?"

My heart is still beating rapidly from the fright. "I'm fine. I'm at the lab and a *coworker*..." I scowl at Jonathan, who's still hovering in my cubicle. "...startled me, that's all."

"Is that your mom?" Jonathan whispers.

I try to shoo him away again, but he's not deterred. Instead, he clears his throat and says, "Mrs. Delaney? Hi, this is the coworker. Sorry to interrupt your call."

The line is silent for so long that I wonder if the call dropped. "Mom?"

"I'm ... here. Molly, will you introduce me to your friend?"

I groan. "Mom, it's just my coworker Jona ... Dr. Stanch. He was just leaving." I glower, hoping Jonathan takes the hint and disappears.

But, of course, he doesn't. He flashes a charming smile toward the phone, even though it's just a voice call, and my mom can't see him. "Jonathan Stanch, Mrs. Delaney. It's nice to meet you."

"Likewise, Jonathan! Where are you from, dear?"

"Originally Ohio, but I've been in Louisiana for a while now. Molly and I were actually in the same cohort for graduate school here at New Orleans State."

"Really? A wonder I've never heard your name before. Wait a minute ... Jonathan, did you say?"

I sigh and close my eyes. I know my mother just made the connection between my coworker talking to her now and the coworker I constantly complain about to my family.

"Yes, ma'am," Jonathan answers. "I'm surprised Molly's never mentioned me." He slides his eyes toward me and smirks. Ugh. He knows, too, that if I have ever talked about him to my mother, it wasn't complimentary.

"Well, maybe in her way, she has. Molly, honey, I'll let the two of you go. I'm sure you have lots of *work* to do," she says slyly.

"No, Mom, it's—"

She cuts me off before I can finish my protest. "I'll text you the details for this weekend. Bye!"

I stare at my phone as she disconnects the call. Just great. Now she's going to think, or hope, there's something going on romantically between me and Jonathan. *Isn't there?* An unhelpful voice inside my head asks. *Of course not*, I argue back.

"Well, that was nice," Jonathan says. "Your parents are visiting this weekend?"

I spin my chair to face him, my hands in fists. "Did you not see me motioning for you to go away?" I stand, trying to minimize the height difference between us.

His smile is soft; he reaches down and tucks a strand of hair behind my ear. "I did, but I wanted to see if you were hungry. You've been working over here for hours without a break."

My stomach growls. I relax my hands and smooth them down the front of my shirt. "And if I am? Hungry, I mean."

He grins. "Then you're in luck. I just so happen to have a picnic ready to go, if you'll join me outside."

A ... picnic? I hesitate, but my stomach growls again, sealing my decision. I'm voting with my tummy. "Okay."

Chapter Twelve

Jonathan

"Yeah?" I ask, barely containing the glee in my voice.

The picnic idea was a gamble. When five o'clock came and went and Molly was still in her cubicle, swiveling in her chair and oblivious that everyone around her had packed up and gone home, I figured she was so absorbed in whatever she was doing that she didn't realize what time it was and that she hadn't eaten since lunch. *Hyperfocus, time blind, internal cues going unnoticed.* Buzzwords from the articles I've been reading on adults with ADHD bounce around in my head. They also say that no two ADHD brains are the same, so without talking to Molly directly to better understand her experience of this "fingerprint" condition, I'm really just guessing.

Tonight isn't the first night I've noticed Molly working for long stretches of time without a break, though. It's why I started coming to the lab more on weekends, when Molly seemed to be fitting a week's worth of work into two days. I knew that if I came in and interrupted her, she would stop and eat something. Maybe drink some water. On the weekend evenings I stopped by and didn't find her in the lab (rare), I just checked on a few things in the lab area and went home. When Molly was there, I stayed longer, even inventing things to do to stick around.

I take Molly's hand and lead her toward the elevator. She doesn't pull away.

When we pass my cubicle, she turns her head to peek inside. "You took it all down."

"Yeah. I'm sorry I had to. I saved all the sticky notes though." I wish I could have left them up. I took plenty of pictures when I got to work this morning because seeing my cubicle, desk, computer monitor, and desk chair covered in sticky notes in perfect rainbow order is something I never want to forget.

It must have taken her hours to place each of the three thousand sticky notes individually. That feels significant. She could have played any prank—something quicker or less thought-out—but she didn't. The prank she chose was tedious to execute and loud in its final product. No one missed seeing my rainbow cubicle this morning. Knowing how Molly values her time and her invisibility, I can't help but think maybe she felt I was worth the sacrifice.

I found something interesting while taking the sticky notes down, too. A tiny heart was drawn on the back of one of the yellow ones. I don't know what that means, but I know what I want it to mean. I want it to mean that Molly is just as captivated with me as I am with her.

I duck into the breakroom to grab the bags of food I stashed there earlier. I had just returned to the lab with food when I heard Molly on the phone.

We go down the elevator, out the front doors, around the side of the building. I gesture for Molly to take a seat on the bench in my grassy alcove spot. We have some time before sunset, though the sunlight is already dimming as dusk approaches.

I sit next to Molly with enough space between us to set the bags of food.

I start pulling containers out of the bags. "It's from Cafe Beignet. I didn't know what you'd want, other than beignets, of course, so I got a few different things."

"Smells amazing." She inhales, and I hear her stomach rumble again.

Better work quicker. "This is the royal croissant: ham-and-cheddar sandwich on a croissant. The Decatur club: turkey, bacon, and Swiss on French bread. Red beans and rice. Jambalaya. And a muffaletta."

Molly chuckles. "That's half the menu."

I dip my head. "Almost. Help me narrow it down for next time."

She scoffs. "You're assuming there'll be a next time?"

I study her expression. Her words are hard, her tone cool, and her eyes guarded. "Hoping, yes. What'll you have?"

"The royal croissant, please."

I hand her the sandwich and uncover the red beans and rice for myself. I watch as Molly lifts the top of the croissant off her sandwich and removes the cheese, setting it on a napkin. She replaces the top and takes a bite.

"You don't like cheese?" I'm gathering intel, gobbling up whatever tidbits I can glean until she lets me in more fully.

She scrunches her nose. "I don't really eat dairy."

"Are you lactose intolerant?"

"No..." She hesitates, blushing. "I just don't really like the idea of dairy products, the texture of them and how they smell. Same with eggs." She takes another bite of her sandwich, chews, and swallows. "I know I sound like a picky five-year-old."

"You don't." I shrug. "I read that a lot of people with ADHD have sensory difficulties, too."

Molly turns her face toward me, eyes wide, before she freezes. Did she forget she told me about her ADHD?

"Oh," she says.

"You told me on the boat, remember?"

"No, I ... I know I told you. But what do you mean you 'read' about it?"

I scratch my chin. "I didn't know a lot about it and wanted to learn more, so I read some articles."

She blinks. "Why?"

I can feel my ears turning red. I didn't think it was a big deal. Molly's acting like learning more about a neurodiversity that affects a coworker is not normal behavior. Okay, *coworker* is understating what I feel about Molly at this point, but still, why wouldn't I want to understand her better?

I shrug again. "I don't know. I thought it would be helpful. For you."

Molly continues to stare at me like I'm a dolphin with six heads. I squirm under the scrutiny. With every other woman, I'm smooth, confident. Some would say charming. Molly disarms me. Nothing in my usual arsenal works with her. The harder I try to impress her, the less impressed she seems to be. "Did I do the wrong thing?" I ask, sure the insecurity I feel is leaching into my voice.

"No," she whispers, her eyes still on me, but glazed over as if she's not really seeing me. She blinks and looks away. "I mean, no, that's fine."

"Are you sure? Because you seem kind of mad? Or something."

She shakes her head, tossing her hair from side to side. "I'm not mad. I'm not. It's just..."

"Just what?"

She forces out a breath. "Just, it was easier when you weren't so nice to me."

I'm taken aback. A million questions zing through my mind. *What* was easier? And why? Also—

"Have I been being mean to you?" The possibility is so distasteful that I set down my food.

Molly screws up her face, her forehead scrunching and her lips forming a grimace. "Uh, no. No, not mean. I didn't say that right. You've never been mean. Just ... annoying?"

"Ouch." Annoying is better than mean, but it's still not exactly a compliment. Actually, I can work with annoying. It means I get under her skin.

She shakes her head, her cheeks flushed. "I'm sorry. It's probably on me, to be honest. I don't always have great tolerance for, you know, people. And, as I told you, I try to avoid distractions so I can focus on my work."

I raise my eyebrows. "I'm a distraction?"

Molly's eyes rake over me from head to toe and back up again. I don't think she realizes she's doing it; she's not trying to be flirtatious or send a message. More like she can't help it. Her raw reaction thrills me—it's guileless and natural, a brief slip of the mask she usually keeps firmly affixed.

When she finally answers the question, her voice is throaty and low. "Oh, definitely."

A shiver runs up my spine. Yep, I can absolutely work with this.

Even so, it won't help to push. I pick my container of red beans and rice back up and steer the conversation around to more neutral topics. "How's your sandwich?"

"Delicious." She peers into my bowl. "Your food smells good. What is it?"

I stare at her incredulously, but she appears to be serious. "Red beans and rice? New Orleans staple?"

"Is it spicy? So much of New Orleans food is seafood or spicy." She shrugs. "I haven't been very adventurous."

"Red beans and rice can be spicy, but Cafe Beignet makes it with the tourists' palates in mind. Flavorful but not spicy. Want to try some?" I push a forkful in the direction of her mouth, raising my eyebrows in question.

She leans her head away, her lips pinched together.

"Come on," I encourage her. "You can't live in New Orleans without at least trying red beans and rice."

She gives a determined nod and takes the fork from my fingers. She slides the bite of food into her mouth and chews carefully.

"Well?" I ask as she swallows.

"I like it. You're right; it's not too spicy. It has a good flavor, and I like that it's dry, not creamy or anything."

I offer her my bowl. "Do you want the rest?" She smiles, and I suppress the urge to buy a hundred more bowls of red beans and rice to present to her. If that smile is my reward, the effort and cost would be well worthwhile.

"Yes, thank you. But only because you have, like, ten other options in that bag." Her eyes sparkle as she teases me.

The grin on my face is automatic. I hand her the bowl. "So, what were you working on so intently this afternoon?"

"Oh, um ... a data model."

I perk up. "What kind of data model?"

She examines my face as if she's determining whether to tell me more. Finally, she says, "I'm looking for a correlation between harmful algal bloom events and tropical activity."

I pause. "You think hurricanes contribute to red tide outbreaks?"

Molly maintains eye contact. "Maybe. The correlation was statistically significant in the model."

Huh. That would mean that the storms change the properties of the water enough to either cause or exacerbate conditions for the growth of harmful algal blooms. Of course, the correlation could just be because storms tend to increase pesticide runoff, which in turn causes harmful algal blooms to flourish. "The correlation might not mean what you think it means, though."

"I know." Her eyes narrow in annoyance. "Obviously I need more evidence. I'm working on it."

I scratch my chin. I didn't mean to belittle her project, but I can see how she might interpret it that way. I change tactics. "That will be a pretty huge breakthrough when you prove it."

She brightens. "Thanks," she says softly.

"I know you've got it, but if you need any help, let me know."

She lifts her chin. "I will."

The sun has fully set at this point, and the night is getting darker every minute we sit out here. "We should probably call it a night."

"It's been a pretty long day." She yawns.

"You look exhausted."

She raises an eyebrow. "Thanks so much," she deadpans.

I chuckle. "Beautiful, as always, but exhausted."

I stand and reach out my hand to help Molly to her feet. After I collect the leftover food and throw away the trash from our picnic, we walk toward the parking lot together.

As we near her car, Molly riffles through her bag. "Hmm."

I stop. "What?"

"I can't find my keys."

I frown. "Did you leave them in your office?"

She bobbles her head. "Maybe?"

Molly goes back to digging through her bag. I lean forward to glance through the window of her car and groan. "Molly."

She looks up, and I point to the front seat through the window. Her keys are sitting right on the driver's seat.

She blushes. "Is it...?"

I pull on the door handle. "Yep. It's locked."

The flush on her cheeks deepens. "Okay. No problem. I can just..." She looks around on the ground, though I'm not sure for what.

I'm certain she doesn't want to wait for a locksmith tonight. That feels like a problem for later. For now, I want to get her home so she can rest. I reach over and place my hand on her arm. "If I give you a ride home, do you have a way to get into your apartment?"

"Yes, but I can walk. It's not far."

I know it's not far, and I know she walks between the lab and her apartment all the time. Still. "It's already dark out, and I'd feel better driving you."

"Okay. Thank you."

I pull my keys from my pocket and unlock my truck.

Molly smiles at me. "Show-off."

I chuckle. "I've locked my keys in my car before, too."

We climb into the truck, and I start driving toward Molly's apartment. "How will you unlock your apartment?" I ask her.

She adjusts her seatbelt and leans back to rest her head on the seat. "Oh, I have a hide-a-key in one of those fake rocks that's hidden in the landscaping by the front door."

I groan. "Molly. Please tell me you don't."

She blinks and looks at me with wide eyes. "Why not?"

I shake my head. "Those things aren't safe. The rocks never look real, and anybody can just take your key."

She fiddles with the strap on her bag. "Even if they did, it's not labeled so they wouldn't know what apartment it goes to. And they couldn't get in the building without a code."

"I still don't like it," I grumble. I turn the last corner and pull up to the curb outside Molly's building. I reach down to unbuckle my seatbelt.

"Don't get out," Molly says. "It'll just take me a second to grab my key."

I shift in the seat. "Okay, but I'm not leaving until you're inside. Do you want me to pick you up for work in the morning?"

"No, I was planning to walk tomorrow anyway. But thank you." She hops down from the truck, shutting the door behind her. I watch out the window as she steps off the sidewalk, squats down, and roots around by the bushes. She straightens, holding up a key for me to see.

I press the button to roll the passenger side window down. "Text me when you get into your apartment," I call to her.

She flashes a thumbs-up before walking to the entry door and typing in a code. The door buzzes, and she pulls it open, disappearing inside.

I wait until her text comes through.

LOVE IN THE LAB

Molly:

I'm inside my apartment. You can stop worrying now

Jonathan:

Thank you. Good night

Molly:

Night. Thanks for dinner

Jonathan:

Anytime

I take a deep breath, placing a call as I pull away from the curb and drive back toward the lab. I'm guessing I can get this taken care of for her in just a couple of hours.

Chapter Thirteen

Molly

Wednesday morning, I lock my apartment door with the spare key, triple checking that it's tucked safely in my pocket before walking to the lab. I know I need to deal with a locksmith for my car today, but all the steps needed to make that happen feel so overwhelming. Just getting started will be a Herculean task I'm dreading.

I wave to my car in the parking lot, noting that the windows still look intact, which means no one broke in overnight. That's a relief.

I trudge up the stairs, wishing I'd taken the elevator. Then, I stash my lunchbox in the fridge in the breakroom and settle in at my desk. I'm following my normal routine this morning and it feels strange. Almost ... boring? *Your day is not supposed to be exciting*, I remind myself. *It's supposed to be stable and focused*.

Still, I'm feeling dissatisfied, which is why I light up when Jonathan approaches my cubicle. He pulls his hands from behind his back and jangles something above my head. Wait, not *something—*

"Hey, my keys!"

The metal keys clank against my desk as he sets them down. "Yes, ma'am."

"How'd you get them?" I reverently pick them up and clutch them to my chest.

He leans his shoulder against the doorway wall. "I called AAA last night. They sent a locksmith out."

I pause, tilting my head as I look up at his face. "They let you call a locksmith for a car that doesn't belong to you?"

"Oddly, yes. Kind of makes you wonder, right?" He chuckles.

"Yeah."

"Anyway, you're all set." He raps a knuckle against the desk and turns to leave.

I'm not ready for him to walk away yet. The fact that he dealt with the locksmith for me is a *huge* deal, making my day infinitely easier. I'm not even sure he realizes how huge. It's the kind of thoughtful service my dad would do for me. Accepting it from Jonathan does funny things to my heart. "Jonathan!" I call after him, more loudly than I intended.

He turns around, a smirk on his lips. "Yes?"

I take a breath. "Thank you. I'm not sure you understand how much agonizing you saved me."

He slides his hands into his pockets and meets my eyes. "I just wanted to make your day easier."

I nod. "You have. Thank you."

His face turns serious. "Listen, I have a weird question that I know I have no right to ask, but it keeps bugging me, and I know it'll bother me if I don't at least *try*."

I laugh nervously. "O-kaay?"

"Can I make a copy of your apartment key?" He grimaces.

"You want a key to my apartment?" I narrow my eyes.

"Not to *use*. But, like, to hold for you, in case something like this happens again. I could be your hide-a-key," he explains.

Is it strange that I believe him? He got pretty worked up last night about how "unsafe" the hide-a-key is. Is it even stranger that I trust him? Jonathan's annoying, but he's never done anything to make me think he's dishonest or unreliable. Is it the strangest of all that the idea of Jonathan protecting me, *wanting* to protect me, stirs up all kinds of butterflies in my stomach?

My bewilderment must show on my face because Jonathan backpedals quickly. "Never mind. That was stupid. It's a stupid idea."

His expression of bald insecurity is one I've never noticed on my coworker before. Usually, he's confident, annoyingly smug. But now, instead of his characteristic smirk, he's wearing a tentative smile. Instead of his typical, relentless eye contact, he's staring at his hands. It feels sincere. It's ... endearing.

Maybe that explains what I do next. I reach into the pocket of my pants and slide out the extra key to my apartment. I hand the key to Jonathan.

His eyes widen. "Wait, really?"

I smirk. "Yeah, I kind of like the idea of you doing my bidding."

His eyes flash. "So do I." He mutters it under his breath, but he's standing close enough that I hear it anyway.

I do the only thing I can think of doing: ignore the comment. Instead, I smile and tease, "But if I catch you raiding my kitchen in the middle of the night, I *will* shoot you."

He scoffs. "Do you even have a gun?"

I tap a finger against my chin. "Hmm, I am from Texas, you know." I don't own a gun. I've never even touched a gun in my entire life.

He laughs. "I'll keep that in mind."

After checking into their hotel late Friday afternoon, my parents meet me at my apartment where we'll make plans for dinner. We exchange hugs all around and I lean in, trying to remember how long it's been since I've been hugged. Probably not since Nicole was here in April. That's probably why physical contact with Jonathan is affecting me so much. Simple human touch deprivation. Humans are meant to have physical contact with other humans. It's not him or his touch specifically; it's a natural biological reaction to touch starvation.

My dad is tall—just under six feet—his long legs providing half that height. His graying hair is mussed from travel, but his gray-blue eyes are bright.

Growing up, my dad always joked that I'm my mother's mini-me. My face still looks like a younger version of hers, except her eyes are blue-green hazel and mine are just plain blue. We're about the same height, but her brown hair has changed to gray, and she's thicker around the middle than I am.

My mom notices the stack of picture frames on the coffee table. I still haven't gotten around to hanging them since the morning, over a month ago now, I had to stop so I could get to work on time. She picks them up, shuffling them to see the photos. "Ooh, pictures! These are so cute. Ben, you should help Molly hang them while we're here."

Neither of them comments on the clutter stacked on every flat surface of the apartment. They didn't nag me about that kind of thing when I was a kid, either, even though my room was always a disaster. I wasn't allowed to leave my belongings in the common areas of the house, but in my own room I could organize or disorganize how it made sense to me.

Still, I can't help but feel a degree of inadequacy when I look around my apartment through my parents' eyes. My deodorant sits on top of the TV. A giant mixing bowl is taking up space on the nightstand next to my bed. My electric toothbrush, cap on, stands upright on the kitchen counter. I really hope neither of them checks the refrigerator or cupboards, because I'm not even sure what's in there. Maybe some shriveled carrots and stale crackers? There's definitely a layer of dust on the lampshades and fan blades.

Now that I've noticed what a wreck my apartment is, it's all I can see. All of a sudden, the space is overwhelming, and I feel the impulse to clean and organize everything. I resist and suppress, forcing myself to focus on my parents, though my fingers are literally twitching to grab a dust rag and get to work.

"Molly?" My dad's voice breaks through my distraction. The way he's watching me with an affectionate smile on his face, I know this is not the first time he tried to get my attention.

I smile ruefully back. "Sorry, what was that?"

"Mom asked where you'd like to go for dinner."

I look between my parents. I have a difficult enough time making decisions when it's something I care about, never mind when the outcome won't really matter. "Oh, wherever you want. There are over one hundred restaurants within walking distance, so..." I shrug.

Dad's eyes light up and he rubs his hands together. "How about some traditional New Orleans food?"

I think of the spread Jonathan provided earlier this week. "Oh, actually I do know a place like that."

I pat my pants' pockets for my phone but don't find it. I wander into my bedroom and see it charging on the nightstand. I unplug it and bring it back into the living room, typing as I go.

"Cafe Beignet. There are several locations. The closest one is a fifteen-minute walk from here."

"Sounds great!" Mom says at the same time Dad exclaims, "Let's do it!"

We walk to the restaurant, my mom chattering about the buildings and people around us. When we arrive, Mom and I grab a table while Dad writes down our orders, so he can wait in line.

"Red beans and rice," I tell him confidently. "With an order of beignets, please."

My parents exchange a look. "You like red beans and rice?" Mom asks.

"You've *tried* red beans and rice?" Dad adds.

I don't tell them I discovered just this week that I like the dish. Instead, I say, "Yes. It's not too spicy here. My ... um, coworker encouraged me to try it."

"Well, isn't that nice?" Mom says and gives Dad her order.

He leaves us at the table to wait in line to order. I'm looking around at the exposed brick, white wrought iron bistro tables and chairs, and shelves against the wall stocked with New Orleans seasonings, baking mixes, and cafe merchandise. This place is cute. And I already know I like at least two things on the menu. The air smells heavenly—a mixture of savory seasonings, coffee, and sugary sweet dough.

I feel my mom watching me and mentally brace for an inquisition. "You tried red beans and rice because of a coworker, you said? Which coworker?" She pauses, waiting until I'm looking at her before adding, "Was it Jonathan?"

"Actually, yes," I say airily. Super casual. Nothing to see here.

"Hmm. That's interesting. Isn't he the coworker you always complain about? He sounded so nice on the phone the other night."

Her eyes are locked on my face, studying, assessing, delving in a way that makes me believe she can really see my thoughts.

I scoff, fiddling with the zipper on my sweatshirt. "That's what he wants people to think."

Her eyes sparkle. "All part of his nefarious ruse, then?"

I set my jaw. "Maybe."

She chuckles. "What do you have against him, anyway?"

"When we were in classes together, he would always rub it in my face if he scored higher than me on exams. When we're in the lab, he interrupts my work, and now, our PI is making me do fieldwork with him, and he's making it as difficult as possible for me."

I realize that though I'm reciting the same complaints I've had about Jonathan from the start, I don't feel the same conviction about them I used to. Also, the charges aren't exactly true. He's not making fieldwork difficult for me. In fact, he's been super accommodating and thoughtful, going out of his way to make the work easier. Other than that first awful day when I fell in the bayou, I've actually been enjoying myself on our weekly trips to collect water samples.

"Maybe he likes you," Mom teases. "Like a little boy on the playground who pulls the pigtails of the little girl he has a crush on."

"Okay, no," I protest, shaking my head emphatically. "First of all, it's harmful to women to suggest that men harass us because they like us. It teaches girls to equate abuse with love—"

"Abuse is a pretty strong word in this case, isn't it?" she interrupts.

"And second of all, Jonathan does not like me," I fume.

She raises her hands in surrender. "Okay, I'm sorry. I just like the effect he's having on you. Trying new foods, having new experiences. It's good for you."

Inwardly, I groan. Not her, too. First Dr. Gantt tells me to get out of my comfort zone, and now my own mother, who arguably knows me better than anyone, says new experiences are good for me? She should know they're not.

"Mom..." I warn.

"Okay. All I'm saying is that playing it too safe can get in the way of living, and I want you to experience all the good things in life—"

Before she can continue, Dad is back, laying our food out on the table. As we eat, the conversation shifts to their travel plans and their eagerness to meet Nicole's boyfriend.

Still, my mom's words run on repeat in my brain, not only her warning about playing it safe, but also her suggestion that Jonathan may like me as more than a coworker or potential friend. If he does, which I doubt, it's only because he doesn't know me well enough yet. So why does the idea send a jolt of anticipation through my chest?

My parents spend the rest of the weekend coddling me. We go to the grocery store so they can stock my pantry. My dad and I hang the photo frames, and he shows me how to stop my toilet from running. Meanwhile, my mom puts together half a dozen freezer meals and labels them with reheating instructions before stashing them in my freezer. They both help me tidy up—dusting, sweeping, reorganizing—and I think my mom even sneaks downstairs to wash a load of my dirty laundry.

It's simultaneously embarrassing and comforting. They helped me with tasks like these all the time when I was growing up. When I was seven and eight years old, getting dressed in the morning before school felt like such a burden some days, literally more intimidating than climbing a mountain. They would help me, even though I was far too old to need help putting on clothes.

When I was in middle school, they helped me keep track of my school assignments and deadlines. They didn't do it for me, but they sat down with me after school every day to review my agenda. They guided me on how to prioritize: *yes, the science assignment is more fun, but the social studies project is due sooner. Why don't you work on the social studies project first?*

In high school, they reminded me to take my medication and spent hours in the car with me while I was learning to drive. It took me a lot of practice to acclimate to all the variables I had to pay attention to at once while driving a car: monitor the mirrors, watch the road ahead, steer, press the appropriate pedals.

And now, they're helping me organize my adult life, too. It's the kind of support I don't have regularly anymore. On the one hand, that's a relief, because I'm an adult and don't want to burden someone I love with taking care of me. On the other hand, taking care of myself all by myself is exhausting.

I remember when I was really young and would melt down from overwhelm and not know how to communicate my feelings except by knocking everything from the table onto the floor. I remember how frustrated they would get when I would not, could not get in the shower because it just felt really hard to do. I remember taking time and attention away from my younger sisters because I just needed so much. I know I could be a lot to deal with. I am a lot to deal with.

My parents and sisters understand. They're family. They know me; they know what to expect. They love me and so don't mind when I need extra support, or forget to call again, or neglect to clean up after myself.

That's another reason I value my work at the lab so much. It's a mutualistic relationship. The lab benefits through my time and efforts that can lead to breakthroughs in our research. I benefit through satisfaction, fulfilment, and, you know, a paycheck. But with a romantic partner, I can't see what I have to contribute. The relationship is bound to be parasitic—like the codependent way copepods cling to the skin and gills of sharks, feeding on them—where I get all the benefits and he is only harmed.

Chapter Fourteen

Molly

Sunday evening after I've said goodbye to my parents and they've gone back to their hotel for the night, I text Nicole to see if she's free for a video call. She answers with a thumbs-up. When her face comes on the screen, she's sitting on a dark brown couch with a dog in her lap.

"You're at Adam's," I say in lieu of a greeting.

"Yeah, but we're fine. He's in the shower. We have a few minutes."

I send her a teasing smile. "Mom and Dad are heading your way in the morning. Is Adam nervous about meeting them?"

"Oh, yes." She grimaces. "It doesn't help that he offered to let them stay in his guest room while they're here."

My mouth pops open. "No! Why would he do that?"

She sighs. "Because he has the extra space and didn't want them to get a hotel room unnecessarily."

"Wow. Adam is such a good guy. I'm not even housing them, and I'm their *daughter*." Also, my apartment is a postage stamp, and Dad says he is well beyond the stage of crashing on somebody's futon while traveling.

Nicole laughs. "Yeah, well. You know them better than he does."

Of course, we're joking. Our parents are pretty much the best. I'm cringing, though, thinking about how uncomfortable it will be for Adam to host his girlfriend's parents whom he's never met before. He must really love Nicole.

A pang of longing erupts in my chest. I am so happy that Nicole and Adam got together. I cheered for Adam the whole time before Nicole admitted her feelings for him, and they really are adorable together. My joy for my sister finding true love is tinged with sadness, though. Despite my bravado about how it's better that I'm alone so I can focus on my work, I'm lonely. Witnessing how meeting Adam has changed Nicole, opening her up and softening her, I wonder if maybe there's hope for me, too. Immediately, Jonathan's ridiculously good-looking face springs to mind.

In the lower right corner of my phone screen, I watch my own face as it twists into a grimace.

Nicole notices, too. She sits up straighter as she peers into her phone screen. "But I'm guessing you didn't call to talk about Mom and Dad. Everything okay?"

I tell her about fieldwork with Jonathan and the pranks we've been playing on each other at the lab. I share my excitement about the data model I've developed and the breakthrough it could be. I explain how severely my daily routines have morphed over the last six weeks.

"So, what's the problem?" Nicole asks. "Mol, it sounds like you're having fun. You sound happy."

I tug on the ends of my hair. "That's the problem! I can't have fun at work. At work, I need to focus on work. I can't afford to get distracted."

"You're doing your best work right now! You said so yourself."

"Yes, but that's in spite of the distractions."

Nicole shifts in her seat, and the dog jumps down from the couch. "Maybe it's *because* you're allowing yourself to take brain breaks."

I shake my head. No. I can't afford Jonathan and his distractions anymore. I'm going to tell him the prank war is done.

Monday afternoon, I watch Jonathan walk to the breakroom and emerge a few minutes later with a lunchbox that he takes out into the hallway. He must be going to eat lunch on the bench outside. I grab my lunch out of the refrigerator as well and follow him downstairs. Now's as good a time as any to talk to him about ending the prank war.

He's getting settled on the bench when I come around the corner of the building. When he sees me, his eyes light up. "Hey!"

"Hi." I wave awkwardly. I'm not sure what to say and feel uncomfortably like I'm about to break up with someone when they have no idea there's a problem. But of course, we're not breaking up because we were never dating.

He gestures for me to come closer. "Come sit down. How was the visit from your parents?"

Small talk first. I can do that. "Great! It was really good to see them. They left this morning to drive to Florida to see my sister."

"Where in Florida does your sister live?" Jonathan takes a bite of his sandwich as he waits for my response.

"St. Anastasia. It's a small town close to Jacksonville." I sit on the bench and unzip the top flap on my lunchbox.

"That's cool. I've never heard of it. Is she younger or older than you? Do you have other siblings?" He chuckles. "I guess I'd like to know more about your family."

Despite my nervousness, I smile as I pick at the wrapper of my granola bar. "I have two sisters, both younger. Nicole is the sister who lives in Florida, and she's closest in age to me. Olivia is the youngest. She lives in Austin with my parents."

"Is that where you grew up? I remember you're from Texas." He's finished his sandwich now and pulls an apple from his bag, shining the skin against his shirt before crunching into it.

"Yeah."

"It's funny that you're one of three sisters. I have three little nieces. My older sister Tamara's girls."

I finally open the granola bar and chew a piece as I consider. "You're from Ohio, I think you said. Right?"

He swallows a bite of apple before answering. "Yep. The Buckeye State. Most of my family still live there."

"What about your parents?"

Jonathan's expression changes, his lips pinching as a wrinkle forms between his eyebrows. He taps his fingers against the bench's armrest. "They're divorced," he says quickly.

"I'm sorry. Do they still live in Ohio?"

His eyes are trained on the last few bits of apple on the core in his hands. "My dad does. My mom lives in New Delhi at the moment."

"New Delhi, India? That's amazing!" I exclaim, but his mood has shifted. He shrugs, and my skin prickles at his discomfort.

I don't push him. Instinctively, I lay my hand on his arm and squeeze. He meets my eyes, and time stops. At first, his gaze is cloudy, his eyebrows drawn together and his eyes narrowed. But the longer we're locked together, the more his expression relaxes until he's smiling again.

I'm not sure what he sees in my eyes, but I know what's happening inside of me. My heartbeat feels erratic. A quiver in my stomach causes a vibration that carries up my spine and exits my body through my shoulders as a shiver. All from a simple touch.

I drop my hand and clear my throat. Awkwardly, I plow ahead to the topic I came out here to talk to him about and which feels more urgent than ever after the moment we just had.

"So, listen," I start. "This thing we've been doing—it's been fun, but I need to refocus on my work."

"What have we been doing?" Jonathan's eyebrows drop in confusion. "Fieldwork? Getting to know each other better? Eating together?"

"No!" I say loudly. Lowering my voice, I whisper, "The *pranks*."

Jonathan rubs his chin, his eyes widening innocently. "What pranks? I guess there has been some weird stuff happening at the lab lately." He gasps. "Are you saying *you* had something to do with all that?"

I huff out a breath. "Jonathan!" I whisper furiously.

His eyes twinkle. "Chill, Molly Wolly Doodle." He rubs his thumb over the space between my eyebrows, smoothing the skin. He trails his thumb above my eyebrow and then between the corner of my eye and my hairline. I hold my breath, watching his eyes as they track the path of his thumb. He continues down my jawline, and goosebumps erupt across my face everywhere he touches. I shiver.

"The air's getting cooler, isn't it?" he asks in a husky voice, his eyes flicking to mine. "Maybe we'll have an early fall this year."

I pull away because it's muggy and at least eighty-five degrees out here. The air around us shouldn't be making me shiver, and he knows it.

Jonathan drops his hand. "I'm going to go back upstairs." He stands. "Enjoy the rest of your lunch."

He walks away without glancing back. My brain fogs up as I try to sort out what just happened. I still feel the whispers of his thumb along my skin, see the ring of green in his hazel eyes.

Wait. I clear my head with a toss of my hair. Did he agree to no more pranks or not? It's his turn, so even if he has one more planned, I don't have to retaliate. I can be the bigger person here, the more responsible one. I finish my lunch and get back to work.

I'm still working at my computer later that afternoon, typing up another report, when Jonathan's voice coming from behind me makes me jump. "It's about time to go home, isn't it, Carrots?"

I check the time—5:45—and swivel in my chair to face him. I'm confused about the new nickname until I realize I have a baggie of baby carrots sitting next to the keyboard on my desk. Jonathan has his computer bag slung across his chest, sunglasses perched on top of his head.

"Are you heading out?" I ask.

"Yeah. You?"

I turn my head to survey the document open on the computer screen. "Soon. I just want to finish this report." I swivel my chair back around.

In a low voice, Jonathan teases, "I'll be in the depths of despair without you."

My mouth drops open, and I freeze, turning my head to see him smirking. I face him and point an accusatory finger. "You said you'd never heard of *Anne of Green Gables*!"

He shrugs. "I looked it up. Couldn't find it streaming anywhere, so I bought the DVDs. Can you believe that? In this day and age?" He shakes his head.

"You bought the DVDs?" I sputter. "*I* don't even have the DVDs!"

He slides a box out of his satchel. "All yours, Carrots." He winks and hands me the boxed set of eight DVDs. Too stunned to argue, I reach out my hand to take it. He doesn't let go of the box. Instead, he pulls the chair and, consequently, me closer, crouching down until his mouth is next to my ear.

"By the way," he rumbles so quietly that I have to lean even closer to hear. "I noticed that Gilbert Blythe and *his* Carrots end up together. Isn't that interesting?"

I gulp and pull back to see his face. Is *that* why he's calling me Carrots? From *Anne of Green Gables*? The corners of his lips quirk upward, but his eyes are devastatingly serious, a whirlwind of green and brown. I'm powerless to look away. He breaks eye contact first, straightening back to his full height and turning toward the door.

"See you tomorrow," he says casually.

"Yeah," I answer in a daze. "See you tomorrow."

When I get home, I open the box of DVDs. One slips out onto the ground, and I pick it up. It's labeled "Bonus Content," but it looks a little ... off. I investigate the box and see that each of the advertised eight DVDs are there, snapped snugly into their trays. There is no empty tray. The Bonus Content is a ninth disc. I study the label on the Bonus Content disc and compare it to the labels on the other eight. It's pretty darn close, but the Bonus Content label is slightly askew, not perfectly centered like on the other discs.

Curious, I slide the DVD into my player. When it starts playing, I groan loudly. It's a video of Rick Astley singing his popular '80s song "Never Gonna Give You Up." I stare at the screen as Astley belts out the lyrics speaking to his commitment.

Before I know it, I'm laughing so hard that literal tears are streaming down my face. He's just too much. I pull out my phone.

Molly:

> You rickrolled me? Seriously? What is this, 2008?

Jonathan:

> [laughing emoji] A prank and a promise

I shake my head, my smile so big it's actually hurting my cheeks. Okay, one more prank. The prank to end the prank war. And I need to make it the best one yet.

Chapter Fifteen

Jonathan

T hursday morning, I know something is up the moment I walk into the office. My colleagues are frantic, speeding back and forth between the office and the lab with piles of papers and straightening up their desks.

Dr. Gantt sees me come in and pulls me aside before I even have a chance to set my bag down in my cubicle. A flush on her cheeks makes her brown skin appear even darker. "Good morning, Dr. Stanch. Change in plans today. We just got word that Dr. Perron will be stopping by this morning. He wants to see how we test our water samples."

Dr. Perron is the dean of the College of Coast and Environment at NOSU. While most of our research is funded through grants, the dean still has quite a bit of power over our purse strings, including our ability to use the building space for our lab. A visit from him likely means he wants to check in on our progress and be sure our research is a worthwhile use of the university's funds.

This is the first Dr. Perron visit I've experienced in Dr. Gantt's lab, but we had them all the time when I worked with Dr. Shepherd, at least before his big research breakthrough last year. After the Society for Conservation Biology honored Dr. Shepherd's work, the visits stopped.

Out of the corner of my eye, I see Molly slip through the door. She observes the frenzied environment and then must notice me talking with Dr. Gantt because she moves closer.

"I know you're scheduled to work with the most recent batch of samples this morning," Dr. Gantt continues. "Do you mind if Dr. Perron and I observe? He should be here any minute." Her phone buzzes and she glances at the screen. "Yes, that's him now. I'll be right back. Can you get the samples set up in the meantime?"

"Of course. It's no problem at all." I flash a confident smile, and Dr. Gantt visibly relaxes.

She claps her hands loudly before announcing to the room, "Alright, team. Dr. Perron will be here momentarily. Please finish with whatever you're straightening and then return to your planned tasks for the morning." She smiles brilliantly to reassure the team. "We're doing good work here, and I know Dr. Perron will agree."

With that, she walks toward the elevator to fetch Dr. Perron at the reception desk downstairs. On my way into the lab area, I stop at my desk to drop off my bag and don my lab coat.

"Jonathan!" Molly hisses from behind me, pulling at my sleeve as I set the bag on my desk.

I turn and look straight into her panicked eyes. "What's going on? Are you okay?" My adrenaline spikes as I scan her for any injuries.

Ignoring my questions, she asks one of her own. "Is Dr. Perron going to watch you test the samples from last week?"

"Yeah, him and Dr. Gantt both. Why? What's wrong?"

She blanches. "I ... didn't know. I thought you would work with them on your own, like normal. I didn't know!"

I put together the pieces pretty quickly and curse. "Carrots, what did you do?"

She winces, her whole face turning red as she admits, "I ... moved the real samples and replaced them with plastic beakers of frozen tap water."

Despite the situation, I chuckle. That's pretty good. If Dr. Perron hadn't surprised us with a visit today, I would have gotten a kick out of finding frozen samples. It's not like Molly would compromise the real samples, or jeopardize the research, for a prank.

"Where did you put the real samples?" I ask, forming a plan in my mind that *might* get us off the hook with Dr. Perron, if not with Dr. Gantt.

"The spare refrigerator in the storage room. I plugged it in and made sure it cooled down to four degrees Celsius before I moved the samples."

I can't help but smile as I regard her with what must be bald admiration. The careful planning and time she put into this prank are such a perfect balance of responsibility and fun. Damn if it's not one of the hottest things I've ever heard.

I think quickly. There's no time to switch out the samples. I have to get in there, divert Dr. Gantt, and make Dr. Perron think it's totally normal to keep important water samples in a storage room refrigerator.

I put my hand on Molly's arm to reassure her. "I'll take care of it, okay? You won't get in trouble."

As I speed walk away, I hear her call behind me, "But what about you?"

Yeah, I'll probably get in some trouble, but I'm not worried about it.

I need to run pesticide testing on the samples using our two standard methods. We usually do a quick QuEChERS test—which stands for Quick, Easy, Cheap, Effective, Rugged, and Safe—followed by a more in-depth analysis of the sample using liquid chromatography-mass spectrometry.

I've only had time to set the solvent on the lab bench when Dr. Gantt approaches with our visitor. I switch on my most charming smile and meet them halfway. "Dr. Perron," I say, reaching out my hand to shake his, "how nice to see you again."

"Yes." He nods. "It's been a while. I heard you left Harvey's lab. Got bored with coastal erosion, did you?"

I flash a plastic smile. "Impossible. No, when Dr. Gantt recruited me to head fieldwork for her research, I couldn't turn down such a great opportunity. The impact her harmful algal bloom work will have on local economies can't be understated." I'm laying it on pretty thick, but Dr. Perron's interest is obviously piqued.

"Why don't you show Dr. Perron how we test water samples from local waterways for pesticides," Dr. Gantt suggests.

"Of course." I lead them over to the lab bench. Dr. Gantt walks toward the large refrigerator nearby where we typically keep our samples as they await testing, and which currently contains Molly's frozen prank samples.

I rush to cut her off, putting myself between Dr. Gantt and the fridge and increasing the wattage of my smile. "I'll go get those water samples from our special project storage."

Dr. Gantt frowns, her confusion evident in the lines on her forehead. I catch her eye. Hopefully, my eyes are communicating my desperate "trust me" message. She must understand because she steps back. "Thank you," she says, guiding Dr. Perron to the mass spectrometer and explaining our process.

I dart back to the storage room and open the spare refrigerator. It's been sitting unplugged in storage since we purchased a newer model a few months ago. The air inside feels plenty cold—not that I doubted Molly's fastidiousness—so I scoop up the containers of water and bring them back into the main lab area.

Though Dr. Perron is waiting next to the lab bench, my boss has just closed the door of the nearby refrigerator. Shoot. That means she's seen the frozen beakers. She regards me with narrowed eyes as I set the sample containers on the counter.

I redouble my smile and focus my attention on Dr. Perron. I smoothly talk through the steps as I prepare the samples. The entire testing process can take anywhere from three to six hours total, so I walk him through what comes next, too. Dr. Perron has some questions, which I answer, and he's on his way thirty minutes later, smiling. As he leaves, he shakes my hand heartily and slaps me on the back. In Boomer language, I understand this to mean he's pleased with his visit.

Dr. Gantt ... not so much. She keeps a thin smile on her face throughout the demonstration and cranks it up as she's bidding Dr. Perron goodbye, but she is *not* happy. She escorts Dr. Perron back downstairs, and I return to the lab area to finish the QuEChERS.

As soon as the elevator doors close behind Dr. Gantt and our guest, Molly's at my side.

"How'd it go?" she asks in a hushed tone.

I shrug. "Dr. Perron didn't know any better, but I'm pretty sure Dr. Gantt is ticked. She looked in the refrigerator."

Molly lays a hand on my forearm. "I'm *so* sorry. What can I do?"

I wave a hand. "Don't worry about it. Dr. Gantt will give me a talking-to, I'm sure. No big deal." I wink. "I'll survive."

As long as Molly doesn't get in trouble, I'll be fine. She doesn't need any more reasons to play it safe in life. She's been so much more relaxed since we started this back-and-forth prank war. More fun. More ... herself. I'm not sure why I have that thought because the Molly I've always known is intense and serious. Still, throughout the years I've caught fleeting glances of softer moments, vulnerabilities that have helped me to know that Molly wears a mask and holds onto it tightly.

"But it's all my fault. I knew I shouldn't have done these stupid pranks..." Her face twists into a grimace, her hand still on my arm.

"There's no reason to regret the last few weeks, Carrots." I catch and hold her gaze. "I don't."

Dr. Gantt clears her throat, and Molly drops her hand like my arm's a tiger shark. As she steps back from me, I silently will her to play it cool, but guilt radiates from her face, turning her cheeks red.

Dr. Gantt studies Molly before shifting her eyes back to me. Instead of the frustration I expect to see there, our boss looks more ... amused. Thoughtful, even. Intrigued.

"Finish testing on the samples—the real samples—and then come talk to me in my office," she instructs me before turning her attention back on Molly. "Dr. Delaney, don't you have reports to write?"

Molly nods and scurries off toward her desk. In my down time between active tasks in the testing, I empty the now only semi-frozen beakers into the sink, wash them, and put them away. I also finish moving samples from the storage room fridge, and, when it's empty, unplug it.

I don't finish testing the samples until late in the workday. Many colleagues have already started trickling out to go home, especially with the eventful start this morning. I peek across the room to see Molly still at her desk when I knock on Dr. Gantt's open office door.

She waves me inside, and I close the door before taking a seat in the chair across from her.

I start with an apology. "I'm sorry, Dr. Gantt. I know I put you and the lab in a precarious position. If Dr. Perron had seen the frozen beakers—"

Dr. Gantt puts her hand up to silence me. "I appreciate the apology and you're right; things could have gone much differently this morning."

I stare at the floor. What I told Molly earlier is true: I don't regret nudging her into a prank war or letting things get this far. The pranks, in addition to our time together during fieldwork, have allowed me to see new sides of her. She's *fun* and having fun too, I think.

I do regret getting caught. That's ... not ideal.

"But," Dr. Gantt continues, "I think I know what's going on here." I lift my head in surprise. She's smiling at me.

"What's going on where?" I ask, my chest tightening.

She chuckles. "I've noticed a difference over the last few weeks in how Dr. Delaney has been showing up to work. She's been more relaxed. Does that have anything to do with you?"

I shrug. I'd like to think so, of course, though I'm not the one who played the first prank, so maybe it mostly has to do with *her*.

"Well, whatever the impetus, it's exactly what I hoped would happen."

I frown. I'm really not following. She *wanted* Molly and I to prank each other? Am I in trouble or not?

Dr. Gantt must notice my confusion because she explains, "I wanted to get Molly out of her comfort zone. I thought that changing her routine, having her go out in the field, would help. I didn't realize working with you would also put her more at ease. Am I right that what happened today with the frozen samples has something to do with the way you and Molly work together?"

"Umm..." I'm not sure what to say. I don't want to implicate Molly.

She holds up a hand. "I don't need details. I want to be clear, Dr. Stanch. Something like this cannot happen again. But, as it appears to be a byproduct of something I think will be valuable to our research, you are free to go."

I rub my chin. "I'm free to ... Are we ... Am *I* not in trouble?"

"Consider this a warning."

"Ah ... okay. Thanks. Thank you. I promise it won't happen again."

I back out of her office, still trying to decode that interaction. I wonder if Molly will understand it better than I do. I make my way to her cubicle to talk to her, but it's empty. My shoulders droop. I was hoping she'd wait for me so we could debrief after everything that went down today. On the other hand, it's getting late, and I'm happy she went home at a decent hour.

I dip into my cubicle to grab my bag so I can go home, too. I'll text Molly when I get there, just to make sure she's okay from today and ready for tomorrow.

We've planned another trip out to the Gulf on the *Pulse* to pick up two gliders that have completed their missions and to collect more samples. We've been traveling to various bayous in the area weekly, wading out to collect water samples. Molly and I have developed a rhythm on these outings, and they've all been miles more successful than that first one, though it would probably be difficult for them to be worse.

Boat trips are special though. They don't happen as often, and unlike the bayou trips, our first boat outing set a high bar. Still, I'm hoping we clear that bar tomorrow.

Chapter Sixteen

Molly

I feel almost criminal as I loiter in the shadows outside the lab building waiting for Jonathan to emerge. I can't believe he's upstairs right now taking the blame for *my* misconduct. I got carried away, that much is clear to me now. Even though I did it in a responsible way, I should have *never* involved the water samples—our research—in my prank.

What was I thinking?

Tired of waiting in the shadows, I walk across the parking lot to lurk near Jonathan's truck instead. I need to talk to him. I need to apologize. I need to thank him.

Soon, I see him exit the building and walk in my direction. He hasn't noticed me yet, so I take the opportunity to study him. The strap on his messenger-style computer bag crisscrosses his broad chest, and his hands are tucked into his front pockets. His eyes, usually warm and playful, are lowered, watching the ground in front of him as he walks. His hair, dark and curly, flops onto his forehead. His gait is confident and strong.

The more I watch him, the more my heart pounds and my stomach flutters, and the more obvious it becomes that I'm not just attracted to Jonathan. I don't want to just apologize or thank him. I definitely don't hate him. Maybe even ... the opposite? Or something close to it.

He's only a few feet from the truck when he sees me. "Hey!" he says, smiling slowly and stumbling back a step. "I thought you went home."

"I wanted to wait for you." I can't look away from him, especially now that he's as focused on me as I am on him. Jonathan has me mesmerized, without even trying. The air between us feels electric, like we're two atoms with opposite charges being drawn together. We're within an invisible force field, and I'm powerless to do anything but drift closer to him.

I don't know if he feels it, too, but he steps forward so we're toe to toe. "I'm glad you did." He takes his hands out of his pockets as his eyes dip to my mouth.

It's all the invitation I need. I launch myself forward and up—he's *so* tall, at least compared to me—my lips crashing into his. For a terrifying second, he freezes, and I'm afraid my impulsive action is yet another mistake. I start to pull away. Jonathan wraps one arm around my back, pulling me closer, while the other arm comes up, his hand cupping the back of my neck.

He's kissing me back. What's more, he's taking control of this kiss, moving his lips against mine with frantic, desperate energy. I reach my hand behind his head, tangling my fingers in his curls, silky against my skin. He groans softly against my mouth.

His lips leave mine, moving to trail kisses across my jawline. "Thank you," I breathe out. "I'm so sorry I got you in trouble—"

"With this reward, it was one thousand percent worth it," he murmurs, running his lips over my neck.

"Something can't be one thousand percent," I say. "Cent means hundred, so—" The rest of my explanation is lost as his mouth covers mine again. I feel him smirking against my lips, and I pull back slightly.

"Are you laughing at me?" I ask. Almost every nerve ending in my body screams at me to lean back in, kiss him again. The self-preservation part of me keeps me in place.

Jonathan leans his forehead against mine, breathing heavily. When he catches his breath, he tilts his face away enough to look me in the eye. "No, I'm not laughing at you. I'm finding you delightful, as always." His hazel eyes are bright and sincere as he lifts his hand away from my back and gently caresses a finger across my cheek. "You're incredible, Carrots. I've wanted this for a while."

All coherent thought leaves my head so quickly I get lightheaded. "A while?" I repeat, dazed.

He chuckles. "Yeah."

"Me too," I admit.

He grins and wraps me in his arms, squeezing my body against him. It feels better than being bundled up in the most luxurious weighted blanket, especially when he presses a kiss to the top of my head. I inhale against his shirt. He has a subtly clean smell, like laundry detergent and the hand soap in the bathrooms at the lab, nothing overpowering.

"Does this mean you don't hate me anymore?" he asks, his voice muffled in my hair.

I smile and nestle my cheek into his chest. "I think it does."

My mantra of the day is "What was I thinking?" I thought it after I learned Dr. Perron was visiting the lab this morning. I thought it as I waited for Jonathan in the parking lot after work. I think it now—a refrain that's looping through my head—as I lie in bed trying to get to sleep after kissing Jonathan Stanch.

Of course, the answer on all counts is that I *wasn't* thinking. I was giving in to my impulses in a way I haven't since freshman year of college. I let Jonathan poke holes in the walls I'd constructed not only around my heart, but around my mind as well. Walls that were designed to keep me on track and focused. Now, layers of regret are filling in the holes like bricks being cemented into place.

Yes, Jonathan is handsome and charming. This, I've always known. He's also, I've learned to my bewilderment, thoughtful and kind and supportive and funny. Add to that his apparent romantic interest in me, and a weaker woman would have given in weeks ago. I take a kind of twisted pride in that. At least I held out this long.

The sad truth is, I don't hate Jonathan. I'm not sure I ever really have, deep down. But I also can't have him.

If I had been focused on my work these past weeks instead of playing games with Jonathan, I'd probably be closer to cracking the proverbial code on my data model. I'd have already worked out a plan to test my hypothesis about the effect of tropical systems on harmful algal bloom outbreaks. I wouldn't have been on the receiving end of that disappointed look from Dr. Gantr.

My phone pings with a text notification.

Jonathan:

> Don't forget we're out on the boat tomorrow. See you in the morning, Carrots

I'm supposed to meet him bright and early by the bench in the grassy area behind our lab building. He's probably picturing a romantic day on the water with some work threaded in between flirtatious looks and hot kisses.

Honestly, that sounds amazing. Imagining his lips on me tomorrow, remembering how they felt against my skin earlier tonight, my heart flutters, and my hands feel jittery. It's desire, and as much as I've tried, I can't control it. Not around Jonathan.

So, I need to control the variables I can: my proximity to Jonathan, my focus on my work, my insistence on staying in the lab.

I text back a thumbs-up, but I already know I'm not going on that boat tomorrow.

Jonathan's already waiting when I arrive at our meeting spot the next morning. As soon as he sees me, his face splits into a huge, authentic smile. Then he must notice the expression on my face, or maybe that I'm not dressed for the boat, because he dims.

I wring my hands as he approaches. "What's wrong?" he asks. "Did something happen?"

I shut my eyes. "Yes. I'm sorry, but this was a mistake. Last night was a mistake."

"No, it wasn't." I force my eyes back open and look right into Jonathan's deep, unblinking gaze. His eyebrows are furrowed, his jaw clenched.

"It was," I insist. "I made a mistake. I don't usually do impulsive things, but—"

"You have ADHD," he cuts in. "Isn't impulsivity a primary characteristic?"

The words sting, but when I assess his expression, he doesn't look angry, just matter-of-fact. I push away the hurt and try to explain. "Yes, but I've gotten very good at suppressing impulsive urges. I purposely fight against them; I don't follow them, no matter what."

His eyebrows pinch tightly together. "Even if it's something you want?"

I shake my head. "It doesn't matter. It might be something I *think* I want in the moment but will derail my long-term goals, jeopardize my work."

Jonathan rocks back on his heels, his expression morphing into hurt. "I get it. You're scared. You're scared of what we could have for the same reason you're scared of fieldwork. You think you'll get distracted and fail."

"I don't *think*; I *know*. It's happened before. I can't risk my work."

He grabs my hands in his. "Freshman year of undergrad was a long time ago! You're so worried about how you've failed in the past you don't realize that when you suppress the characteristics of your ADHD, you're losing yourself. Over the last two months you've shown me this amazing side of yourself; a side that's funny and fiery and nurturing and sexy. Why don't more people know this about you? Why did you show *me*? I'm more than a distraction; *we're* more than a distraction, and you know it. And it scares the hell out of you."

It does scare the hell out of me. Everything he says is hitting its mark, striking me right in my heart. There's another piece of this puzzle, though. The piece that tells me he deserves better, even though he doesn't realize it yet.

"I like you," he continues, impassioned. "Just the way you are. You. Whether you're locking your keys in the car or creating complex data models or scowling or laughing. I'm ... I'm falling for you. I want *you*." His voice breaks, and he looks away.

I shake my head. He may think so now, but when it's day after day of picking up after me and dealing with my issues, how quickly will that feeling fade? No, it's better for me and for him, even if he doesn't realize it now, to stick to the plan. No dating, no distractions. Focus on work. Control what I can control to stay afloat.

"I'm sorry," I say softly. "I just can't."

"Can't or won't?" His eyes cut back to me.

"It's not that simple," I protest, pulling my hands away from his.

"It is if you let it be."

"We can still be friends. Partner up on our projects at the lab." Even as I say it, I know it's impossible.

His eyes darken. "I'm not interested in being friends. I ... can't. It's all or nothing for me. Either take this risk with me, or we go back to being semi-cordial colleagues. Your choice."

Why is he making this so hard? I swallow a sob, willing myself to stay stoic, at least until I'm alone. "I'm sorry," I say again, voice cracking despite my effort.

Jonathan's shoulders tighten. "I have fieldwork to do. I guess I'll see you around the lab. Goodbye, Molly."

As I watch him walk away, a quiet whimper breaks through my facade, and tears start dripping down my cheeks. My legs are suddenly weak; I drop onto the bench when I'm not sure they'll continue to hold me upright.

If this morning is about correcting the mistake I made when I kissed Jonathan, why did I feel so at ease in his arms last night, and why do I feel so heartbroken now?

Chapter Seventeen

Jonathan

I plug in the GPS coordinates for the glider I'm picking up today and steer the *Pulse* out toward the Gulf. It was only a month ago that I was following this same path through the Rigolets into Lake Borgne and then through the Chandeleur Sound with Molly onboard with me. The day she first opened up to me. The day I realized how strong my feelings for her were becoming. The day we almost kissed.

I imagined then what it would be like to kiss her for real, and last night I learned reality is better than my imagination.

Kissing Molly was a perfect moment. We have so few of those in life, don't we? Moments where we're intensely present, deliciously engaged, and thoroughly happy. When Molly kissed me, though, that's where I was. I should have known it would be fleeting.

I should have seen this coming. I knew she was a flight risk. But she kissed me last night, and I thought all my problems were over, that I finally won her trust, and now we could be together.

Naive? Maybe. I prefer the term "optimistic." I'm not feeling so hopeful now, though, more ... confused. And hurt.

Alone on a boat in a vast expanse of water is either the best place to be in my state of mind, or the worst. The best because it's gorgeous out here, and there's really no bad time to be out on the water. The worst because it leaves a lot of time for thinking, reflecting, and obsessing.

For some reason, though, it's my parents more so than Molly who are on my mind. As much as I threw the "distraction" excuse at Molly this morning, haven't the pranks, fieldwork, and my focus on Molly over the last couple of months been a distraction for me? An excuse not to reflect too much on my dad's upcoming wedding and my unresolved feelings around my parents' divorce.

I still haven't come to terms with either. Last time I talked to her, Tamara suggested seeing a therapist to help me work through it. It's a good idea. I'm not sure why I didn't think of it years ago. Probably because I've been living and working far from Ohio since my high school graduation and haven't had any real reason to grapple with my childhood issues until now.

As I pilot the *Pulse* back to shore, I resolve to make an appointment. Nearing the marina, my phone starts going crazy with notifications. I glance at the screen, telling myself it's not because I'm hoping Molly called or texted while I was out at sea today.

Mostly the notifications are from social media apps. I dock the boat, turning off the engine before I look more closely.

Interestingly, I have an email from Dr. Perron with the subject line "Opportunity." I'm intrigued. The email itself gives a phone number, with Dr. Perron asking me to give him a call.

I pocket my phone and finish gathering the equipment and performing final inspections of the *Pulse* before putting her back in storage. We store the gliders here, too, so I need to hose down and dry off the one I brought in today.

When I finally return to my truck in the parking garage adjacent to the dock, I call Dr. Perron.

He picks up right away. "Derek Perron."

I clear my throat. "Hi, Dr. Perron, it's Jonathan Stanch. You asked me to give you a call?"

"Jonathan! Hello. Can I call you Jonathan?" He pushes forward without waiting for my answer. "Listen, I wanted to talk to you because I was impressed with how you comported yourself at the lab the other morning."

"Thank you, sir." I didn't "comport" myself in any particular way as far as I'm aware. I was just trying to keep Molly out of trouble and make sure Dr. Gantt's lab looked good.

His voice slips into a confidential tone. "There's an ... opportunity that's come up in another lab that I want to discuss with you."

"Okay. What kind of opportunity?" I love working on Dr. Gantt's team, but with my feelings for Molly and her rejection this morning, I can't help but think a change might be a good idea. It doesn't hurt to hear more.

"Can you meet me tomorrow for dinner? There's a place on Conti Street. I'll send you the details."

I hesitate. Conti Street is known for its nightlife and bars, especially on Saturday nights. It doesn't have quite as wild a reputation as Bourbon Street, but it's not a likely choice for a business meeting. "What time?"

"Around six thirty, if you're available."

That's early enough that whatever restaurant or bar Dr. Perron has in mind won't be too lively yet. "Sure, I can do that. I appreciate you thinking of me."

"Great! I'll text you the details."

"Looking forward to it, sir."

We hang up, and I wonder what kind of opportunity would have Dr. Perron speaking so vaguely and wanting to meet on a Saturday night on Conti Street.

I don't know Dr. Perron well, only that he's been the dean of the college for the past five years and tends to watch the research projects happening in the College of Coast and Environment at NOSU a little too closely, in a way that implies he doesn't trust the principal investigators, the PIs, who are in charge of the labs. He gets antsy when a lab hasn't produced any flashy findings that can be touted to the press.

I'm not savvy enough to understand the larger political landscape of the colleges and departments at NOSU. I just want to keep my head down and pilot boats. If Dr. Perron's mysterious "opportunity" can help me do that farther away from Molly Delaney, all the better for my heart.

Saturday evening, I opt for jeans and a dress shirt for my meeting with Dr. Perron at a bar. Conti Street is in downtown New Orleans, and the restaurant where Dr. Perron asked me to meet him is near Jackson Square. Even though I live in Metairie rather than New Orleans proper, it's only a twenty-minute drive. Parking is a challenge though; I pay to park in a garage and walk the last half a block to the bar.

When I arrive, Dr. Perron is already sitting at a tall pub table with a bottle of locally-brewed beer in front of him. The place is busy, but it looks like it's still a normal dinner crowd. I hold my hand up in greeting as I sit across from Dr. Perron.

A server materializes out of nowhere. "Something to drink?"

"Ah, just a root beer, please." I don't have anything against drinking; it just feels weird when I'm meeting with my boss's boss. This isn't exactly a night out on the town.

As the server disappears again, Dr. Perron shakes my hand across the table. "Jonathan! How's your Saturday going?"

"Pretty good," I lie. *Was rejected by the woman of my dreams yesterday, so, you know, two thumbs up.*

"Good, good. Did you eat yet?" He takes a swig from his beer bottle.

I force a smile. "I can always eat."

He hands me a menu, and I look at the options: typical bar-and-grill fare with a lot of local flavor. I haven't had much of an appetite today. When the server comes back with my root beer, I order some chicken wings and fries. Dr. Perron orders red beans and rice, which of course makes me think of Molly.

Who am I kidding? Everything makes me think of Molly.

"So," I start, hoping to prompt Dr. Perron to cut to the chase.

"So, tell me about your research interests."

I talk a bit about my PhD topic—the ecological consequences of urbanization on marine life—then about the research teams I've been on the last few years. "To be honest, Dr. Perron, mostly I like being in the water or on the water. Fieldwork is my favorite part."

He nods his head. "Call me Derek, please."

"Okay." Feels unnatural, but fine.

The restaurant is getting more crowded, with new groups of people coming in and sitting at the bar. A live band starts setting up in one corner, and the mood grows festive. I'm not at all in the right headspace for any of it.

Dr. Perron leans in, so I mimic his movement, leaning my forearms against the table. "Listen, we are on the cusp of receiving a large grant to research blue carbon offsetting. I'm looking for a PI to head things up. That could be you."

I frown. "Carbon offsetting?" It's a practice in which large corporations try to compensate for their greenhouse gas emissions through projects that supposedly remove equivalent amounts of carbon dioxide from the environment. Blue carbon offsetting is more specific to coastal wetlands, with corporations funding projects to compensate for carbon in the ocean, like restoring mangroves or seagrasses.

Blue carbon offsetting has been gaining popularity, but there are still questions about how effective it is and how much is just corporate posturing.

"Yessir. Could be huge for the university and for your career. What do you think?"

"What's the funding organization?" I start to ask when my phone pings, and I'm distracted by a text message. "Uh, you know what? I'm so sorry, Dr. Perron, but I have to go. Can we talk more about this another time? Bit of an emergency." I gesture to my phone.

Dr. Perron holds up his hand. "Sure thing. I'm interested in bringing you in for this, though. Let's talk details another time."

I pull out my wallet to cover my root beer and uneaten food, but Dr. Perron waves me away. "I've got it," he says with a wink. "Business expense."

I nod my thanks and speed toward the door holding my phone to my ear.

Chapter Eighteen

Molly

Another lively Saturday night for Molly Delaney, I think dejectedly as I slump on my couch and queue up the next *Anne of Green Gables* movie. I'm torturing myself, of course.

I couldn't find the energy to go to the lab today, my hard-won routine failing me at a time when my work is all I have left. By choice. I chose this.

So, it's a couch day. Honestly, as much as getting out of bed this morning felt insurmountable, I'm surprised I made it all the way to the couch. Some days are like this, and I've found that, despite all my instincts telling me to fight through the malaise, giving in produces better results. I can wallow for a day and then be back on track the next. The ache in my chest is new, though, since yesterday morning.

Unfortunately, wallowing isn't conducive to even the most basic parts of adulting, like feeding myself. The only food I have left in my kitchen from my parents' visit requires preparation, and I'm certainly in no place to do that today.

But I *can* make ready-to-eat food appear on my doorstep with my phone in just a few presses of a button. I order chicken tenders, my lifelong comfort food, and watch Anne while I wait for them to arrive.

Twenty minutes later, a notification on my phone tells me that the delivery person can't get through my apartment building's front entry door. I groan. I'll have to go all the way downstairs to get the food. I briefly consider if it's really worth it until my stomach growls. Fine. I heft myself up from the couch. I don't bother to put on shoes as I walk out the door while messaging the delivery person to wait for me.

Soon I'm back upstairs, bag of food in hand. I twist the knob to open my apartment door, but it doesn't turn, and the door doesn't open. It's locked.

My apartment door has two locks, and they both use the same key. One is a deadbolt that I have to remember to turn to the left to lock the door from the inside before I go to bed at night. From the outside, it can only be locked or unlocked with the key. I didn't bring a key with me, and therefore, the deadbolt can't possibly be engaged. The second is a doorknob lock. This one has a button on the doorknob on the inside of the apartment that I can press to lock the door from the outside. The door will still open from the inside when the lock is engaged but then requires the key to open it from the outside.

I drop my head into my hand. I must have forgotten to unlock the doorknob on my way out. Now I have to go all the way back downstairs and outside barefoot to grab my hide-a-key from the bushes—

Except I don't *have* a hide-a-key in the bushes anymore, do I?

I groan. There has to be another solution. My brain cycles through ideas. The building super is out of town this weekend, and their backup lives an hour away. I don't know any of my neighbors. I pat my pockets. I definitely *don't* have my keys, right?

I consider calling to Beaker through the door and somehow getting her to bat the doorknob enough to swivel the button. I'm scraping the bottom of the barrel for ideas that don't involve the man I rejected yesterday morning.

I don't really have a choice. As embarrassing as it is to have to text Jonathan to let me into my apartment, a part of me thrills in anticipation of seeing him. If he's even willing to come.

Molly:

I know you're mad at me but I need help

My phone immediately starts to ring. I answer, and before I can say anything, Jonathan's voice echoes into the hallway. "What happened? Are you okay?"

I hear loud music and talking in the background. He's out, not sitting around his apartment alone like I am. I sigh, rubbing my knuckles against my chest. The ache there has only expanded upon hearing his voice. "I'm okay. I locked myself out of my apartment, and I don't have a hide-a-key outside anymore."

Jonathan's silent for a few seconds, likely remembering, like I am, how he insisted on holding onto my spare apartment key. "Are you somewhere safe?" he asks.

"Yes. I'm in the hallway with my food order." I sheepishly explain how I came to find myself in this predicament.

"Okay. I'll be right there."

"If you're busy, I can figure something else out," I hedge. I'm not sure what that "something else" would be, but I've inconvenienced Jonathan so much already. He's a handsome, single man out on a Saturday night. He doesn't need to interrupt his evening to rescue his ... whatever we are to each other. Just plain coworkers? Frenemies?

He *should* be out, meeting people. He deserves to meet a nice, uncomplicated woman without all my baggage. He deserves everything he wants.

"No, I'm not far away. I can come," he insists. I puff out a relieved breath and give him the code for the front entry door.

The call disconnects, and I sit on the floor with my back against my apartment door. I open the bag of food and eat my chicken tenders while I wait. When I finish, I lean my head against the door and close my eyes.

It's not long before I hear Jonathan's familiar footsteps coming up the stairs. I open my eyes and jump up as the footsteps start to echo in the hallway itself.

"Hey," I greet him breathily as I drink in the sight of him. His black button-down shirt is slim cut through the torso, tucked neatly into dark-wash jeans that contour to his hips and legs. His black derby shoes are different and more stylish than the leather work shoes he wears to the lab. His curls look neater than normal, as if he put product in them.

It's a study in contrast with me clearly dressed for a night on the couch. He looks like he could have been on a date. Was he on a date?

"Were you on a date?" I blurt.

Jonathan doesn't answer my question, instead asking one of his own. "Is that my shirt?"

I glance down at my holey leggings and baggy red T-shirt, which yes, is indeed the one I borrowed from him that first day of field-work. The material is so soft and feels so cozy against my skin. Add to that the fact that it's a piece of Jonathan, and wearing it makes me feel less alone.

It's a guilty pleasure. I never expected him to see me in it. My face heats, and I'm sure it matches the shirt when I lift my head. I can't read Jonathan's expression. His eyes are guarded, his face aloof.

Something feels weird about the interaction. I know I'm the one who inserted this emotional distance into our relationship—and for good reason—but I miss the back and forth. I miss *him*. And something else is missing, something I can't put my finger on.

Jonathan pulls his keys from his pocket and singles out the one for my apartment. He slides the key into the keyhole and turns it until we hear the clicking noise that indicates the lock is disengaged. He removes the key and hooks his finger through the key ring.

He takes a step back, but I don't move to open the door. "Jonathan—" I start. I have no plan for what I want to say; I just know that my heart has been weighed down and miserable these last couple of days without him.

He interrupts me. "I hope you've been keeping an eye on the potential hurricane that's in the Caribbean. They say it might come this way."

I haven't been keeping an eye on anything. I haven't even heard about it. I realize, though, what's so different about tonight, why Jonathan feels all wrong. He hasn't smiled once since he got here.

Not a grin or even a smirk, and certainly not the wide relaxed smile that makes my knees wobble. The ache in my chest grows to a throb. I scrabble for anything he might be willing to give me. "Jonathan, please." I hate how querulous my voice sounds, how vulnerable. "Can we please try to be friends?"

He shakes his head, his expression shifting from the restrained indifference he's shown since he arrived to a weariness that matches the way I feel. "I can't be friends with you."

"Can't or won't?" I ask, echoing his challenge to me from the other morning.

Finally, here's a ghost of a smile, just the smallest uptick at the corners of his mouth. "It's not that simple."

"Why not?"

"I can't just take what I feel for you and stuff it into an undersized box."

The implication being that I can. After all, he's seen me do it. I took my joy at being out on the water and crammed it into a box labeled "fear of the ocean." I funneled my loneliness into a box called "dedication to my work." Now I want to take whatever this big soft emotion I'm feeling for Jonathan is and force it into a box, slapping the word "friendship" onto it, after calling it "hatred" for years.

Jonathan runs his hands through his hair. "Caring for someone else doesn't follow strict rules or schedules. You know, with the way you obsess over couples like your sister and her boyfriend, and Anne and Gilbert, and Matthew and Marilla—"

"Matthew and Marilla are brother and sister," I can't help but correct.

He pauses. "Really? That's, um ... weird. I could have sworn... Anyway, what I'm trying to say is that I find it surprising that you don't seem to believe in love."

I drop my eyes to the floor. I can't face him as I say possibly the most vulnerable thing I've said to anyone ever. I owe him this much. "I do believe in love. I just don't believe it's meant for me."

I hear his sharp intake of breath and raise my eyes to take in his expression. He looks stunned. He shakes his head and opens his mouth as if to argue, then closes it again. He steps closer, backing me up against the wall next to the door. Slowly, he slides a hand behind my neck, his fingers tangling in my hair, and leans forward. His lips brush mine in the softest, sweetest kiss. A few seconds of contact and it's over, much too soon. I want to fist my hand in his shirt and pull him back to me, beg him to kiss me for real. It wouldn't be fair to him.

He rocks back on his heels, his face inches from mine, not touching. His eyes, dark and intense, bore into mine. "You're wrong," he whispers in a broken voice.

He reaches behind me and twists the doorknob, swinging the door to my apartment open.

As he turns away, I stop him. "I ... I need my spare key back." I try to keep my voice steady, though my heart is pounding.

Without turning around, he answers me in a rough tone. "Not yet." Then he walks away.

The interaction guts me, and I feel the full weight of the decision I've made to live a solitary life focused on my research. It's a heavy weight, situated primarily on top of my heart.

But Jonathan's parting words ignite a flicker of hope deep within me. Why do those two words, despite my insistence that love is not for me, make me so inordinately happy? He came here tonight to help me, no questions asked. He didn't have to.

Keeping the key feels like a declaration. He wants to be there for me, and he's not done with me yet.

I wake up Sunday morning feeling ready to take on the day. I shower, get dressed, and go grocery shopping—with a list and everything. In the afternoon, I head to the lab to get started processing the water samples Jonathan collected without me on Friday.

As afternoon turns to evening, Jonathan doesn't come to the lab. Not that I expect him to after our interaction yesterday. It's just that he's become such a part of my routine over the last few weeks. I've gotten used to seeing him at the lab on weekend evenings.

He usually arrives right around the time I should be taking a break, and though two months ago I would have said his timing interrupts my workflow, now it seems fortuitous. I never forget to eat dinner on the nights when Jonathan comes into the lab while I'm working. I don't tonight either, but not because Jonathan comes in. It's because I never get to hyperfocus; I'm so distracted by watching the door.

The disappointment is a palpable sludge I feel inside my body, oozing from my heart into my stomach and weighing down my legs. I trudge home while it's still light out.

At home, I go to the kitchen to get a glass of water. I'm planning to go to bed early and dissociate by scrolling on social media for a while before I fall asleep. At least I'll see Jonathan tomorrow at work though I'm not sure how to act around him. Smile politely? Ignore him? Surreptitiously watch him out of the corner of my eye all day while not approaching him directly? That seems like the most realistic option.

The thoughts distract me from seeing the piece of paper on the front of my refrigerator at first. Once I notice it, it's all I can see. An indigo-colored sticky note hangs on the refrigerator door with the message "You are beautiful" written across it in messy handwriting.

I know that handwriting. I recognize that sticky note in the hard-to-find indigo color. And who else even has access to my apartment?

Jonathan was *here*, sometime today while I was out. Maybe I should feel indignant, angry even. He doesn't have permission to use the key to enter my apartment, after all.

Instead, I'm elated he hasn't given up on me, which is selfish because I'm not going to change my mind. I can't tell him we can't be together one day and then secretly want him to continue pursuing me. I don't want to play games with his emotions. I care about him too much for that.

Still, I feel lighter as I get ready for bed. When I'm finally situated under the covers, phone in hand, I remember that Jonathan said something about a potential hurricane in the Caribbean.

I open a web browser app and search for information. Sure enough, there's a tropical storm named Hernando southeast of Cuba. The track forecast cone has Hernando potentially continuing northwest into the Gulf, making landfall as a low category hurricane somewhere between the Florida panhandle and coastal Texas within a week.

Of course, my mind instantly goes to my research. If Hernando comes close enough to New Orleans, I could try to gather data on how the properties of the water change because of the storm. Although, it would be too dangerous to be out in the Gulf collecting data in the middle of a hurricane. How else could I get real-time data about the water as a hurricane passes through?

An idea sparks in my brain, and I kindle it, letting it grow to an ember and then a small lick of a flame until the fire is burning hot and bright. It *could* work. I just need to convince Dr. Gantt. It's going to be a long night.

Chapter Nineteen

Jonathan

I walk up the stairs to the lab on Monday morning with Molly Delaney on the brain. So what else is new?

My first big plan—to win Molly over—was a success, I would say. After less than two months, she no longer hates me. In fact, she likes me, maybe more than likes me if I'm reading between the lines correctly. So, my new big plan is to help Molly Delaney love herself.

When we were standing in that empty hallway outside her apartment, and Molly admitted that she doesn't believe love is meant for her? It broke me. Molly's amazing, and I'm not sure how she doesn't know that. Any man in his right mind would want to be with her. I know I do.

So, I broke into her apartment yesterday. Well, is it really "breaking in" if you have the key? I entered her apartment with the key she gave me, and I left her a note. And I plan to do it again today and every day as long as it takes, even if I use up each one of the three thousand something sticky notes left from when Molly covered my cubicle.

She needs to see herself the way I see her: beautiful, bold, creative, nurturing, dedicated ... I could go on.

Even if she never reconsiders us being together, I desperately want her to believe she's worthy of an amazing partner—someone who loves, respects, and supports her—if she wants one. And if she doesn't want a partner, I'd like to know she's making that choice because it's what she really wants, not what she thinks she deserves.

I swivel my head to check Molly's cubicle as I move toward mine. She's not here yet. Will she be mad about the sticky note? Acknowledge it, or me, at all?

I don't have time to dwell too much on her reaction. I have a meeting with Dr. Gantt this morning about the ocean gliders. Three of the five in our fleet are currently sitting in storage at the dry dock in Slidell, ready for their next missions. We need to decide what we want those to be. The consistent data from the Gulf are valuable to track baseline information and even trends over time, but we need to do more to make the gliders worth the investment.

I hope Dr. Gantt has some ideas, because I haven't come up with anything yet.

I settle into a chair in Dr. Gantt's office. Instead of jumping right into talking about the gliders, she starts us off with another topic.

"How is Dr. Delaney doing with the fieldwork?" she asks, leaning her chair back slightly as she regards me from across the desk.

I swallow uncomfortably. "Great," I answer honestly. "She's a natural. She settled right in, and we work together well."

Dr. Gantt narrows her eyes. "I'm looking at your face, and I'm sensing there's a 'but' coming."

"*But*," I start, shooting her a smile, "I think I work better solo, and Dr. Delaney has probably learned enough about the fieldwork processes by now, right?"

I clasp my hands together in my lap and then unclasp them and try to slide them in my pockets. I'm fidgeting. I can't tell Dr. Gantt the real reason Molly won't work with me anymore. *Yeah, so after a string of super unprofessional pranks we played on each other right here in the lab, the last of which almost resulted in our team losing funding, Dr. Delaney and I kissed in the parking lot, and then she freaked out because a relationship is so outside of her comfort zone, and now I'm wallowing and pining, and she's back to following her strict life rules.* I'm sure that explanation would inspire our boss's confidence in us.

"You don't want Dr. Delaney to work with you anymore?" Actually, I desperately want Dr. Delaney to do everything with me forever, but it's not up to me.

I rub my chin. "That's not exactly what I meant—"

Before I can finish the thought—fortunately, because I have no idea what I'm going to say—the door to Dr. Gantt's office bangs open, and a disheveled Molly stands in the doorway.

Her hair is wet, slicked back into a messy ponytail. She's wearing yoga pants as normal, but her T-shirt is inside out and backward. Dark circles rim her eyes, and I wonder if she slept at all last night.

I jump to my feet in concern. Is this because of me?

Even as I stand, I notice further details. She's clutching a notebook in her hands; it's flipped open to a page filled with calculations and notes in her sloppy handwriting. Her eyes, though tired, are bright. Her expression is one of excitement and determination.

Dr. Gantt also stands up. "Dr. Delaney! This is a private meeting."

"I'm so sorry to intrude, but you have to hear this. It's the breakthrough we've been looking for!"

Dr. Gantt and I exchange a look, and she props a hand on her hip. "Well, I'm intrigued." She smiles and gestures Molly forward into the room.

Molly closes the office door behind her and takes a seat in the chair next to me. She's practically buzzing with energy as she sets her notebook on Dr. Gantt's desk.

"There's a hurricane coming, probably. Hopefully!" A laugh bubbles up out of her mouth like she can't stop it. Her cheeks turn pink.

"Hey," I say soothingly, laying my hand on top of hers. "Tell us what's going on."

Molly turns her head and meets my eyes. She takes a deep breath, in and out, and faces forward. "I'd like to send the ocean gliders out before the hurricane to collect data in real-time as it passes through."

I sit back in my chair. She told me she was working on proving a correlation between hurricanes and red tide outbreaks. I can see how live data that track the properties of the water in the Gulf before, during, and after a hurricane would be useful. Even potentially game-changing.

Dr. Gantt tilts her head, her braids swinging with the motion. "Tell me more," she prompts.

Molly explains her hypothesis that the changes tropical storms and hurricanes cause in the ocean, or in this case, the Gulf, might be so severe as to create conditions for outbreaks of harmful algal blooms. "I created and ran a data model that compared our Gulf water samples from the last two years with weather data. It showed a statistically significant correlation between hurricanes, or even just tropical storms, and the conditions for an outbreak."

Dr. Gantt smiles, clearly catching on to the idea. "So, if we deploy the gliders during the upcoming hurricane, we could see in real time how the storm changes the water."

"Exactly."

Dr. Gantt drums her fingertips on the desk. "It's a risk though. Gliders are expensive equipment. Could they be damaged?" She looks at me.

I clear my throat. "Of course it's possible, but—"

"But there's documentation of gliders at sea during storms. NOAA uses them to collect data to help improve hurricane forecasts. A university in Florida left a glider out unintentionally during a category four storm last season. They set it to avoid surfacing to send data until the storm passed. It was safer underwater. It survived, and it was the same model we have."

"But they didn't use their data to make any connections with red tide?" Dr. Gantt asks.

"No, it wasn't their focus. But it is ours." Molly wears a hopeful expression as she answers Dr. Gantt's questions.

Dr. Gantt turns to me. "What do you think, Dr. Stanch?"

I don't hesitate. "The bigger the risk, the bigger the reward," I respond with a grin. "Let's do it."

Molly squeals and claps her hands. Dr. Gantt breaks in. "Okay, okay, it's not a done deal. We still have safety to consider. We'll want the gliders as close to the center of the storm as possible, but we might not know where that is until just a few days out. Can we safely launch the gliders before the storm gets too close?"

Molly points to the calculations in her notebook. "I've been watching the forecasts and, yes, based on the current expected track and speed, we should be able to go out and deploy the gliders using the *Pulse* before the water gets too rough."

Dr. Gantt frowns. "Do we have to deploy them by boat? Why not on the shore, and program them to travel into place?"

I shake my head. "It would take too long. If we launched the gliders from the dock, it could take them days to get into position. They wouldn't be ready in time for the storm."

"What timeline are we looking at then?"

Molly jumps in. "Right now, Hernando is forecasted to make landfall, probably in or near New Orleans, late on Thursday. That gives us roughly three days. The track should be more predictable by tomorrow night after Hernando passes over Cuba into the Gulf. If we deploy the gliders Wednesday, we have the best chance of accurate positioning and a safe voyage."

"Okay, then. I'm officially green-lighting this expedition with the caveat that it must be done safely. If anything changes significantly, let's come back together and reevaluate."

I bounce my right knee, my foot slapping the floor in a way that reminds me of a dog during a satisfying scratch behind the ears. I'm fidgety now for a whole different reason. This is going to be so much fun.

"Now, what kind of team do you need?" Dr. Gantt continues. "Dr. Stanch will obviously pilot the *Pulse*. You'll want at least one other person with you on Wednesday. Then when the data start coming through, you can have all the grad students at your disposal, Dr. Delaney."

"I'm going with Jonathan on the boat Wednesday," Molly throws in.

Dr. Gantt and I both freeze and turn our attention to Molly. "Really?" I ask, at the same time Dr. Gantt prompts, "Are you sure?"

Molly focuses her eyes on mine, her lips pressed together firmly. She lifts her chin, a glint in her eye. "I'm not missing this."

Why does my heart pound with the hope that she means more than just a boat ride?

Over the next day and a half, I live out all my old *Twister* dreams as Molly and I learn everything we can about soon-to-be Hurricane Hernando. Granted, tornadoes and hurricanes are vastly different—strong, rotating winds really being their only similarity—but the vibe's the same, the rush of facing off against Mother Nature and the risk of losing it all.

As Molly watches for track developments in the forecast, I focus on preparing the gliders. I notice when an email comes in from Dr. Perron on Monday, but I don't have time to do more than skim the message. It's crunch time on possibly the most significant breakthrough of my career, and, more importantly, Molly's.

With all the activity, there's really no time for Molly and me to talk, though I do make it to her apartment each day to leave a note on her refrigerator. On Monday, I wrote "You make the impossible look effortless" on a blue sticky note. And today on my way to Slidell to make sure all three gliders in storage there are functioning properly and ready for a new mission, I stop by her apartment and leave a red one that says, "You meet challenges with courage and strength."

She hasn't mentioned the notes to me, but I know she's seen them because she moves them. When I stick the third note, the first two are sort of diagonal to each other, lined up bottom right corner to top left corner. I don't know if she has an end goal in mind for their placement, but I like the idea that she sees a note, maybe, hopefully, it makes her smile, and then she unsticks it and carefully sets it in place.

As expected, after Hernando passes over Cuba into the Gulf on Tuesday night, the spaghetti models start to align. By Wednesday morning, the probability is high that Hernando will intensify into a Category 1 hurricane before the end of the day and then slowly move toward New Orleans, making landfall here Thursday night.

Chapter Twenty

Molly

Waiting on a hurricane really is like stalking a turtle. That's the phrase Dennis Jackson, a popular local meteorologist, uses. Dennis and I have become good friends over the last two days. Well not like real friends, but I've watched all his broadcasts, read all his social media posts, and pored over every map and track he's shared about Hurricane Hernando.

I think Dennis must be living at the Channel Nine headquarters this week. Even though the changes to the track forecasts have been minimal and Hernando is creeping along at just ten miles per hour, Dennis is up on the screen, giving live updates every couple of hours and posting to his public social media accounts with details in between on-camera appearances. Does the man even sleep?

If not, I'm right there with him. I'm slamming down coffee and Dr. Pepper as I check and recheck the coordinates for the gliders against each shift in the forecasted storm track. I'm planning to have each of the three gliders take a slightly different path, hoping we'll get data from the center and the edges of the storm as it passes through.

Jonathan's been busy prepping the gliders. Gah. That man. I've returned home each night this week to a new note stuck to my refrigerator. Three days, three notes, each one sweeter than the last. He's not only running full force on my research project right now, he's also finding the time to melt my heart. He must really believe I'm worth all this effort.

I'm waiting at my apartment now for him to pick me up to drive to Slidell and head out on the water with the gliders. In the meantime, I'm sitting on my couch with a laptop propped up on the coffee table, watching Dennis's latest live-streamed forecast.

"Remember, everyone, today is the day to finish all your preparations. Make sure you're stocked up on nonperishable food and clean water. Charge your devices in case we lose power. Bring any loose items from the yard inside. If you're evacuating from any of our lower-lying areas, remember you don't need to go far. We're expecting Hernando to make landfall as a Category 1, which is definitely not something to ignore, but there's no need to panic, either. One of our best rules of thumb for these storms as you're deciding whether to evacuate or ride it out is: run from water, hide from wind. If you're in an area that floods easily, which is a lot of us here in Orleans Parish, consider going to higher ground at a friend or relative's house, or at one of the public emergency shelters set up in the area."

The rotund Black man in a bow tie has such a soothing voice, yet it's authoritative at the same time. No wonder I, and most of the rest of New Orleans, consider him *the* person to listen to in a potential weather emergency. He's famous for his reassuring hurricane "rules" that counsel residents to be prepared and alert in the face of a forecasted hurricane, but also not to get sucked into the hype. His most quoted rule is: "Don't panic until I tell you to panic."

He's not telling anyone to panic now, though he would probably advise Jonathan and me against going boating today. I peek out the back window. So far, the day is bright and sunny and will likely remain that way for hours yet. We'll be fine.

Jonathan texts that he's parked downstairs, so I grab my bag and kiss the top of Beaker's furry little head. After ensuring I have the key and locking my door, I walk down the stairs to the front entrance. Before I open the door, I take a deep breath to fortify myself against what's bound to be a long, awkward ride out to Slidell.

The truck's parked at the curb. I open the passenger side door and slide into the front seat. Without meaning to, I inhale the now-familiar smell of Jonathan and his truck. The clean smell, mixed with hints of cinnamon and citrus, instantly makes me feel comfortable and safe. I've missed this.

Jonathan is on the phone with Dr. Gantt, her voice projecting into the cab through the speakers. "And no major changes to the forecast?"

He glances at me, so I answer. "Hi, Dr. Gantt. I've been religiously tracking the forecast, and all the models are in agreement about Hernando's path and intensity."

"Okay. That sounds fine, then. But you always have an out today, okay? Your lives are more important than the research. If it feels unsafe at any point, you turn back. Is that clear?"

"Yes, ma'am," Jonathan and I reply in unison.

"Alright, then. Be safe out there."

We say goodbye and Jonathan disconnects the call. He smiles at me nervously before pulling out onto the road and driving toward I-10, but at least it's a smile.

We've been en route less than ten minutes when my phone pings, and I see a notification from the National Weather Service.

"Hernando is officially a hurricane now," I announce.

Jonathan drums his fingers on the steering wheel. "Already?"

"Yeah." I study my phone. "No changes to the track or forecasted intensity at landfall. We're officially under a hurricane warning. It's kind of exciting and nerve wracking. I've never experienced a hurricane before."

Jonathan raises his eyebrows. "How have you never been through a hurricane before?" he asks. "As long as you've been in New Orleans."

We're doing small talk. This is fine. I can handle this. I shrug. "If any ever got close, I just went to visit my parents for a few days."

He keeps his face forward, but his disbelief is evident in his voice. "But you grew up in Texas."

"I grew up in Austin," I clarify. "Not much major hurricane action there."

"What about tornadoes?"

I remember that Jonathan's favorite movie is *Twister* and wonder if he's been thinking about that these last few days. Not that hurricanes and tornadoes are very similar. "It's not a real hot spot for those either."

"Hmm," he hums.

We both fall silent again. I yawn, trying to ward off the soothing effects of the truck's motion. I anticipated the awkwardness. How could it not be? We have so much we could say to each other, so much we're not saying, but also, we need to focus on the task at hand. This could be huge for both our careers, not to mention Dr. Gantt's reputation. It's best to push our personal drama to the side for today.

"Why don't you believe love is for you?" Jonathan asks suddenly, his eyes on the road.

I heave out a loud sigh. I'm too tired for this conversation. "Do we have to talk about this now?"

"Yeah, I think we should talk about this now," he answers, his tone indicating that it's not up for debate.

My stomach flutters. Why do I find him so hot when he's stern and bossy? I'm not sure, but maybe it's why I answer him instead of deflecting. "It's just ... I'm not what you would call a catch. I'm messy, disorganized, forgetful—"

He interrupts me. "First of all, I would definitely call you a catch. Second of all, you are creative, bold, empathetic—"

"Okay, I get it. You think I'm wonderful. For now." I roll my eyes. "I've just had years of practice controlling the variables in my life because it helps me stay on track."

"No distractions," he supplies.

"Right. Plus, I don't want anyone feeling obligated to take care of me when my life is a mess, which it often can be."

"So instead, you're living half a life." His jaw ticks, and he squeezes the steering wheel.

My shoulders tense, and I fold my arms across my chest. "When I first told you about my ADHD, and you lectured me, it was none of your business. Why do you think it's any of your business now?"

"Maybe it's not!" he snaps back. "Maybe it's none of my business. But I can't just sit back and watch..." he trails off, his voice cracking. He swallows and starts again in a gentler voice. "Molly, I care about you. You're the most amazing woman I've ever met, and it kills me, literally keeps me up at night knowing that you don't realize how amazing you are. That you're punishing yourself for having a brain that works a little differently instead of embracing who you are and enjoying the things that make you happy."

Warmth fills my whole body. I blink back tears, rubbing my gritty eyes. Before I can stop them, the words, "Like you?" slip softly out of my mouth.

Jonathan darts his eyes over to the passenger seat. "*Do* I make you happy?"

"Of course you do," I whisper. I lean my head back against the seat and close my eyes. They're so heavy all of a sudden.

"I'm glad. I love when you smile."

I drift off, snoozing the last twenty minutes of the drive, and waking up again only when the truck pulls to a stop in the parking garage at the marina.

I look around, tossing my head to feel more alert. We're the only vehicle in the garage. I hop out of the truck and follow Jonathan toward the office.

"They should have the *Pulse* ready for us," Jonathan says, "I called ahead, and they know we're coming."

He makes no mention of our conversation in the truck before I fell asleep, so I don't bring it up, either.

Jonathan smiles and shakes hands with a man in a polo shirt with the marina's logo on it. The man points us toward where he has the *Pulse* out of storage and waiting for us. "Are you sure you want to go out today?" he asks.

"We'll be fine," Jonathan answers. "We actually need some data about the storm, so we have to do this ahead of Hernando."

"Okay. I'm the only one here today. I'll wait until you get back so I can put the boat back up for you."

"Appreciate it, man." Jonathan shakes his hand again.

We walk down the dock to our boat. Three gliders are strapped onto plywood pallets, taking up most of the space on the back deck. The platforms are about two feet high, bringing the tops of the gliders even with my waist. Behind the gliders is the door leading to the enclosed control area where Jonathan will pilot the boat.

Jonathan checks all the instruments and whatever else needs to be checked. Like last time, he leads me through the safety procedures, reminding me where to find flares, life vests, and other equipment.

Before we set off, I check my phone for one last Hernando update while we're still in range of cell towers. I read the latest post from Dennis.... Well, that's not good.

"Jonathan."

He finishes punching coordinates into the GPS and lifts his head to look at me. "Yeah?"

"Hernando has almost tripled in speed since this morning. The track and intensity are the same, but now they're saying landfall tonight, not tomorrow night."

"So, when will we start seeing the outer bands?"

I peer up at the sky—the sunshine has started to make way for clouds, though none yet indicating a storm on the way. "This afternoon."

Jonathan breathes out forcefully. "Alright. That complicates things."

I study his expression carefully. "What should we do?" I doubt this expedition is still in the range of what Dr. Gantt would consider "safe," but scrapping it now would be disappointing.

Jonathan shrugs, watching me as deliberately as I'm watching him. We're each waiting for the other to show what they're thinking. "It's your call. This is your project."

I debate sharing my thoughts. Finally, I admit, "I don't want the responsibility of this decision to be mine alone. You'll be out there, too. Please. What do you think?"

Jonathan nods. "I think it will be more dangerous. I also know I can pilot the *Pulse* even through bad weather. Collecting these data would be huge. We've come this far, so … let's do it."

I smile. "It's what Bill and Jo would do, right?"

He bursts out laughing. "Absolutely. For science."

"For science," I agree.

Chapter Twenty-One

Molly

Before we leave the relative safety of the Rigolets for the Gulf, Jonathan advises me to put anything I don't want to get soaked or washed overboard down below. His words make the risks of this trip feel suddenly real, and my stomach flips with uneasiness.

He stops the boat and lowers the anchor so we can prepare. I take my bag, which contains my wallet and phone, below deck and secure it in a cabinet.

Jonathan comes down and meets me at the bottom of the steps. He slips a bright orange life vest on me from behind like a sweater and spins me around to adjust the straps and buckle it in the front. Though his motions are brusque and purposeful, the tender attention and concern behind them stir my heart.

Jonathan cares about my safety. He cares about my happiness. He cares about my work. He cares about *me*.

"Do you get seasick?" His voice cuts into my thoughts. I blink to refocus my eyes and see Jonathan strapping on his own life vest.

"What?" I ask.

"Do you know if you get seasick or have motion sickness?" he repeats.

I lift my shoulders. "I'm not sure."

He hands me a large brown capsule and a bottle of water. "Take this," he instructs. "It will help keep you from getting seasick." He reads the question in my expression and answers before I even have a chance to ask it. "The water is going to get rough. Between the wind and the waves, we'll be pitching and yawing like crazy."

"Okay." My voice is faint, even to my own ears. What am I getting us into here? I've never done *anything* like this before. I swallow the pill with a gulp of water.

"It's not too late to turn back," Jonathan says, like he's reading my mind. He brings a hand to my cheek and strokes his thumb across it. His eyes lock onto mine. "Are you sure this is what you want, Carrots?"

I think back to the sticky note waiting on my refrigerator for me last night: "You meet challenges with courage and strength." I'm not sure that's true, but I'd like it to be. I've been so afraid for so long—afraid to let my guard down, afraid to try something new, afraid to be myself. My fear and caution haven't gotten me where I want to be. I need to step into the unknown.

I push down my doubts, lifting my hand and placing it over Jonathan's on my face. "The bigger the risk, the bigger the reward, right?"

His eyebrows flash up. He smiles with his whole face, his eyes gleaming. "Attagirl," he murmurs, almost to himself.

We return above deck to find that the wind has picked up. Metal clangs rhythmically against metal as the shackles of the dock lines hit on the railings. The boat leans to the side and a spray of water comes up over the railing. We're in the control center of the boat where the steering wheel sits. It's enclosed, with all the windows closed; a safe haven as the waves outside turn gray and foreboding.

"Stay here in the helm until we need to go out to launch the gliders," Jonathan instructs.

He doesn't need to tell me twice. I wait as he ducks outside and to the front of the boat to pull the anchor up. He flips a switch, and I see the anchor chain start to move. Though it comes up automatically, he has to reach over and untwist it every so often.

Soon he's back at the wheel, and we're on our way under the bridge and through Lake Borgne. The weather holds until we reach the Gulf, where the waves are so strong, they make the boat lurch.

Jonathan sets his jaw. "Hold on," he says, not taking his eyes off the front of the boat as we climb the swells in front of us and then plummet back down with a splash. Water crashes across the front of the boat.

I grab onto the railing next to me as we bounce up and over waves. As we travel farther from shore, the waves don't crest as often or as high, so the ride smooths out some. For now. I still feel the wind rocking the boat back and forth, though.

Because of the conditions, the trip takes longer than normal. It's another hour before we reach the location I calculated as the most ideal to launch the gliders. We're still fifteen minutes out when the rain starts. The waves are back now, too, buffeting us from every direction.

Finally, we're in place. Jonathan turns off the engine and motions for me to stay put while he lowers the anchor. Between the rain and the crashing waves, he's soaked within seconds of stepping out of the control area.

I groan to myself, knowing I'm next.

When Jonathan returns, he closes us in the control area. "It's pretty rough out there," he tells me, clenching and unclenching his jaw. "Stay with me. You turn on each glider, and then we'll work together to unstrap them and get them into the water."

I nod, but Jonathan shakes his head. "Answer me with words, Carrots. I need to know you understand."

I clear my throat. "I understand. I've got it."

"Okay." He takes a deep breath, pulling me to my feet. "Are you ready?"

I shoot him a weak smile. "As I'll ever be."

"Let's go." He takes my hand, then opens the door. Though the control area isn't remotely soundproof, I immediately discover how much sound those thin walls and windows were muffling.

The sound of the waves is deafening, layered below the splash of raindrops and the roll of thunder. Every so often, lightning cracks across the sky, electrified light cutting through the heavy clouds. Really, if it wasn't so loud and terrifying, the sound alone might be soothing—a day at the beach and a thunderstorm rolled into one.

I don't realize I've stopped moving until Jonathan tugs on my hand. *Focus, Molly*, I scold myself. We carefully slide our way to the gliders. Trying to walk while the boat pitches back and forth reminds me of the bounce houses I played in as a child. One minute, the ground is beneath my feet and the next it's gone, and I'm floating until the deck finds the bottom of my feet again.

By the time we've made it the few feet to the first glider, I'm drenched. My board shorts stick against my thighs, my boat shoes squelch with every watery step I take, and my glasses are dotted with beads of rain. I shiver against the wind whipping through my now-wet clothes.

I let go of Jonathan's hand, bending over the gliders so I can flip the switch on each one to power them on.

My hair is soaked, and the feel of it sticking to my neck irritates me. I toss my head back and forth and roll my shoulders to push it back without using my hands, which are busy on the gliders. I wish I'd thought of putting it up before we came out here.

I feel Jonathan at my side, his warm body temporarily blocking the stinging rain. "I'm going to tie your hair back!" he shouts.

"I don't have a hair tie," I call back.

I tilt my head enough to see him take a black hair tie from his pocket. Wordlessly, he pulls the hair away from my neck and gathers it in his fist. He brings his other hand up and gently combs his fingers through the hair on the top of my head, smoothing it down.

Forget about the buttons on the glider. Jonathan has my full attention. I'm frozen, slack-jawed as he twists the hair tie around my ponytail twice. When he's done, I stand and face him, my back to the boat's control center.

His eyes meet mine with a sheepish expression. He puts his mouth close to my ear, so I can hear him when he says, "I started carrying them after I noticed you never have one when you need it."

I ... have never heard anything so thoughtful in my life. But that's business as usual for Jonathan Stanch—accommodating, empowering, and bolstering me at every turn.

Before I can react or think of a response, the boat bobs again, pitching Jonathan toward me. With impressive reflexes, he puts his arm up in time to catch himself against the roofline of the control area so we don't collide. It does mean that I'm boxed in between the wall and Jonathan's body, which is mere inches from mine. My eyes are aligned with his life vest, his shirt dripping and sticking against his shoulders and biceps.

When the deck steadies, I expect him to move away, but he doesn't. I lift my head, and he's staring down at me, fire in his eyes.

Blame the adrenaline, or his proximity, or even the motion of the boat—I feel that fire down to my very core. I don't know who leans into whom, but the next thing I know, our mouths are fused together. Our lips, slick from the rain and ocean spray, slip against each other as we struggle to gain purchase.

Jonathan moves his free arm behind me, settling it between my shoulder blades and pushing me closer to his chest. Our bulky life vests bump, but I hardly notice, save the annoyance of not being as close to him as I'd like.

As I link my hands behind his neck, my vision narrows. All I see is Jonathan. All I hear is his heavy breathing. All I smell is his clean, citrus scent. All I taste are his lips. And all I feel is his skin sliding against mine.

Then the sky flashes, and our surroundings funnel back into my consciousness. Water sluices down my back. The waves crash against the side of the boat.

A laugh bubbles up inside my chest. What starts as a soft giggle against Jonathan's lips intensifies until I'm laughing so hard, I can barely breathe.

Jonathan cocks his head, still inches from my own. "Something funny?" he asks into my ear.

With my hand, I gesture wildly around at the rain pelting us, the crashing waves, and the deck pitching beneath our feet.

"I can't control any of this," I shout. I also mean my feelings for Jonathan—the unrestrained way my body craves his nearness, and my heart demands his attention.

He raises his eyebrows. "No, you can't," he agrees.

I laugh again. "And I'm okay!"

I have no control over any variables right now. I'm out of the lab. I haven't had a consistent schedule in days. And while I *am* focused on work, I'm also allowing myself to enjoy a bit of distraction in the form of one very handsome, very drenched co-researcher. The story I've built up in my mind for years, the "truth" I've held onto, would suggest I should feel overwhelmed and dysregulated, but I've never felt stronger in my life. I've never felt so powerful.

It's no small part because of Jonathan.

He grins at my epiphany. "Yeah, you're doing great."

He brings his mouth back down to mine and kisses me slowly and deeply, like he's drinking me in, savoring the taste of my lips. When he pulls away, he hugs me to his life vest and wipes the water from my face with the sides of his hands.

"You're amazing, you know that?" he yells above the commotion around us.

I don't know that, but I'm beginning to hope it's true.

After deploying the gliders, it takes us twice as long as normal to get back to the marina. Jonathan pilots the *Pulse* like a pro, but I'm sure he must be exhausted, battling the wind and waves like he is.

He radios ahead to let the marina worker know when we're close. As we near the shore, the rain lets up, though the waves become more intense in the shallower water. Finally, we reach the dock.

I stand under an awning while Jonathan helps the marina worker get the *Pulse* lifted into its dry dock, strapped down, and covered. Jonathan promises to come back in a few days to check on it and dry it out properly.

It's a relief when we make it back to Jonathan's truck in the marina parking garage, the roof overhead a respite from the steady deluge of rain now falling as Hernando's outer bands come ashore.

Standing next to the truck, Jonathan peels off his shirt. I couldn't move my eyes away even if I wanted to. "What?" He shrugs. "It's soaked."

I look down at myself and, using my thumb and pointer finger, pluck the wet shirt away from my skin. "Wish it were that easy for me," I mutter.

"Hey," Jonathan smirks. "I wouldn't complain." I scoff and shake my head.

He opens his truck door and pulls out two towels, handing one to me. After dabbing it across my body to absorb as much of the water as possible, I wrap the towel around my shoulders, reveling in the soft warmth. Opening the passenger side door to the truck, I move to spread the towel on the seat, but Jonathan stops me.

"I have a couple more towels for the seats," he says. "Keep that one."

I nod, and he lays a giant striped beach towel on the passenger seat. I climb into the truck and settle into the seat. Jonathan does the same. We're cocooned in the cab of the truck, the air warm around us.

"Where to now?" Jonathan asks.

I sigh, looking beyond the walls of the open-air parking garage to the wind and rain beyond. "Can you drop me off at my apartment?" I ask. "I know it's out of your way."

Jonathan scoffs. "You misunderstand," he says. "I mean where are *we* going now? I'm not leaving you alone for the storm."

I startle. "No, I'll be fine."

Jonathan sets his jaw, his eyes holding mine in a level glare. "I'm not leaving you alone," he repeats. "Either I come home with you, or you come home with me. Your choice."

I drop my eyes. Though I'm plenty warm now with the towel draped over me and the heat pulsing out of the vents into the truck cab, I shiver. Dark ringlets of hair are plastered against Jonathan's forehead. I watch a droplet of water form at the end of one curl, getting heavier until it drops free and rolls down his cheek and onto his neck. I swallow thickly before meeting his eyes again.

It's clear there's no point in arguing with Jonathan about this, and honestly, I don't think I want to. Facing my first hurricane, even a low-category one, by myself is not appealing.

Finally, I say, "My cat is at my apartment."

He frowns. "What flood zone are you in?"

"X."

He nods. "Me too. In Metairie. Do you have a hurricane kit or emergency supplies?"

My face warms. "I do not." See, these are the kinds of things I don't think about.

In one decisive motion, Jonathan shifts the truck into reverse and starts backing out. "We'll go to your apartment first and pick up your cat, and then we'll hunker down at my place."

I slump back against the seat, feeling one hundred pounds lighter.

"Sounds good," I say. One less decision I have to make. One less plan I need to formulate. One less thing for my brain to consider. I study the profile of Jonathan's face, his jaw still set in determination. Yep. A decisive man is a sexy man.

Chapter Twenty-Two

Jonathan

T he thirty-mile drive to Molly's apartment takes double the normal time despite most of the traffic heading east away from New Orleans rather than west toward it like us. Our area is in the squall line now, which means we're seeing strong gusts of wind and heavy rain off and on. I drive slowly and carefully on the slick roads, which are fortunately free from debris so far.

I finally pull up to the curb outside her building, and we run through the rain to the entry door. Molly types in her code, and we step inside.

What a day. What a *week*. I don't know what that kiss on the boat meant, but I also can't dwell on it right now. I need to get Molly and her cat to my apartment and keep them safe. That's the only thought I have room for in my brain at the moment.

As we walk up the stairs, I ask, "How did I not know you have a cat?"

Molly shrugs. "She doesn't like strangers. She usually hides when someone she doesn't know comes in."

"What's her name?"

"Beaker."

I smile. "That's cute."

We get to her apartment door, and I wonder if it's too soon to tease her by asking if she's sure she has her key. Yeah, probably too soon. Instead, I instruct, "Just grab the cat and whatever you'll need overnight: a change of clothes, toothbrush, whatever."

She looks over her shoulder at me. "I don't have time to change?"

I shake my head. "We need to be off the roads as soon as possible. You can shower and change when we get to my apartment."

Molly looks like she's about to say something else. Her mouth hangs open, and her forehead furrows with an unanswered question. But she closes her mouth and disappears into the back part of the apartment.

She comes out a few minutes later with an overnight bag, a litter box with its lid on, and a cat in her arms.

I chuckle. "You have a black cat."

"What's wrong with that?" Molly frowns.

I grin. "Nothing at all. It's very spooky season."

"Oh no." She groans. "You love Halloween, don't you?"

My smile widens. "I *love* Halloween. You don't?"

She wrinkles her nose in disgust. "Costumes and rowdy parties? Pass."

Molly locks up her apartment and we're back on the road. She holds Beaker on her lap, which the cat does not seem happy about, considering how she's growling. My apartment is only about ten miles away, but I drive slowly. The weather is getting worse, and because Hernando sped up at the last minute, people who wanted to evacuate didn't get as early of a start as planned. My nerves ratchet up, needing to get Molly somewhere safe before the storm gets any worse.

A few hours later, we're all three tucked in safe and dry at my apartment: me, the woman I'm pretty sure I'm in love with, and her cat. Hernando is predicted to make landfall around one in the morning, but its outer bands are no joke and have been bearing down on us for hours. The wind outside has kicked up, and the rain has been steady. At least the apartment complex still has power.

Objective met, I allow my mind to wander. Today was incredible. Like my own *Twister* moment. We braved the storm, launched our Dorothy, and watched the data come pouring in. Well, no data yet, but I'm sure we'll see them soon.

I was Bill Paxton, Molly was Helen Hunt, and we even had a sexy makeout session in the pouring rain. Actually, in *Twister* it's a broken sprinkler or something, not rain, and certainly not early-bands-of-a-hurricane rain, so looks like Molly and I win there. Damn, she was amazing, both at the science stuff and the kissing stuff. My pulse kicks up just thinking about it, and I look across the dark living room toward my bedroom door.

Like a gentleman, I gave Molly my bed while I toss and turn on the couch, the material scratchy against the bare skin on my back. Why did I buy such an uncomfortable couch? I make a mental note that next time I'm couch shopping, I should lie down on each one to test it for sleepability. You never know when a hurricane will necessitate inviting the woman of your dreams to sleep over platonically, forcing you onto the couch for the night. It's good to be prepared for that type of scenario.

I chuckle dryly to myself and shift positions again. My eyes are just getting heavy when a popping explosion from outside rouses me. The ceiling fan above me slows to a stop. Power's out. A transformer must have blown.

As my eyes adjust to the new darkness, I think I hear a soft whimper through the bedroom door. Molly. I freeze and wait. I hear it again.

"Molly?" I call. "Are you okay?"

"Uh huh," comes the whimpered response.

I'm on my feet and at the door in seconds. Without pausing to put a shirt on or knock, I push into my bedroom and cross the floor to the bed in several long steps.

I kneel softly by the side of the bed so I can see Molly's face through the inky darkness. Her eyes are open, and she's lying on her side, clutching the blanket up to her chin.

"Carrots," I say gently. "Are you all right, sweetheart?"

She shakes her head. "No," she whispers hoarsely. "Did you hear that?"

I reach up and stroke her hair. "Yeah. It was a transformer exploding outside. It's why we lost power."

Her eyes widen. "Exploding? Are we safe here?"

I lean forward and press a soft kiss to her forehead. "Yeah, baby. We're safe here. We might get a little warm without the air conditioner, but we're safe. I promise."

The tension drains out of her muscles as she sinks deeper into the bed. Her eyes flutter closed and then open again, the fear in them tempered. A slow ache builds in my chest as I realize I did that for her. She believes me when I promise her safety. More than anything, I want to be worthy of her trust, although I'm certain I'll never be fully worthy of her.

Her eyes close again, and her breathing evens out. I stand and slowly turn, tiptoeing back toward the door.

"Stay." I hear the hushed voice behind me and turn on my heels. Her eyes are open, watching me. "Stay with me, please," she repeats. The way she says "please," soft and guileless, tears at my heart.

"Are you sure?" I whisper into the dark.

"I need you with me," she says, and whether she's just talking about tonight in the face of the hurricane, or she's talking about forever, I'm all in.

I creep around to the other side of the bed and climb under the covers. I roll toward Molly, pulling her into my arms and aligning her back to my chest. I nuzzle my nose into her neck, placing a soothing kiss below her ear. She sighs and drops her head against my chest. Within minutes, her steady breathing tells me she's asleep.

Every nerve ending in my body is on high alert as I revel in the feel of her skin against mine. I inhale the scent of her hair, and it's my shampoo from the shower she took in my bathroom shortly before going to bed. I close my eyes and focus on the soft inhale and exhale of her breath lulling me to sleep.

I wake the next morning sticky with sweat. One of my arms is tucked beneath Molly's hip, the weight of her body leaving my skin prickling and numb. My other arm curls around her, my hand resting on the T-shirt over her stomach. Our legs are tangled in the most blissful knot I've ever experienced.

Oh, and there's a cat practically sitting on my face. I turn my head to try to dislodge her, but she doesn't move. I lift my arm from Molly's stomach and push Beaker off. She growls and resettles at the foot of the bed.

I slide my other arm out from under Molly and stretch it out to get the blood flowing again. I left my phone in the living room when I came in here last night, and the digital clock on my nightstand isn't working. The power's still out. I try to gauge what time it is based on the amount of light coming through the window, but I'm really terrible at that.

Since I'm up, I roll out of bed as quietly as possible and tiptoe out of the room. I retrieve my phone from the coffee table and my shirt from the back of the couch. Seven in the morning. My phone battery's at 54 percent, which isn't bad, considering. I have a portable power bank fully charged in the kitchen. I made sure it was ready to go before the storm. I'll check with Molly when she wakes up in case her phone situation is more dire than mine, though.

I walk into the kitchen to figure out what I can offer Molly for breakfast, my shirt flung over my shoulder. I try to remember what I have in the refrigerator without opening it up and letting what might be left of the cold air out. How long does the air stay cool in a refrigerator without power? I can't remember, but I do know the freezer will stay cold longer.

Motion in my peripheral vision causes me to turn my head in time to watch Molly shuffle into the kitchen. She's still wearing her pajamas—striped, loose-fitting shorts that hit about mid-thigh and a T-shirt so oversized that it almost covers the shorts completely—and her hair is tousled from sleep. It's a heavenly combination, and I'm still pinching myself, wondering if I was really fortunate enough to spoon with her all last night.

Her cheeks are flushed pink, and she won't quite meet my eyes, though I notice she peruses my naked chest before dropping her gaze. I play it cool. "Good morning, Carrots." Giving her space, I lean my butt against the kitchen counter next to the refrigerator.

"Good morning," she mumbles. Still looking at the floor, she shuffles her feet. "We probably need to talk."

My heart seizes. Is she going to walk our second kiss back the way she did the first? I'm not sure I can stand that. I pull my shirt over my head, covering my torso. "We absolutely should talk," I agree. "But not before we eat breakfast. How do fruit pops sound?"

She lifts her head in surprise, finally looking me in the eye. "For breakfast?"

I grin. "Yeah. They'll melt soon if we don't eat them." I scrunch my forehead in thought. "I think I have strawberry and lemon."

The corners of her lips tick up. "I'll have lemon, please."

"Yes, ma'am. Coming right up." I straighten and open the freezer, pulling out the boxes of fruit pops as quickly as I can so I can shut the door again. Still cold. That's a good sign.

I gesture to my small kitchen table, and she takes a seat. I set the boxes of fruit pops in the center of the table. Both boxes have already been opened, with three lemon and two strawberry remaining.

I move back toward the refrigerator and open the door to grab a couple bottles of water. They're room temperature, which tells me I'll have to throw out the half bottle of milk, pound of raw ground beef, and package of deli turkey in there. I have two or three containers of leftovers, too, but I probably should have already thrown those out weeks ago.

I hand a bottle to Molly and sit in the chair next to hers. She's already helped herself to a lemon fruit pop, her tongue popping out from between her lips as she licks it. The sharp memory of the feel of those lips on mine, that tongue in my mouth, forms like a movie reel in my head. My heart pounds. Maybe popsicles were a bad idea.

I gulp and tear my gaze away from her mouth. "How's the charge on your phone?" I ask.

She frowns and looks down at her phone on the table in front of her. "Twenty percent," she answers. "Oh, and I have a text." Her eyebrows scrunch together as she reads it. "It's a notification from my apartment manager. No damage to the building, but the power is out."

I nod. "Same as here, then. Do you want me to take you home, or...?" *Please say no. Please say no.*

"No." She locks eyes with me. "Like I said, we should talk today."

"Yeah," I agree reluctantly.

"But first, can we walk outside? Is it safe? I want to see what it looks like."

"Sure. It's safe. Hernando came and went quickly. It's sunny this morning."

We finish our fruit pops, me using all my restraint to keep my eyes fixed firmly on the kitchen cabinets above Molly's head. Then, as Molly goes into the bathroom to change her clothes, I plug her phone into the power bank to charge.

Molly reappears in leggings and a fitted T-shirt. We both put on shoes and make our way out of the apartment and onto the sidewalk below.

The first thing I notice as we walk down the block is that it's much cooler outside. The temperature must have dropped at least ten degrees since yesterday morning. I shiver in my basketball shorts and T-shirt.

The second thing I notice is the fallen tree branches and clumps of Spanish moss littering the sidewalk and street. The fabric of my building's awning is tattered, strips of it hanging off the frame.

The third thing I notice is Molly slipping her hand into mine, intertwining our fingers. I turn toward her, my mouth hanging open in surprise. "You're holding my hand."

She smiles shyly, looking up at me through her eyelashes. "Yeah. Is that okay?"

I squeeze her hand. "For the record, I'm always okay with you touching me." I stop walking and turn my body to face her fully. I bring my free hand between us, enclosing her hand between both of mine. I study her face. "Are *you* okay with it? I mean, what does this mean? We kissed again yesterday. Well, 'kissed' is probably an understatement, but I know adrenaline was running high, and maybe you regret it now. And then last night, you were scared, so I understand if I was just a source of comfort."

"Jonathan," Molly says in a soft voice.

I recognize that I'm rambling, but I can't seem to stop every thought in my head from pouring out of my mouth. "Molly, you have to know that I'm so into you. I don't ... I don't know if I can handle it if you brush me off again." I swallow. "But if that's what you feel you need to do, I respect that." I clamp my mouth shut.

"Are you done?" Molly asks, her eyes sparkling.

My ears warm. "I think so ... except to say I think you're amazing and beautiful and you smell really good, and I can't stop thinking about your mouth on mine—"

Stepping onto her tiptoes, Molly brushes a kiss across my lips. "Jonathan," she says again.

"Yeah?" I croak.

"I'm really into you, too. I want to date you, and kiss you, and spend as much time together as possible. Only with you."

"Only with me," I repeat dumbly. Then, as the words sink in, a slow grin creeps across my face. "You mean, like, exclusively? Are you asking me to be your boyfriend, Carrots?"

She smirks, pulling her hand away from mine and turning forward again, ready to continue walking. "I mean, if you don't want to label it..."

"No," I say quickly, catching her hand in mine again. "Let's use all the labels. I love labels. The more official, the better."

She stops walking again and smiles at me. "I like you better like this."

My eyebrows pull together. "Like what?"

She tilts her head thoughtfully. "Messy. Vulnerable. Real. It makes me feel like you're just being you, rather than trying to trick me into something."

I shake my head. "I was never trying to trick you into anything. I just wanted your attention, whether positive or negative."

"I gave you *a lot* of negative attention." She grimaces, and I pull her against my chest in a hug.

"Why *did* you hate me? What did I do?"

Molly's cheeks turn red, and she hides her face in my neck. "Honestly?" she asks in a muffled voice.

"Of course."

She lifts her head and looks me in the eye. "I've always been attracted to you, from our first class together. But that attraction was a threat to my routine and my rules. You were a threat." She shrugs. "It was easier to hate you. Plus, you were kind of a reminder of what I thought I could never have, what I was depriving myself of in pursuit of my goals."

I smirk. "I was too much of a temptation, so you had to cut me out completely?"

She rolls her eyes. "Something like that."

I pinch my lips together as I turn serious. "But not anymore, right?"

"No," Molly says, curling one hand behind my head and pulling my mouth down to hers. "I'm done denying myself. You're mine now."

I swallow a moan, heat creeping down my spine. I like the sound of that. A lot.

Chapter Twenty-Three

Molly

After our walk around Jonathan's neighborhood, during which we saw minimal damage and lots of other people escaping their stuffy, dark buildings for the cool weather outside, we open the apartment windows and cuddle on the couch.

I meant it when I told Jonathan I'm done denying myself. Something happened to me on that boat yesterday—Was that only yesterday?—that changed me. A realization. An epiphany.

I can exhaust myself trying to control what I can control, but I'll never be able to control enough. Maybe a better use of my energy is to continue excelling at my work while *also* embracing joy in my life. Nothing brings me more joy than Jonathan. Except maybe beignets.

Speaking of things I can't control, I'm *dying* to see if the gliders have transmitted any data. No electricity means the shore station can't receive the satellite transmissions from the gliders, though.

Even if the server could receive the data, I can't get online to check it. I'll just have to be patient.

We spend the day on the couch, talking, laughing, and kissing. At one point, Jonathan pulls my feet into his lap and traces the small tattoo on the top of my foot. It's the letters MNO in script.

"I wouldn't have guessed you'd have a tattoo," he says.

"It wasn't my idea, and I don't plan on getting another," I glare almost accusingly in his direction.

He holds up his hands. "I wasn't going to ask you to. What's it mean?"

"The first initials of my and my sisters' first names: Molly, Nicole, Olivia. We all went and got the same one together after Olivia turned eighteen. A little against my will."

"I like it." He grins. "It looks hot."

I chuckle, but my face warms. I'm still getting used to the idea of someone, especially someone as handsome as Jonathan, thinking *I'm* hot.

In the late afternoon, the power blinks on in Jonathan's apartment. As the fan starts spinning, and the appliances beep in the kitchen, I leap from the couch to boot up my university laptop.

Jonathan chuckles. "Give it a minute, Carrots. The router has to reconnect first."

I carry the laptop back to the couch and sit, snuggling into Jonathan's side. He loops an arm around my shoulders.

Finally, I'm able to get online and log in to our lab's servers where the data from the gliders should be relayed. There's nothing newer than yesterday morning and nothing at all from the three gliders we programmed to cross paths with Hernando.

I slump back against Jonathan's arm. I can't believe it. All of that for nothing? I risked my life, and Jonathan's for that matter, for nothing?

Peering at the screen, Jonathan leans his head against mine. "Do you want to hear my long list of possible explanations?" he asks.

"It doesn't matter because the explanation at the top of the list is that the gliders all got damaged in the storm, and we have no data." This was supposed to be a big break for my research and a huge bump for my career—and Jonathan's.

"Okay, Gloomy McDoomy. *Or*, the gliders haven't resurfaced yet. Or they did resurface, but the shore station still hasn't powered back up enough to receive the transmission. Or—"

I groan, throwing my head back against the couch cushion. "I get it, Mr. Sunshine."

He chuckles, his lips tickling the skin on my exposed neck as he nuzzles closer. "Patience. Give it some time. Nothing's for sure yet."

"I hate waiting," I mutter.

My phone pings with an incoming text, so I distract myself with my phone. "It's another text from my building manager," I tell Jonathan. "Electricity's back up at my place, too."

My phone pings again, at the same time Jonathan's makes a chiming noise. It's a group text from Dr. Gantt.

Dr. Gantt:

> Anyone who is still in town, please meet at the lab tomorrow morning at ten for a team meeting to debrief after the storm. Anyone who evacuated, please travel home safely, and we'll see you next week.

Jonathan's phone chimes again. He squints at the screen. "Dr. Gantt wants me to check in with the marina in the morning before the meeting to make sure our equipment there is in good condition."

"Like call them? Or—"

"No, she wants me to go in person." Now it's his turn to groan. "Do you know how early I'll have to wake up to get to Slidell and back before the meeting at ten?"

"Okay, message received. Beaker and I will get out of your hair." I try to sit up, but Jonathan keeps his arms in place, holding me down. "Don't you need to drive us home now?"

"Noooo," he pouts, sticking out his bottom lip and clutching me tighter.

I giggle. "We'll see each other at the lab tomorrow."

His eyes spark. "I can't do *this* at the lab." He leans in and captures my mouth with his.

After a while, I break away. "I really should get home."

Jonathan exaggerates a sigh. "Fine. Let me grab my keys."

I make it to the lab by 9:45 the next morning. Like in Jonathan's neighborhood, the extent of the damage in downtown New Orleans seems to be downed tree branches. On my walk to the lab, I see a few shingles loose on buildings with older roofs in the area. I caught Dennis Jackson's broadcast this morning summing up Hurricane Hernando. It ended up making landfall as a weak Category 1, with sustained winds at eighty miles per hour. Dennis explained that because Hernando sped up so much, the damage was minimal. It didn't stick around long enough to cause flooding issues or wind damage, and even storm surge wasn't an issue. We were all pretty fortunate.

I don't see Jonathan's truck in the parking lot, so he must still be on his way back from Slidell. He texted me earlier this morning with a message that said, "My bed was lonely without you last night." Even though I wasn't near a mirror, I know my face blushed bright red. Anyone else seeing that text would *so* get the wrong impression.

Although, truth be told, *my* bed felt pretty lonely last night, too, after being curled up against Jonathan's delicious bare chest the night before. I shake my head. I don't know how I went from hating him to wanting him this much in just two months.

Through the front doors and up the stairs, I pause before scanning my badge to enter the lab. I take a deep breath in through my nose and out through my mouth to help shift my brain into work mode. My badge beeps against the scanner, and I pull open the door.

I've taken barely three steps inside when Dr. Gantt rushes over to me. "Molly!" she exclaims, putting a hand on each of my shoulders. "Congratulations!"

"Um..." The back of my neck prickles as my thoughts swirl. This isn't about Jonathan and I dating, is it? That would be weird, right? "Congratulations?" I echo.

"The gliders, Molly! The data started pouring in early this morning."

I gasp, my heart pounding. "They did?"

Dr. Gantt bobbles her head. "You haven't checked?"

"I ... I checked yesterday afternoon, but when nothing was there..." I trail off, the news sinking in. The gliders are transmitting data from the storm! Tears prick at the back of my eyes. I close them, bringing my hand up to cover my mouth.

I have to see for myself. My eyes pop open again, and I rush past Dr. Gantt to boot up my laptop at my desk. She follows, laughing.

I log in to the servers and navigate to the glider data. Dropping into my chair, I study the rows and rows of gorgeous numbers. A chuckle sounds, the reverberations tickling my throat. It's me; I'm laughing. I sit back in the chair, running both hands through my hair.

"It worked!" I whisper between giggles, awestruck.

Dr. Gantt rests her hand on my shoulder. "Good work, Molly. I haven't delved deeply into the data yet, but all three gliders have reported, and the data are continuous since yesterday afternoon. It's comprehensive."

Comprehensive. "Do you know what this means?" I ask.

She beams at me. "Not fully, not yet. But we're bound to find some interesting patterns, hmm? This is it, Molly! Thank you. You did it. I'm going to start gathering everyone for the meeting. We have big news to share!" She walks away, leaving me at my desk, staring into the computer screen.

I did it. With Jonathan. He should be here, celebrating with us. I want him to be here.

Knowing a text will be useless if he's driving, which I hope he is, I pick up my phone and call him.

"Good morning, beautiful," Jonathan's cheerful voice echoes in my ear.

"Where are you?" I ask.

"Almost there. Is something wrong?" His tone has shifted, but I'm too focused on getting him here to pinpoint the change.

"No," I answer, my throat too thick to elaborate. "Just get here, to the lab, as soon as you can. Please."

"Moll—" I hear him say as I hang up the phone.

I jump to my feet, knees trembling, and join Dr. Gantt and about fifteen colleagues who are gathered in a circle near the entrance to the office.

Dr. Gantt calls everyone to attention. She starts with some platitudes about how she hopes everyone made it through the storm okay. A few of our coworkers share about small trees down in their neighborhoods and minor flooding in their backyards. I half listen, most of my attention focused on the glass entry door, watching for Jonathan to arrive.

Finally, I see him burst through the stairwell door and rush toward the lab, just as Dr. Gantt says, "As you know, we launched a risky project in tandem with the hurricane. Drs. Delaney and Stanch led the charge, and I'm excited to announce—"

Jonathan erupts through the door, his eyes on me, assessing and cataloging through furrowed brows. He pushes his way through our colleagues and across the center of the circle to stand in front of me. Ignoring—or maybe not even seeing—everyone else, he runs his hands over my arms, then lifts my chin while spinning me around.

"Are you okay? What's wrong?" he demands gruffly.

I take a step back, my face and neck flushed from a mixture of embarrassment and eager desire. Probably 70 percent desire, 30 percent embarrassment.

"I'm fine!" I insist breathlessly.

His face and posture relax as he lets out a long breath. "When you called, you sounded upset." He cups my face in his hands. "I got here as fast as I could."

"Ah. Well..." I hedge. I clear my throat and lift my gaze to the rest of the circle.

Jonathan freezes as if just realizing we're surrounded by our boss and nearly all our coworkers. He drops his hands and takes two steps back from me. He looks around the circle at our colleagues, some gaping with wide eyes, some smirking and laughing. His ears turn adorably red.

He waves to the crowd, then shoves his hands into his pockets. He flashes an abashed smile. "Sorry, all. Carry on."

I bring my fist to my mouth to cover my grin. Jonathan may have just outed our relationship to our boss and most of our research team, but the way he stormed in here, single-mindedly focused on my well-being? That might be the most attractive thing I've ever seen in my life.

Dr. Gantt clears her throat, laughter dancing in her eyes, though the rest of her expression remains impassive. "As I was saying, the project using the gliders to collect ocean data during the hurricane was a roaring success—"

Jonathan zeroes in on me again. "It was?" he asks, eyes locked on mine.

I move my hand away from my face and let him see my beaming smile. I nod.

He whoops, rushing toward me again. Circling his arms around my waist, he lifts and spins me around. Before I can stop him, he smacks a kiss against my lips.

I'm laughing as he sets me back down on the floor. So are most of our audience.

"Yes, Dr. Stanch, we're all quite excited," Dr. Gantt says dryly.

"Sorry, again." Sheepishly, Jonathan stands behind me, as if my accomplishment can hide his embarrassment.

Dr. Gantt claps her hands. "In any case, it means we have a lot of work to do. Anyone trained in data science, please see Dr. Delaney. We'll want those data processed as soon and accurately as possible. Anyone trained in fieldwork, please see Dr. Stanch. All the gliders need to be retrieved from the Gulf and thoroughly checked for damage."

Some people crowd around me, congratulating me and expressing their eagerness to see the data. Others filter toward Jonathan. Soon, we're on separate sides of the office, but I glance up to see that Jonathan hasn't taken his eyes off me, admiration and pride evident in his expression as he watches me from across the room.

The next few weeks are a blur of data analysis and interpreting findings, all while spending as much time with Jonathan as I can. We leave work together at five each evening and grab dinner, either out somewhere or at my apartment where Jonathan cooks. After dinner, we watch a movie, or play board games, or just talk until Jonathan reluctantly drives home before it gets too late.

Somehow, he manages to add a sticky note to the growing collection on my refrigerator every night without me noticing. He writes messages like, "You make every day brighter," and "I'm so lucky to have you." The note I love the most says, "You're my favorite person." It's a simple message but rocks me to my core. I've never been someone's favorite person before. I continue to unstick each new note and add it to my arrangement. I'm using the sticky notes to make the outline of a heart.

One topic we talk about is some sort of job that Dr. Perron is recruiting Jonathan for. Jonathan tells me about the phone conversation and the Saturday night meeting before the hurricane. Since then, Dr. Perron has emailed Jonathan with enough information that his interest is piqued but not enough to make any sort of solid decision.

"Blue carbon offsetting is an interesting emerging field, but as PI, I doubt I'd be able to do as much fieldwork as I am now. Plus, Dr. Perron's been vague every time I've asked about the source of the grant funding," Jonathan tells me.

I like working with Jonathan, and I'd miss him if he moved to another research team. I don't want to influence his decision, though, and it would make some aspects of our relationship easier if we didn't work together.

I thought there might be some fallout at work over Jonathan and I dating, but it's a nonissue. Neither of us supervises the other, so as long as we continue to act professionally and avoid disrupting anyone's work, including ours, Dr. Gantt and the university's human resources department are fine with it.

During the day at work, I'm collaborating with Terri, our team's primary biostatistician, on the glider data. Though all three gliders were knocked off course by the storm, we still had one that roughly aligned with Hernando on its east side, one that was about on its west side, and one that fell about in the middle, even if it wasn't exactly the eye. We're still working on connecting the data to harmful algal blooms, but the real-time information about how the Gulf water changed before, during, and after Hernando is valuable in its own right.

Fortunately, none of the gliders were severely damaged during the storm. Unfortunately, I'm too busy processing the data to go with Jonathan to retrieve them. He takes a small crew out to bring the gliders back to the lab to inspect. They find they're a little banged up but still work.

In the midst of all this, I get a text from my sister, Olivia.

Olivia:

> Can Annie and I stay with you while we're in New Orleans the weekend before halloween?

Molly:

> Of course. It'll just be an air mattress on the floor, but you're welcome to it

Olivia:

> Beggars can't be choosers [laughing emoji]

Literally everyone in my family has come to visit this year at one time or another, which I suppose is a benefit of living in a city that's a major travel destination.

What I don't do is tell my family that Jonathan and I are dating. I'm not ready to explain the relationship, or defend it, or deal with the surprised and smug comments.

The day after Olivia texts, Dr. Gantt encourages Jonathan and me to get a full research article manuscript written up as soon as possible. The four of us—me, Jonathan, Dr. Gantt, and Terri—spend time discussing and writing the paper. We're hoping to have it far along enough to post it to a preprint server called EarthArXiv for earth and environmental science research by the end of the month. Preprint servers are a first step in disseminating research findings quickly, while letting other scientists know with a date stamp that we have priority and credit for the findings. From there, we'll watch for the reaction of our colleagues around the world, make adjustments to the data analysis or write-up, and then submit the manuscript to a scientific journal for peer review and publication.

The submission, peer review, and official publication process can take months, so posting to the preprint server sooner rather than later will hopefully get people talking about our findings now.

So, with the countdown on to Olivia's visit and posting to the preprint server by the end of the month, October flies by.

Chapter Twenty-Four

Molly

Halloween in New Orleans is a pretty big deal; any excuse to dress in costume and celebrate is a worthy one here. Every year on the Saturday before Halloween, the Krewe of Boo! hosts the official parade with marching bands, dance crews, and the over-the-top floats New Orleans is known for.

The parade is why my sister Olivia and her friend Annie are in town this weekend, and why I'm trying to entertain them as they sit in my living room. Or I'm holding them captive, more like. Insert evil laugh here. Okay, not really, but I am letting them stay in my tiny apartment, so they kind of owe me.

"Actually," I tell them, "the history of parades in New Orleans is fascinating." Olivia groans, but I ignore her and continue. "In the 1800s, the city didn't have a lot of governmental resources, so communities formed mutual aid associations to bridge the gap.

These were usually formed around cultural groups as immigrants with shared language and tradition gathered together."

Olivia's eyes have started to glaze over while Annie politely smiles and nods her head.

"When a member of one of the societies died, their group honored them with a grand celebration of life, which evolved into parades with bands and mourners marching down the street," I finish.

"That's really interesting, Mol," says Olivia dryly, "but we came here to watch a parade, not learn about them."

"Fine." I chuckle. "What made you guys decide to come this year?"

Annie has been Olivia's best friend since middle school. By then, I was already away at college, so even though I know Annie, I haven't spent very much time with her. She seems soft-spoken and calm, in stark contrast to my baby sister who thrives on being the center of attention and the life of every party.

Olivia looks away, and Annie clears her throat. "Uh, my brother invited me and then his, um...." Annie glances quickly at Olivia, who is focusing intently on the messy stacks of books and papers on my coffee table, her jaw tight. "His girlfriend decided to tag along, so I asked Delaney to come so I wouldn't feel like a third wheel."

Everyone outside of our family calls Olivia by our last name, Delaney, which is a nickname she switched to sometime around high school, I think. I'm not sure why.

I decide to ignore the weird vibes happening right now and instead ask, "Oh yeah, you have a twin brother, right?"

Again, Annie glances at Olivia, who is still acting like she's not part of this conversation. "Yes. Gage."

I smile. "I remember seeing the three of you running around together whenever I'd come home for a visit."

Annie's expression turns wistful. "Yeah."

Olivia tosses her hair, her blonde ponytail swishing on top of her head. "That was a long time ago," she says in a stony voice, her face impassive.

I narrow my eyes and swivel my attention between the two friends. "This is weird, right? There's a subtext here I'm not understanding?"

Annie's eyes widen, and she shrugs. Olivia pinches her lips together. Neither of them answers, so I let it go, for now.

After all, I'm not exactly showing my whole hand, either. I'm not ready to share Jonathan and my fledgling relationship with my family yet. Last night, snuggled on the couch together after watching *You've Got Mail*, I told Jonathan he needed to make himself scarce this weekend while my sister is visiting. I also reclaimed my spare key from his key ring—at least for the next few days—so Olivia can use it.

He flashed that ever-present smirk of his. "What, are you ashamed of me?"

"No, it's just that as far as my sisters know, I hate you. I'm not ready to explain everything yet. They will definitely have ... opinions." I scrunched my nose, thinking about the merciless teasing Nicole and Olivia would dish out.

Jonathan tilted his head, the corners of his mouth turning up. "You never actually hated me, though, did you?" As he asked, he twirled a strand of my hair around his finger in a way that made my whole scalp tingle.

It was my turn to smirk. "I thought I did." He continued twirling, and I felt a shiver travel up through my shoulders and escape out the top of my head. I closed my eyes at the sensation. "But I don't hate this."

As the girls and I finish dinner, Annie asks, "Are you sure you won't come to the parade with us?"

We're at a restaurant in the French Quarter about a twenty-minute walk from my apartment, close to where the parade will pass through. The end of the parade route is actually only a couple of blocks from my apartment, but Olivia and Annie are supposed to meet up with Gage and his girlfriend at Jackson Square.

I shudder involuntarily thinking about the chaos and crowds surrounding the parade. "No. I'm good."

Olivia's eyes soften as she nods. She gets it.

New Orleans is a party city, but I am *not* a party girl. The noise by itself is formidable, loud drums and brass instruments from the marching bands, people cheering and shouting in the streets, but the real struggle for me is the press of the crowd around me. In a New Orleans parade situation, there is no such thing as personal space.

The one and only time I tried to watch a parade with a group of friends back in graduate school, I enjoyed it at first. The buzz of excitement in the air and the novelty of the experience had my full attention. Then as the floats came through, the riders throwing plastic cups, beads, and MoonPies from above our heads, the crowd surged together closer to the street, and I felt suffocated. From all sides, people pressed into me—the smell of body odor, alcohol, and vomit overwhelming.

One friend saw my distress and helped me get to a stoop in the doorway of a closed real estate office. I spent the rest of the parade sitting on the cold concrete with my knees pulled up to my chest and my head resting on my folded arms. Even then, all my senses remained heightened, and the stoop smelled strongly of urine.

Obviously, I'm not eager to repeat that experience, so I am 100 percent fine with heading home to my quiet apartment while Olivia and Annie enjoy themselves.

"Will you be okay walking home by yourself?" Olivia asks outside the restaurant as we prepare to go our separate ways.

I wave my hand as if swiping away her concern. "Oh yeah. It's not far."

Olivia slips on the Mardi Gras-style, feathered peacock mask she brought to complement her, in my opinion, *way* too revealing costume, but that's probably my overprotective older sister instincts talking. Olivia is an adult, after all. She wears tight green-and-blue-patterned bicycle shorts under a long open-front mesh skirt designed to look like peacock feathers. Her top is cropped just below her chest, leaving her stomach exposed down to her belly button. Though the top covers up to her neck, a keyhole cutout on her chest shows some cleavage, and it's open in the back. The top has the same peacock feather design as the skirt. She looks hot. I guarantee more than one set of eyes will be on her tonight, but that's probably the point. Olivia loves the attention.

Annie is in costume, too, though hers is much less "look at me." The friends clearly coordinated, because Annie is a bird, too—a swan. The skirt of her white dress flounces out with layers of tulle down to her knees. Her mask is also in a masquerade-style with sequins and white feathers.

The sidewalks are already filling up with other people in costume, and as I look around, I begrudgingly admit to myself that Olivia's outfit is relatively conservative in this crowd.

I wave a quick goodbye and walk in the direction of my apartment. The sun is starting to set and though it's not dark yet, shadows overtake the sidewalk in front of me.

Despite my reassurances to my sister just moments ago, I feel uneasy as the dusk creeps in. Even more so when my skin prickles with the awareness that someone is watching me. I pick up my pace, wrapping a fist around the keys in my pocket so that one of them sticks up through my fingers like a claw.

I walk even more quickly when I hear footsteps behind me. I'm not alone; groups of people ramble past, but I'm definitely swimming upstream as I head away from the parade route. I turn my head subtly to glance behind me and make out a hulking man, encased in shadows and reaching toward me.

I scream just as a familiar voice says my name and a hand clamps down on my shoulder.

My hand flies to my chest as if I'm trying to keep my heart from exploding out of my body. It takes a minute for the adrenaline to dissipate enough for me to recognize my "assailant."

"Jonathan! What the heck! You scared the crap out of me!" I smack his chest, hard.

"Oof!" he grunts as my hand hits his sternum. "Sorry."

"What are you doing here? And why are you following me like some sort of stalker?" I narrow my eyes and take in his dark wash jeans and the black T-shirt that's tight around his biceps. Okay, a very sexy stalker, but still.

He rubs his chest where I hit him. "Sorry. I'm not trying to be a stalker. I knew you were walking by yourself, and I wanted to make sure you got home okay."

I raise my eyebrows. "And how did you know I was walking home by myself?"

Jonathan chuckles. "You told me. Remember?"

I think back. Oh, yeah. I did tell him, including which restaurant we'd be at. Still, I make a show of sighing deeply before I say, "Fine."

Jonathan smirks and pulls me into a hug. I melt against him.

"How was dinner?" he asks as we start walking toward my apartment again.

"Fun, if a little crowded."

Jonathan's eyes wander to the people funneling around us. I can't see his face, but I feel his distraction.

"Where's your truck?" I ask, nudging his side with my elbow.

"Hmm?" He looks down at me. "Oh, I parked at your apartment."

I smile. "That's your idea of making yourself scarce, is it?"

We hear the blare of a trombone in the distance behind us, and Jonathan twists his head around to look back.

I stop, and Jonathan's chest bumps my shoulder when he continues walking. He gives me a sheepish smile.

"You want to go to the parade, don't you?" I ask. It makes sense. Jonathan loves Halloween. He's a fun person. Why wouldn't he want to go to a fun Halloween parade?

"I don't have to go," he says quickly.

"But you *want* to go," I press.

He doesn't answer, but I see the yearning written plainly on his face. He pulls me into another hug. With my nose smushed against his chest, I smell the mixture of cinnamon and citrus that always clings to him. It's subtle; it doesn't overwhelm even my sensitive olfactory nerves.

His mouth is against my hair, so his voice is muffled when he asks, "Would you come with me?"

I pull away and look into his face. He grimaces, knowing what he's asking me.

"I ... no." I take a step back. It's just not possible.

He takes my hand. "What if I stay with you the whole time? Like a bodyguard?"

A quiver of thrill runs through me. Could I do it? Could I watch the parade like everyone else? It *does* look fun, and Jonathan doesn't ask me for much.

Jonathan sees the indecision on my face, so he plows forward. "Please? Carrots, if you can brave a boat in the middle of a hurricane, you can watch a parade. You're strong and spunky and amazing." His grin is cajoling, but his eyes are certain, locked on mine in a way that ignites my confidence.

"You won't leave me?" I ask.

He quakes his head back and forth. "Not for a second."

"And if it's too much, and I want to leave?"

"We're out of there immediately," he confirms. "No questions asked."

"Okay." I nod, and his eyes light up like fireflies over the river. My heart swells that I can do this for him or at least *try*.

He swoops down, smacking a kiss against my lips. "Thank you! You won't regret it. Trust me."

And I do trust him.

Chapter Twenty-Five

Jonathan

I pull Molly by the hand through the crowd, trying to get to Tchoupitoulas Street before the parade. We bob and weave around tourists and locals alike, adults dressed in a variety of barely-there costumes and children decked out as superheroes and princesses.

I glance back at Molly, worried I might be rushing her along, but she's laughing. My whole body is vibrating, an internal buzz that starts where Molly's hand touches mine and radiates down my arm and throughout my nervous system.

I know Molly told me to lay low this weekend while her sister is here. Even though I just saw her yesterday at work, it wasn't enough. I couldn't stay away.

I find us a spot along Tchoupitoulas Street that's not too crowded yet. The parade has started, but it will take time to reach us here toward the end of the route. Before long, the space around us fills with groups of people, many in costume, and we hear loud music filtering down the street toward us.

I love this parade. It's not as wild as the Mardi Gras parades, but it has all the other hallmarks of New Orleans celebrations: colorful, loud, fun, and a little rowdy. I'm breathless, energized as we wait for the parade to reach us.

As the parade approaches, the crowd thickens, and people unintentionally jostle us from every direction. I widen my stance and maneuver Molly so that her back is against my chest. I wrap my arms around her shoulders, folding them in front of her. I'm a human forcefield, encasing Molly in my embrace and deflecting the chaos around us—at least that's my goal.

Police motorcycles signal the beginning of the parade, and Molly jumps when one of them sounds their siren right in front of us. She leans one side of her head into my arm, her ear against my sleeve to muffle the noise. As the floats and dancers amble past, the street overflows with Lady Gaga songs, drum corps, and cheers from the enthusiastic crowd.

Ducking my head so my mouth is next to her ear, I ask, "How are you feeling?"

She twists her neck so she can look up at me, a grin on her face. "Safe," she answers. "I'm having fun."

Warmth oozes through my chest, spreading like melted butter until it pools in the tips of my fingers and toes. I have a sense of how much it means to her to be out here enjoying the parade, how significant this is for her. Playing a role in making it possible for her to enjoy the parade and sharing this experience with her, knowing she feels safe with me, it's a rush. I'm proud of her for taking a risk, trusting me. At the same time, I feel a responsibility to guard and protect her.

It's astounding how quickly I've fallen for Molly. I've always recognized her beauty and intelligence; now I also know how funny she is, how nurturing, how bold and creative. When I'm with her, I experience everything in dazzling saturation; ordinary scenes are more vibrant and resonant. Before we started working together, my life felt full and satisfying. I didn't realize anything was missing. Now that I know what life is like with her beside me, I can never go back to the sensory deprivation of life without her.

By the end of the parade, Molly feels confident enough to leave my arms. She still stays close to my side, our elbows linked. We laugh and dance, grabbing for the candy and other swag falling from above our heads. Her eyes light up at the impressively designed Krewe of Boo! float showcasing a spooky skull the size of a small car, flanked by dancers in extravagant costumes.

Tonight, I'm falling in love with the parade all over again, because watching Molly experience it is a blast of dopamine like I've never felt before.

After the last of the festivities roll past us and the crowds of people start to disperse in every direction, Molly and I walk back to her apartment hand-in-hand. We don't have far to go, and when we get there, I don't want to leave.

Standing on the sidewalk next to my truck, I scratch my chin. "Do you think your sister is home yet?"

"I doubt it. They were watching the parade closer to Jackson Square, so even if they were coming straight home afterward, it would take them a while. And I'm sure they aren't coming straight home."

I raise my eyebrows and give her an expectant look.

She knows exactly what I'm suggesting. She puffs out a breath. "I'm not inviting you up, Jonathan. Not tonight."

I consider exaggerating a pout, making her laugh, but I need her to see how serious I am about her, that I'm not just a prankster.

So instead, I tilt her chin up until her eyes meet mine. "I don't want to say goodnight."

"Me neither," she whispers. "We could sit in your truck and talk for a while."

I unlock the doors, and we climb in, settling into the seats.

"What did you think of the parade?" I ask.

"It was amazing. So much fun. No wonder you love Halloween."

I chuckle. "And other reasons, too. How about you? I know you're not a big fan of Halloween. Does that mean you're one of those Christmas-obsessed people?"

Molly smirks and shifts her gaze from side to side. "Maybe," she says, elongating the word.

"What's your favorite thing about Christmas?"

Before she can answer, the cab light clicks off, dropping us into a murky darkness. Beams from the streetlights shine in through the windows, but the half-light feels cozy and private.

"My favorite thing about Christmas. Hmm ... I'd have to say opening my stocking on Christmas morning."

"What do you mean, opening your stocking?"

"Well, my family's rule for Christmas morning was that when me and my sisters woke up, we weren't allowed to open gifts right away. We had to wait for our parents to get up, and then we opened presents one at a time. That always felt like a lot of pressure to me. Everyone was watching me, rushing me, especially if one of my sisters was eager to open their next present." She grimaces. "Opening presents felt like a performance. As excited as I was for whatever toys Santa brought, I wished I didn't have to experience them with an audience."

I bob my head. "That makes sense, though I would have guessed you would like the orderly, one-at-a-time method better than the chaotic mass-unwrapping method." I grin. "We're a chaos family."

She scoffs. "Why doesn't that surprise me?"

"So, you didn't like all eyes on you while you opened your presents, but you did like opening your stocking?"

"Yes. The stocking was different. That we were allowed to open as soon as we came downstairs, no waiting for our parents or going one at a time. My parents figured it would keep us occupied until they woke up. Anyway, even when all three of us came downstairs at the same time, my sisters were so preoccupied looking through their own stockings that they didn't pay me any attention as I opened mine. I was free to pull out each item at my own pace, and I stretched it out as long as I could. It felt peaceful and ... magical."

I reach over the center console and find her hand, interlacing our fingers. I remember magical Christmases. When I was really young, Christmas *was* magical and peaceful—my parents and sister and I would be together all day, playing with our new toys and eating sweets. Then we'd go to my grandmother's house for a big family Christmas dinner. But after my mom left and I was angry with the world and taking it out on my dad, the day always felt haunted with thoughts of what I didn't have.

Some of this must be showing on my face because Molly asks, "Do you not like Christmas?"

I squeeze her hand. "I ... do. I mean, sure I do. But Christmas is such a family-oriented holiday, and after my parents divorced, I had a tough time feeling like I still had a family. My mom was gone; I was angry with my dad. I think that's why I gravitated toward Halloween—it's a friend holiday, you know? Not a lot of pressure to go home and see the family."

Molly shifts in her seat and leans closer to me. Her eyebrows are pinched together, creasing her forehead. "I've noticed..." She hesitates before continuing. "I've noticed that you don't talk about your dad much. When he calls, you send it to voicemail. I feel like I know a lot about your mom and your sister, your nieces, and even your brother-in-law, but not your dad."

My chest tightens and my instinct is to deflect, make a joke or flippant remark and move the conversation along. I almost do, until I feel Molly's hand caress my shoulder, squeezing with the perfect amount of pressure to unfurl the tension I'm holding in my muscles. She moves her hand to the back of my neck and runs her fingers through the hair at the nape.

I let out a whoosh of breath and start talking. "My parents got divorced when I was twelve. You know that. My mom got an amazing opportunity to move to Switzerland and work for the World Health Organization. Dad didn't want to go. I feel like he abandoned her, like he refused to support her dreams. I blame him for breaking up our family."

Molly rubs my back as she responds. "That sounds hard."

"It was. Nothing was the same after that. I couldn't look at my dad the same way. He should have been willing to follow her to keep our family together. We only saw Mom about once a year after she moved."

She makes a humming noise in her throat. "You and your sister stayed in Ohio with your dad?"

"Yeah. Until I graduated. I took a gap year and spent it with my mom in Egypt. She's moved around to a few different offices over the years. Then I went to college in Florida before coming here for grad school."

"Why didn't you and Tamara move with your mom?"

I consider the question. "I'm ... not sure. I don't remember it even being a conversation. Maybe she didn't think she could take care of us on her own with her new job?"

"Your dad's job was less demanding?"

I frown. "Well, no. He was an engineer and had intense deadlines that kept him plenty busy."

Molly makes the humming sound again, and I'm suddenly disoriented. Why wasn't there a conversation about Tamara and I moving to Switzerland with Mom? Did she not want us to come with her?

As if she senses my impending existential crisis, Molly pivots the conversation back into safer territory. "Anyway, after the parade tonight, I might be coming around on Halloween. Are you doing anything Friday for Halloween night?"

I shake off my thoughts and focus on Molly. "Trick-or-treating is usually pretty lively in my complex, so I'll be busy handing out candy. And then a friend of mine is having a party. Would you want to join me?"

"For which part?"

"Either. Both."

She scrunches her nose as she thinks. "Handing out candy sounds fun. Count me in for that. And I'm a hard maybe for the party. Can I see how I feel day of?"

"Of course. You'll need a costume, though."

She grimaces. "Do I?"

I grin. "Yes. I'm not budging on that. It's Halloween. You need a costume."

Her eyes light up, and she smiles smugly. "Okay."

"Not a scientist."

She flings her head back against the headrest and groans. "Ugh, Jonathan! Why not?"

I laugh. "You *are* a scientist. Halloween is about dressing up as something you're not. It's fun!"

"If you say so," she grumbles.

We're quiet for a few minutes, and I check the time on my phone. "It's getting late. Time for you to go inside?"

She sighs. "I suppose."

"I'll walk you to the door."

I circle the truck and meet her on the sidewalk. Catching her hand, I pull her into me. "By the way, I really loved sharing the parade with you tonight."

She rests her head against my chest. "I had fun, but it also drove me a little crazy."

I peer down at her in concern, pulling back enough to see her face. She's smiling. "What do you mean?"

"You did such a great job of blocking out the smells around us that might have overwhelmed me." Her nose crinkles. "The problem was being surrounded by *your* scent all that time. It had me thinking ... things." Her eyes spark, holding my gaze.

"Yeah?" I ask, my voice coming out huskier than I intend.

She nods slowly, looking up at me through her lashes.

"What kind of things?" I ask, sliding my hand to the back of her neck. "Things like this?" I duck my head and kiss a trail up her neck and down again.

"Hmm." She wraps her arms around my neck, pulling me closer. "More like this."

She crashes her lips against mine, and I walk us backward until I'm pinned between her and the truck. She controls the kiss: the pace, the intensity. She leads the way, and I'm an eager follower.

I run my hand through her hair, nestling my palm against the back of her head. Her lips are soft and insistent, but I break away from them to kiss along her jawline. She nudges my cheek with her nose, and I chuckle, making my way back to her mouth. We dive in again, tongues tangling, battling for command.

Molly kisses me, not with the polished, standoffish mask she presents to the world, but with the reckless and impulsive determination she hides underneath. And I'm here for it. I relish every second, each taste of her tongue, every nip from her teeth. Her hands slide down my sides, wrapping around my waist and ducking under the hem of my shirt. I'm on fire where her fingers touch my bare skin.

We're full-on making out on the sidewalk, and while we've got a modicum of privacy tucked away in the shadows next to my truck, we're very much in a public setting. I can't fight my smirk. Dr. Molly Delaney, the queen of control, coming undone for *me*. Damn, that makes me feel good.

Of course, I've been losing my head over this woman for weeks now, so it's about time I get my turn to drive her a little crazy, too. It's heady and addictive, being with her, and I want more.

Yeah, definitely no turning back now. She's stuck with me; I'm all in.

Chapter Twenty-Six

Molly

I open the door to my apartment, not bothering to fight my giddy smile, and almost jump out of my skin. Olivia sits on the couch, arms crossed and scowling. Jeez Louise, that's twice in one evening I've been jump scared. 'Tis the season, I suppose.

"Where have you been?" Olivia demands.

I quickly school my expression before closing the door. Did she see me with Jonathan outside? I'm not exactly sure how long we stayed out there, making out against the cab of his truck, but I don't think it was so long that Olivia and Annie would be home already. I gave them the spare key so they could let themselves in, knowing I'd likely be fast asleep.

"Why are you back so early?" I counter. "And where's Annie?"

Olivia's shoulders droop, her expression shifting from annoyance to something more raw, and I suspect, more truthful. She washed her face and changed out of her costume into joggers and an over-sized T-shirt. Her eyes look red and swollen, as if she's been crying. Before I can catalog further, she turns her face down, staring at her hands in her lap.

I settle onto the couch next to her and loop an arm around her shoulders. She shifts until she's leaning into me, her face hidden in my neck.

I flashback to when my sister was five years old and I held her on the couch after the "pet lizard" she brought inside from the backyard was crushed on the tracks of the sliding glass door. I was twelve, and Olivia was my shadow and sidekick. As I held her tiny body racked with sobs, an uneasiness seeped into my own psyche. It wasn't the first time I felt like I was absorbing the emotions of people around me, but it was the most profound for me at the time. Not only did I feel Olivia's anguish, I felt an almost uncontrollable surge of protectiveness and helplessness that left me disoriented.

That protective instinct returns now, full force, but I'm no longer twelve years old. The helplessness I felt then has been replaced with unfamiliar new confidence, almost like a dress I'm trying on for size and admiring in the mirror of the department store fitting room.

"Livvy, what's wrong, honey? What happened? Did you and Annie have a fight?"

In a flat voice, Olivia answers. "No. Annie's fine. She's still with her brother. They walked me home after the parade. I just … couldn't stay with them."

I feel my forehead furrow as I try to puzzle this out. "Why not?"

Olivia pulls away, swiping her eyes with the back of her hand. "Never mind. It's stupid."

I frown. Obviously, she's not telling me the whole story, but I know from experience that if I press, she'll shut down even more.

"I'm going to get ready for bed," she says now, and I let her go.

After she shuts herself in the bathroom, I text Nicole.

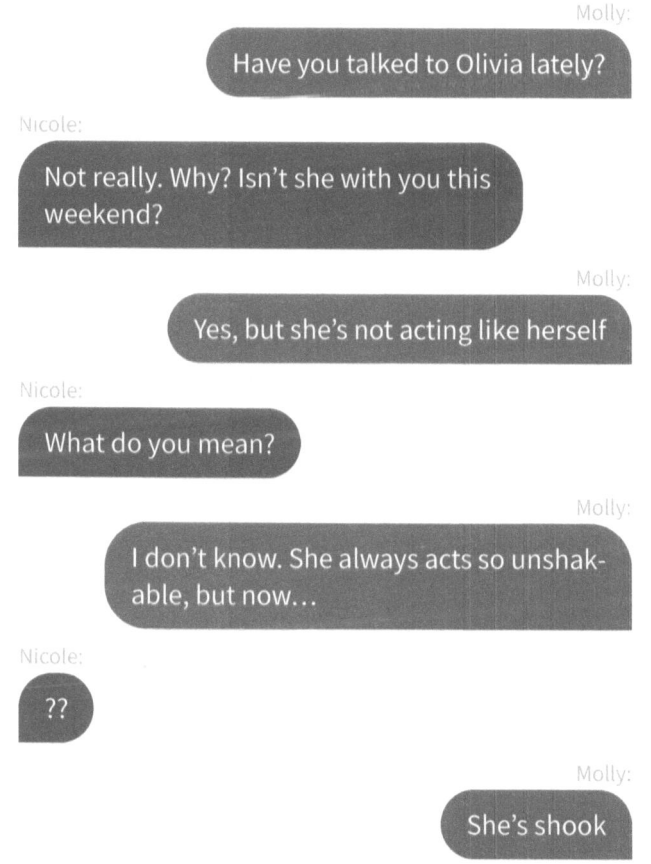

Molly:
Have you talked to Olivia lately?

Nicole:
Not really. Why? Isn't she with you this weekend?

Molly:
Yes, but she's not acting like herself

Nicole:
What do you mean?

Molly:
I don't know. She always acts so unshakable, but now…

Nicole:
??

Molly:
She's shook

Nicole:
Hmm. Let's talk to her together when we're home for Thanksgiving

Molly:
Good idea

Molly:
You're bringing Adam, right?

Nicole:
Yes! He's excited

I answer with a thumbs-up then busy myself setting up the air mattress for Olivia. I'm not sure who won the coin toss between the love seat and the air mattress, but one of my guests will need it.

Then I change into my pajamas while I wait for my turn in the bathroom. Before long, Olivia slips out, avoiding eye contact. It's best to give her time and space when she's upset, so I go to the bathroom and brush my teeth.

When I'm done, Olivia is sitting on the couch in the dark living room.

"Goodnight, Livvy," I call out.

I hear the smallest sigh, and then she answers. "Night, sissy."

I've just gotten comfortable under the covers when Olivia quietly climbs into bed next to me.

"Can I sleep with you?" she whispers.

"Of course," I whisper back.

As we settle in, I'm again transported into my memories of Olivia as a child and the many nights she would sneak into bed with me after lights out. Though brave and bold in the daylight, even as a child, Olivia always seemed her most vulnerable at night. I'm not sure Nicole, or even our parents, knew how often she would snuggle up with me like this. She's never been great about sharing her feelings, but if I can support her through this simple comfort, I'll take it.

I don't know what happened tonight to upset Olivia. Maybe Nicole and I can get to the bottom of it when we're home for Thanksgiving in a few weeks.

After the weekend, when Olivia and Annie go home, I still don't know why my sister was so upset. It's a busy week at work, though, and I have to put it out of my mind.

After putting the finishing touches on our manuscript, we submit it to the preprint server. The week passes, and it's suddenly Halloween. As promised, I drive to Jonathan's apartment to help him pass out candy to trick-or-treaters. I don't wear a costume, but I have a festive T-shirt. It's orange with a picture of Charlie Brown covered in a sheet full of round holes, with the phrase "I got a rock" printed at the top. Add to that the jack-o'-lantern earrings I have on, and I hope Jonathan will be satisfied.

He opens the door, and I laugh. He's dressed as Gilligan from the old TV show *Gilligan's Island*. He's wearing light blue jeans with a red long-sleeved, collared shirt, and of course a white bucket hat on his head.

"Ahoy!" I greet him.

He grins. "Right back atcha, Charlie Brown."

I look down at my shirt and tug on the hem. "Is this okay?"

"You look beautiful. Come on in." He leans down to give me a peck on the lips.

I hold up the paper sack in my hand. "I brought dinner from The Saucy Wing." Before I knocked on the door, I set two glass bottles on the floor. I nudge them with my toe. "And root beer."

He takes the sack, and I bend down to pick up the root beer bottles.

"That's perfect," he says, his eyes bright as he opens the bag to investigate the contents. "I was planning on candy for dinner, but wings are probably a better idea. Thank you."

The simple gratitude warms me from the inside out. As much as he makes sure I'm taken care of, I want to make sure he's okay, too.

"You know," I say, following him into the apartment, "I always thought Gilligan and Mary Ann would end up together."

Jonathan wags his eyebrows. "What a perfect couples' costume. You can be Mary Ann. We'll put you in short shorts and a crop top, your hair in pigtails."

I slap his arm while fighting off a smile. "Stop."

He shrugs. "Maybe next year."

I shuffle through the big bowl of candy he has on a table near the front door. "What candy did you get for the kids?"

He pulls my hand away from the bowl. "Stop that. You'll mess up my system."

I laugh. "What's your system?"

"I layer the candy in the bowl based on my preferences. See, at the top I've got the Mounds and Crunch bars, then the Snickers and Cookies 'N' Creme, and at the bottom, the Milky Way and Twix. That way, I give out the candy I don't like first, and if there's any left at the end of the night, it's all the stuff I like."

I put a hand on my hip. "And what about the candy I like?"

"Oh, no, my dear. I got something much better than candy for you." He winks. "I stopped by Cafe Beignet earlier. The bag's on the kitchen table for you."

I squeal and duck into the kitchen to find my beignets. "You're the best!"

"Don't forget it!" he calls after me.

After two hours of bouncing between the couch and the front door for a steady stream of trick-or-treaters, the doorbell finally stops ringing.

I flop onto the couch cushion next to Jonathan and rest my head against his shoulder.

"Don't get too comfortable," he warns. "I'm about to stand up. Are you still feeling up to going to the party?"

I groan. "No. I'm sorry. I think I'm just going to head home. You go ahead though."

"Maybe," he hedges. "They are expecting me."

"And you want to go. So, go. You'll have fun."

He looks at me warily. "Is this a trick? Or a test of some kind?"

I laugh and pat his leg. "Not at all. You want some people time, so go to the party. I want some alone time, so I'll go home."

"Okay," he agrees. "But don't go home. Stay here and have your alone time. Then I can see you when I get back. I won't be too late."

Even though the drive home will be easier now than later tonight when I'm tired, I am pretty comfortable already on Jonathan's couch. "Word of warning: if you leave me alone in your apartment, I *will* snoop around."

Jonathan chuckles and presses a kiss to my forehead before standing up. "Go for it. What's mine is yours, Carrots." He grabs his keys. "I'll be back in a couple of hours."

After he leaves, I *do* snoop, but not too invasively. In a desk drawer, I find the stack of sticky notes I put up in Jonathan's cubicle and that he's been using since to leave notes on my refrigerator.

Though we've been officially together almost a month now, this is my first time back at his apartment since Hernando. My apartment is closer to everything, including the lab, so we tend to hang out there. Being here now makes me think of that night and how safe I felt, despite the risk we were taking out on the boat. I think of the collection of sticky notes on my refrigerator, each sweeter than the next. Every little and big way he's shown me I'm special to him.

Maybe it's time to leave a note on *his* refrigerator. But what to say?

I've been happier this month with Jonathan than I've ever been before in my life. He pushes me out of my comfort zone while making me feel safe. He helps me remember my good qualities instead of always dwelling on the bad. He encourages me to find more balance in my life, embracing joy in addition to work.

When I think about it, there's really only one thing to write that encapsulates everything I want to say.

I sort through the stack of sticky notes until I find the sunshine yellow one with a tiny hand-drawn heart on the back. I jot down the words and stick the paper on the front of Jonathan's refrigerator. Then I curl up in his bed to watch a movie.

I must fall asleep, because the next thing I know, Jonathan settles into bed next to me, spooning me with his chest against my back and his arm over my side with his hand resting against my stomach.

He nuzzles his nose into my neck, then whispers softly in my ear, "I love you, too."

Even half-asleep, I smile. Maybe Halloween isn't such a bad holiday after all.

Chapter Twenty-Seven

Jonathan

I wake up smiling, holding Molly in my arms. I swear I sleep better when she's in bed with me, when my skin is in contact with hers. It calms everything inside me, and I relax into the sound of her rhythmic breathing. I could 100 percent get used to this.

She loves me.

I sit up slowly, careful not to disturb Molly, and slide off the bed to walk to the bathroom. Then, I move to the kitchen to get coffee started. I lean back against the kitchen counter and stare at the bright yellow sticky note on my black refrigerator. I can't see my own face, but I'm sure the grin there could only be described as goofy. But something's missing.

I need to hear her *say* it.

I turn around and finish getting the coffee ready. I open the refrigerator door to see what I can offer Molly for breakfast. Last time she was here, we had fruit pops, but I'm sure I can do better than that this morning. *She doesn't like eggs*, I remind myself. I wonder if that would extend to French toast? Pancakes are probably a safe bet. I've seen her eat pancakes.

A noise behind me catches my attention, and I spin to see Molly walk into the kitchen. I grin and emphatically close the refrigerator door so that the sticky note is on display.

Gesturing toward it, I ask, "Can you read this note for me, please?"

She shakes her head, a smile playing across her lips. "Good morning to you, too."

I take one long step toward her and smack a kiss against her cheek. "Good morning. Now, please read this note?"

She smirks and stares at the note quietly.

"Out loud, Carrots!"

She giggles. "Ohhh. You didn't say that."

I throw up my hands. "Molly!"

She laughs and takes my hands in hers. Her hair is mussed, her clothes sleep-rumpled. Those deep blue eyes I love are bright. A soft smile lights her face as she holds my gaze. "I don't need to read it because I have it memorized. It's written on my heart. I love you, Jonathan."

I pull her against my chest and wrap her in my arms, burying my face in her hair. After several minutes, I release her and tap my thumb underneath her chin to lift her face toward mine. "I love you, Molly."

Her lips form a tight smile that doesn't quite reach her eyes. My heart sinks. "What?" I ask.

She shakes her head and drops her gaze to the floor. "Nothing. It's just sweet of you to say."

I frown. "You don't believe me?" I flash back to the night last month when I left my dinner with Dr. Perron to unlock Molly's apartment door. *I don't believe love's meant for me*, she said. Is that still true? Clearly, I need to up my sticky note game.

She hesitates before responding. "I believe you believe it's true."

I brush a strand of hair off her forehead and cup her face in my hands. "That's because it *is* true," I insist. "Look at me." I wait until she reluctantly meets my eyes. "You. Are. Extremely. Lovable."

Between each word, I press a soft kiss on a different part of her face—first her forehead, then each cheek, and finally the tip of her nose. The last one makes her smile.

"Okay," she says.

"That's right, okay. Never argue with me when I'm trying to tell you how amazing you are."

Another small smile. Each one feels like a victory. "Noted. Now, I need to get home."

"Noooo!" I pull her into another hug and tighten my arms. "At least stay for breakfast."

"I will, but then I need to go. I didn't plan to stay over, and I don't have anything with me."

"I'm sure I have an extra toothbrush."

She's grinning now. "Jonathan."

I grin back at her. "Molly."

She shakes her head in exasperation. "I need a shower and to change my clothes."

Oh, really? I raise my eyebrows with a smirk, then open my mouth to respond. Before I can say anything, she claps her hand over my mouth. "That was not an invitation." The glare she shoots me lights up my whole body.

💕 💕 💕

After breakfast, Molly heads out. I putter around the apartment, straightening up and throwing away empty candy packages from last night.

Feeling restless, I stretch out on the couch and check my phone. I have a new email from Dr. Perron. The guy's relentless. He quoted me an attractive salary and promised a large research team with state-of-the-art equipment. All that costs money, and he hasn't said where the funding is coming from. That makes me uneasy. If the grant is coming from the National Science Foundation or the Environmental Protection Agency, why wouldn't he just say so? Why the cloak and dagger?

The primary attraction of the position when I started talking to Dr. Perron was avoiding Molly. My priority is the exact opposite now.

I don't know. The extra money would be nice. A principal investigator position looks good on a CV. Honestly, though, I'm happy piloting boats and wading through bayous for a living.

Dr. Perron is pushing me for an answer. The position would start in the new year. I keep putting him off, especially since we've been so busy with the hurricane data from the gliders.

The data show everything Molly hoped. In addition to water temperature and pH, the gliders collected data on the water turbidity—that is, how cloudy the water is—and changes in salinity, which can all affect the possibility of red tide outbreaks.

The manuscript we uploaded to EarthArXiv just before Halloween included the real-time information in addition to the results of Molly's data model. I've never been prouder to be involved with a research project before.

I navigate to the preprint server site on my phone and take a peek at our article. *What the—*

There are a ton of comments on our preprint already. We're trending—well, at least among other coastal environmental scientists.

I text Molly.

Jonathan:

We're going viral

Molly:

????

Jonathan:

[laughing emoji] The preprint's blowing up on the site

Molly:

Really??

Molly:

Omg I just looked. How did people even find
it so quickly??

Jonathan:

Dr. Gantt's name carries a lot of weight

Jonathan:

Almost as much as Dr. Molly Delaney

♥ ♥ ♥

Monday morning, I pick Molly up on my way into the lab. She sits
in the passenger seat refreshing the browser on her phone over and
over again. The online conversation around our preprint has grown
even more.

Molly reads a comment aloud for me. "The analysis of the
real-time water property data during the hurricane provides valuable
insights that haven't been well-documented before."

I hardly have time to react when she smacks my arm excitedly.
"Listen to this one! 'The discussion section effectively highlights the
broader implications of these findings for coastal management.'"

I chuckle. "Are you just cherry-picking the positive ones?"

"No," she grumbles. "Here's one giving a suggestion. 'The study
focuses on one tropical event. It would be valuable to discuss the

potential for variability across different tropical storm and hurricane characteristics.'"

I scratch my chin. "That's a good point. Can we add that before we submit it to a journal?"

"Sure. We haven't even decided which journal we want to submit to yet."

Those are our next steps: choosing a journal and making edits to our manuscript before we submit.

Molly's still glued to her phone as we park, walk through the parking lot, and ride the elevator up to the second floor.

As if she's been waiting for us, Dr. Gantt catches us the moment we walk into the office. She ushers us into her office and closes the door.

"Is everything okay?" I ask as I slide into a chair. Molly sits down next to me.

"Very much so," Dr. Gantt answers with a smile. "I take it you've seen the reactions online to the preprint?" We both nod. "I just received a call from the head of the conference committee at CERA."

Molly and I exchange glances. The Coast and Estuary Research Association is one of the major nonpartisan organizations whose mission is to promote research in the coastal environmental sciences. Their annual conference is coming up in just a few weeks.

"They're inviting us to come to the conference to share our findings," Dr. Gantt finishes.

I check Molly's expression before I let myself react. Her eyes are wide and glowing. "Are you serious?" she squeals.

"One hundred percent," Dr. Gantt answers.

I grin at Molly's excitement. I don't love conferences, even just attending. They feel so stuffy and pretentious to me. And if you're presenting, the pressure is high. It's a great opportunity, though, so I'll grin and bear it. Especially for Molly.

We discuss logistics. The conference is in Las Vegas the week before Thanksgiving, just two and a half weeks away.

As soon as I hear the location, I can't help but laugh. "A coast and estuary conference in the middle of the desert? Are they all sick of scenic ocean views, or what?"

Dr. Gantt makes a disapproving face. "More like they want easy access to gambling and alcohol."

I chuckle again. Scientists gone wild. Got it. Maybe the conference won't be as stuffy and pretentious as I fear, though drunk and rowdy isn't exactly my scene, either.

Preparations for the conference take up a lot of our work time over the next couple weeks. We have to outline the presentation and practice it, plus arrange travel logistics like booking flights and finding a nice cat hotel for Beaker. The conference starts first thing on a Wednesday morning and goes through Friday late afternoon. Our presentation is on Friday.

Because of a prior commitment, Dr. Gantt can't get to Las Vegas until Thursday, which means Molly and I fly in without her on Tuesday.

While I don't enjoy conferences, I love traveling. I've never been to Las Vegas. Apparently, the conference center is right on the Strip, so we should have plenty of opportunities to sightsee in between conference sessions.

Our flight is only about half-full—I guess Las Vegas is not as much of a destination in the middle of the week—and Molly and I end up having a row to ourselves. After we stow our carry-ons and settle into our seats, Molly makes a quick call to her mom. I hear only her side of the conversation, but it rankles in more ways than one.

"Yes, Mom, I'll be safe... Well, I can't really control the flight, but I'll be careful walking around the city once I get there." She glances at me. "Yes, of course. He's one of my co-researchers." Her cheeks turn pink. "No, not really... Um ... maybe? ... I know." She sighs. "Okay. Yes, I'll see you next week for Thanksgiving... I love you, too."

Reason number one the short phone call annoys me is that Molly still hasn't told her family that we're together. Her sisters and parents are the most important people in the world to Molly, and I'm sour that she's keeping us a secret from them. We've discussed it several times, and she keeps going back to the excuse that she doesn't want to deal with their teasing. I think it's more than that. I think she's waiting for me to get tired of her or something, and if that happens—which it never will—she'll feel less embarrassed about it if her family never knew about the relationship in the first place.

My family knows all about her. She's talked on video calls with Tamara a few times. I even mentioned the relationship to my dad—though it *may* have been as part of an excuse as to why I can't come to Ohio for Christmas. Only my mom, who I haven't talked to in a while, hasn't heard about my girlfriend.

Reason number two it bothers me that Molly calls her mom right before we take off is the sweet simplicity of the love between them. Guilt over how I've continued to duck my dad's calls niggles at me. I've been trying, and I just can't find a way to be okay with him marrying Sharon. He wants an answer about Christmas, and as much as I'm certain I'm not going to Ohio, I'm also reluctant to tell my dad that. I know when I do, I'll feel even more like an ungrateful brat.

These two reasons are why, when Molly switches off her phone and curls into my side, I'm already defensive. When she asks, "Do you need to call your dad before we take off?", I downright bristle.

"No," I say flatly. "He doesn't even know I'm going anywhere."

Molly sits up, her hand against my chest, and stares at me in disbelief. "He doesn't know?"

I shrug. "I haven't told him." I did tell Tamara, and she likely told our dad, but explaining that fact doesn't suit my mood at the moment.

Molly searches my face. I'm not sure what she sees written on it, but she rests her head back on my shoulder rather than forcing a conversation.

I shut my eyes and lean my head into hers. It's hard to stay grumpy while I'm breathing in the subtle lavender scent of her hair. We sit this way, quietly leaning on each other, while the plane takes off and climbs higher until it reaches cruising altitude.

I clear my throat, and without changing position, I say, "My dad's getting remarried." Molly doesn't respond, except to take my hand and link our fingers together, silently encouraging me to continue. "He and Sharon have been dating for two years. I feel like he's betraying my mom. I know that doesn't make any sense. They've been divorced for over a decade. I don't know why I revert to a surly preteen with anything to do with my dad. It's like I'm still sitting in that fog of hurt and confusion after my mom left."

I stop talking, and after a moment, Molly tips her head up. "Is that why you've been ignoring his phone calls?"

I sigh. "Yeah. He wants to have the wedding in Ohio just after Christmas, and I haven't told him for sure if I'll make the trip home for it."

"Will you?" She presses a sweet kiss to my neck, her lips feather soft against my skin.

"No. I can't seem to tell him, though."

Molly makes a humming noise that sounds from the back of her throat. "If you change your mind," she says carefully, "I could go with you. Be your backup."

That makes me smile. Molly's all of five foot three, but her words make me picture her as a burly bodyguard with a neck tattoo. Molly *can* be ferocious with her biting retorts and barbed insults when she wants to be—I've been on the receiving end enough times. Even so, I know she means more like emotional backup, and no one is more perfect for that job than she is.

"Thank you. I'll keep that in mind." Her sweet offer leaves a bitter aftertaste. She's open to spending her favorite holiday with me and my family, but her own family still thinks I'm her archnemesis or whatever.

As if she's reading my mind, Molly's face twists into a frown. "And actually—" She hesitates, but when she continues, she's resolute. "Will you come to Texas with me next week? To see my family for Thanksgiving?"

Warmth radiates through my chest. "As what, Carrots?" I ask, only partially teasing. "Your co-researcher? Your friend? Your arch-nemesis?" I say the last word pointedly, but I'm grinning.

Chagrined, Molly bites her bottom lip and blushes. "As my boyfriend."

"Are you sure?" I probe. "You'll tell your family?"

"Yes," she says. "I should have told them weeks ago."

"No arguments here." I lift my arm and loop it around her shoulders, pulling her closer to me.

She puts a hand on either side of my face and looks into my eyes. "I'm sorry. I didn't mean to make you feel like you aren't important to me. The truth is, you're everything to me, and honestly that feels a little scary."

"For me, too," I murmur. "I love you."

Her eyes shine. "I love you."

I close the gap between us and kiss her tenderly and slowly, like we have all the time in the world.

Of course, we don't, which the middle-aged flight attendant makes apparent when she clears her throat disapprovingly before asking what we'd like to drink. I flash her my most charming smile, and before she moves on, I've won her over. She promises to bring me the entire can of root beer when she comes back instead of the little plastic cup that's mostly ice with a swallow of soda.

The rest of the four-hour flight is uneventful. When the captain asks us to put our seats and tray tables in the upright and locked position, I peer out the window. Rugged, snowcapped mountains jut up below us. I grew up in Ohio, was in Florida a while, and have lived in Louisiana ever since. Mountains are a beautiful novelty.

Molly must feel the same—growing up in Texas and living in Louisiana—because she gasps as she leans closer to the window.

Soon the mountains give way to a flat grid of buildings and roads that grow larger as the plane dips closer to the ground. We've arrived.

Chapter Twenty-Eight

Molly

The first thing I notice about Las Vegas is the noise. Even in the airport, the chiming bells of slot machines echo through the corridors. When we step outside, the next thing I notice is the lack of humidity in the air. It's probably ten degrees cooler here, and I'm instantly grateful I packed layers for the conference.

Jonathan and I take a taxi to the conference hotel, passing neon billboards on the short trip. I watch the tall, shiny buildings grow closer as we near the Strip, but our hotel is right on the edge, so we can't see many of the landmarks yet.

Though we've been traveling for more than four hours, it's two hours earlier here, so it's actually not much later here than when we left New Orleans. The conference starts tomorrow morning, which gives us all afternoon to explore.

The first step is to get checked into the hotel so we can ditch our luggage. As we approach the front entrance, my head is on a swivel. Across the street is a shopping plaza with a giant Coca-Cola bottle and large M&M's characters adorning the front. Down the street, a roller coaster looms almost as tall as the hotels around it. I shake my head. New Orleans is known as a fun city, but Las Vegas is next-level.

At the front desk, Jonathan convinces the clerk, whose name tag says Justin, to give us rooms near each other. He chats with him about exploring the Strip.

"You know about the monorail, right?" Justin asks.

Jonathan's eyes jump to mine, and I grin at him. A monorail sounds fun.

"No. Can you tell us about it, please? It's our first time in Vegas."

"Sure! There's a monorail that runs the length of the Strip. You can get on and off at various stops. It's a great way to get an overview of the area, especially if you've never been here before."

We thank Justin and head to the elevator to find our rooms.

"Drop off our bags and then monorail?" Jonathan asks as the elevator doors close behind us.

"Sounds like a plan. I want to take a shower and change first, though. I feel like I smell like airplane." I scrunch my nose.

Jonathan raises his eyebrows and opens his mouth, but I put my finger over his lips. "Still not an invitation." I laugh, shaking my head.

He smirks. "One of these days..."

I pat his chest. "You'll be the first to know," I promise.

Jonathan's room is right next door to mine, and I leave him with a quick kiss while I get settled.

I close the door to my hotel room, then lean against it, closing my eyes and smiling. It's so *fun* to be traveling with Jonathan, exploring a new city with him before giving the biggest presentation of my career to date.

Despite the heavy conversation on the plane, I feel light. I acknowledge that it's at least partly because Jonathan needed me, and I was there for him. I contributed to the relationship in a way that benefited Jonathan, despite my fears about symbiosis. It makes me think maybe I can do this. I can be a scientist, a daughter, a sister, *and* a partner, balancing it all. I can allow myself to be loved the way Jonathan wants to love me and love him in return.

I shower and change, texting Jonathan when I'm finished. For this trip, I decided to switch things up from my normal leggings and T-shirts, at least for a few outfits. I may have ended up dropping down the rabbit hole of the internet when I searched "women's outfits las vegas november" and spent several hours poring over the results. Most of the outfits weren't for me; they looked uncomfortable, or revealing, or just too flashy. I bought a couple pairs of dark, stretchy pants—it's really amazing the kinds of pants you can get with elastic waistbands these days—and a few long-sleeve blouses with subtle patterns and dark colors. The one I'm wearing now has swirls of black and silver against a cream background.

Moments later, there's a knock on my hotel room door. I open it to find Jonathan standing in the hall, holding out a single flower with one hand, his other hand behind his back.

"What's this?" I ask, my face splitting into a smile. The flower is a rich red color with a trumpet shape that reminds me of lilies. The long stem has vibrant green leaves angled off it.

It's beautiful, but I find myself staring more at the man holding it. He changed his clothes, too, and is now wearing black fitted jeans with a maroon long-sleeve button-down shirt. I chuckle. Looks like we both decided to dress up more while we're here.

Jonathan eyes me up and down, and grins. "You look ready to take on Las Vegas," he teases.

"So do you. What's the flower for?"

His eyes turn serious. "I know our presentation isn't until Friday, but I want to say how proud I am of you. This is a big deal, and I'm so happy that you're getting the recognition you deserve."

I take the flower from his hand. "It's beautiful. Thank you. It's your project too, though, you know."

He grins. "I know. But I was following your lead. You're the mastermind. I'm just the work grunt." He winks so I know he's kidding.

I gesture for him to come inside, and he does, keeping a hand behind his back. "What's in your other hand?" I ask, trying to peek behind him.

"Ah," he says, holding up a finger. "It's our ultimate Las Vegas travel kit." He pulls out a sling crossbody bag and places it on the end of the bed. He unzips it and starts cataloging the contents. "We have reusable water bottles, sunscreen, a portable phone charger, a map of the Strip, lip balm, Advil, blister bandages, a microfiber cleaning cloth for your glasses, noise-canceling earbuds, and..." He smirks at me. "Hair ties. And the best part is, I'll carry it, so you can just sit back and relax."

I laugh. "That's perfect."

He shrugs. "I like to be prepared."

We head out and follow the hotel signs to the monorail station. Jonathan buys our tickets at a kiosk in a space that reminds me of a subway station, except we're high above ground, not below it. Within five minutes, the monorail arrives, and we shuffle on with the rest of the crowd.

I'm glued to the window as I list the sites I'd like to see. "The Bellagio fountain, The Venetian, and the Sphere."

Jonathan tracks each suggestion on a map on his phone. "How about we ride this to the end and then hit all the spots on our way back?" he asks.

"Fine with me." I settle into my seat next to the window. Though the monorail is almost full, it doesn't feel stuffy or loud. We ride all the way down to the SAHARA station, each of us pointing out what we see: lots of hotel pools, a Ferris wheel, plus some unglamorous parking lots. We pass right by the Sphere, lit up and pulsing a rhythmic pattern. A lush, green golf course looks out of place among all the concrete.

Jonathan plans out our return stops. Most of what we want to see is at the Harrah's station, so that's where we hop off. New Orleans also has a Harrah's casino, which is maybe why, in addition to proximity, I decide this casino is the one I'm going to try. Even though the whole idea of a loud, crowded, chaotic casino makes my skin crawl, I promised myself before we even got on the plane that I would at least enter a casino while in Las Vegas. It's part of the experience, after all.

I take a deep breath and tell Jonathan that I want to go inside Harrah's.

"Are you sure?" he asks, with a tilt of his head and concern in his eyes. "I'm not a casino person, so don't worry about me missing out."

"Yes," I say resolutely. "We can't come all the way to Vegas and not go into a casino."

He smiles widely, all his teeth showing. "Let's do it." He takes my hand, and we walk up to the glass doors. They open automatically. Gleaming marble floors give way to a tacky dark-purple carpet where tables and chairs and gaming machines sit. Nearly all of these are glowing with bright and blinking lights. A long bar with tall stools, huge television screens, and shelves of bottles stretches out to our left.

The strong smell of cigarette smoke mixed with some sort of cloying citrus fragrance assaults my nose, making me immediately want to walk back out. Instead, I press my face against Jonathan's sleeve, and we continue on.

It's so *loud*. Music, beeping, alarms, and the tick-tick-tick-tick sounds of the roulette wheel clamor around us, plus the sound of conversations and laughter from the crowds of people.

We walk halfway through the room, past a pizza parlor. All the while, I can feel Jonathan's eyes on me.

"Seen enough?" I ask brightly, glancing sideways at him.

Jonathan smirks. "More than."

We turn around and make our way back out the glass doors. I exhale in relief when we get to the sidewalk outside. It's not exactly calm and quiet on the streets of Las Vegas, but at least the noise can escape into the desert sky instead of being trapped next to my ears.

Jonathan grins at me. "We can check that one off the bucket list."

"Yep," I say, pinching my thumb and pointer finger together as if I'm holding a pencil and miming a check mark in the air. "Check and check."

Next, we walk to The Venetian, passing a group of women dressed like showgirls, including feather plumes swaying behind their leopard-print cowboy hats.

I pull Jonathan to stand next to the railing that looks out over the hotel's re-creation of a canal in Venice, Italy. Gondoliers push their boats along with long poles while tourists enjoy the tour.

Jonathan nudges my shoulder, and I look up at him. He has his eyebrows raised expectantly. "Wanna ride?"

I grin. "Definitely."

We learn there are two options: outdoor gondola rides and indoor gondola rides. I kind of want to try them both, but I settle on the indoor option; I figure that an indoor canal is more of a novelty than an outdoor canal.

We follow the signs inside to the ticket booth and buy tickets. I look around and am suddenly glad we chose the indoor gondola ride. It looks amazing in here. On either side of the canal, the shops are set up to look like Italian cafes with arches and balconies. The ceiling is painted to look like a bright blue sky with fluffy cirrocumulus clouds.

When it's our turn, we're ushered onto a gondola. We sit side by side facing the gondolier, who wears black pants with a black-and-white horizontal-striped shirt and a bright red ascot loosely tied around his neck. On his head, he has a flat-brimmed straw hat with a red ribbon around its base.

An older couple takes the bench facing us. Once everyone is settled, the ride operators take a photo of each couple, and we're told we can purchase ours at the end of our ride. Then, the gondolier pushes off, and we're floating down the man-made canal.

I snuggle closer to Jonathan, who has his arm wrapped around my shoulders. I peer up at him. He's looking everywhere, trying to take everything in. When his gaze lands on me, he smiles and presses a kiss to my cheek.

"Will you take our picture, please?" the woman across from me asks. She looks to be about my mother's age, with light brown skin and curly gray hair coiled short on top of her head. The laugh lines around her eyes are pronounced, creasing the skin at the corners like beams of joy radiating from her face.

"Oh, sure," I agree.

She hands me her phone. I snap a couple of shots, being careful to position it so the background is mostly canal, rather than people-filled sidewalk or gondolier.

"Thank you," she says when I give the phone back. "Want me to get a few of you?"

I look at Jonathan. He grins and nods. "Sure, thank you." I fish my phone out of my pocket and open the camera app for her.

We take one with our faces pointed toward the camera, and then the woman says, "Now look at each other."

We do, and I can't help but notice the happy shine in Jonathan's eyes. Warmth fills my chest. He really does love me. Maybe even as much as I love him, which is saying something, because my feelings are deep and wide like the ocean. Now that I'm in, I'm diving farther and farther down, love compressing my body and soothing my senses. I'm suspended, floating weightless.

The woman holds out my phone, drawing my attention back to her. "Here you go. I'm Angela, by the way, and this is my husband, Luther."

"Molly and Jonathan," I respond.

"How long have you two been married?" she asks.

I flash Jonathan a panicked look, but, laughing, he gestures for me to answer. "Oh, um, we're not married." I stutter.

Her eyes twinkle as she tilts her head. "No?"

I shake my head in confirmation, feeling my cheeks turning red. Next to me, Jonathan quakes with silent laughter.

"Too bad," she says with a broad smile. "But you're certainly in the right city to fix that problem."

My eyes widen just as Angela's husband speaks up. "Angela and I got married right here in Las Vegas thirty years ago this week. Best decision I ever made." He shoots Jonathan a wink.

"Happy anniversary," Jonathan says with a grin. He squeezes my shoulder.

Talking about marrying Jonathan is making me feel nervous, but curiously, not in a ready-to-panic kind of way. It's more of a flutter-in-my-stomach kind of way, almost ... excitement? I'm too self-conscious about how I'm feeling to look at Jonathan, so I focus on the sights around us.

Small fountains on the brick walls lining the canal shoot streams of water behind us as we travel under bridges and around corners.

Then, the gondolier starts to sing! His clear baritone voice belts out an Italian aria as he pushes the pole around the bottom of the canal to propel us forward.

I'm enchanted, at least until Jonathan leans down to whisper in my ear. "Look at his name tag."

I do and immediately bite back a laugh. The name tag says, "Chet" in a swooping cursive font. I press my face into Jonathan's chest to stifle my mirth.

An Italian gondolier named Chet. I lift my head until I'm looking at Jonathan. "Only in Vegas," I say, matching his gleeful smile.

When our ride is over and we disembark, we wander over to the photo stand where we can view and purchase the photo the ride operator took of us when we first boarded. It's a cute picture of us, and we consider it, but I scroll through the pictures Angela took.

I'm fixated on one where Jonathan and I are gazing at each other, starry-eyed and looking very much in love, with the scenes of fake Venice behind us. We don't buy the overpriced photo. Jonathan agrees this one is perfect.

We finish our first day in Las Vegas at the Bellagio Fountains, then head across the street to Paris Las Vegas where we see the Eiffel Tower replica and grab a casual dinner at a French bakery that sells sandwiches and pastries.

It's been a long day, between traveling and sightseeing, and we'll be busy again tomorrow when the conference starts. We head back to the hotel early before the famous Vegas nightlife kicks off.

When we get there, though, we linger in the hallway outside our rooms, neither of us wanting to say goodnight. Today has been perfect, and I don't want it to end. I lean my head into Jonathan's chest, and he wraps his arms around me. We stand snuggled into each other for what could be five minutes or five hours. I've lost all track of time.

Finally, Jonathan sighs. "We have a busy day tomorrow. I should let you get some rest." He makes no move to loosen his embrace.

I sigh in response. "I suppose so," I say, nestling deeper into his chest.

He kisses the top of my head, and I lift my chin, angling for a different kind of kiss. Jonathan presses his mouth to mine, slow and lingering, like sweet molasses on my lips. He kisses me like he can't stop, but also like there's no rush, despite the early morning we have tomorrow.

We finally say good night, disappearing through the doors of our separate rooms. I fall asleep with my lips warm and tingling.

Chapter Twenty-Nine

Molly

The next morning, we need to be up, dressed, and at the conference registration desk by eight. Jonathan must have woken up even earlier than me, because he knocks on my door with an orange juice and croissant that he picked up for me at the hotel cafe downstairs.

"Stop reading my mind!" I tease, grateful for the boost the orange juice will give me.

"Never." He grins, and we walk toward the elevator.

The croissant is no beignet, but it's good, and I can probably do without the extra sugar making me feel wired today anyway.

We check in and get our badges, along with a printed-out copy of the conference program. Once conferences go to mobile apps for their programs, I don't understand why they continue to print a copy for every attendee and include it in their welcome packet. Most of us will be accessing it on our phones anyway.

However, I'm grateful for the solid, professionally-printed program this time. My name is in it! I may collect discarded copies from the other attendees to bring to my family at Thanksgiving next week.

As Jonathan and I step away from the registration desk, the first thing I do is find the Friday lineup and scan for my name. I actually spot Jonathan's name first, as the second author listed right after mine. It even says, *Invited Presentation* instead of *Accepted Presentation*, broadcasting that the conference organizers reached out to *us*, not the other way around.

I've presented at conferences before, of course, but this presentation—this project—is special. It aligns with my own research interests, rather than only those of the lab's PI. It developed as a side project out of my own brain. Possibly most importantly, I worked on it with Jonathan. Also, it doesn't hurt that our results are generating a lot of interest from our colleagues.

Jonathan leans over my program and taps my name. "Look at that. 'Molly Delaney, PhD, New Orleans State University.' I can say I knew you when." He pretends to wipe a tear from the corner of his eye, but underneath the theatrics I know how genuinely proud of me he is. He's only told me about a hundred times.

The feeling is mutual. I tap *his* name. *Jonathan P. Stanch, PhD, New Orleans State University*. "Right next to mine."

He grabs my hand and brings it to his lips. "As it should be."

I chuckle and redirect him. We are here to work, after all, not canoodle. *Though there's always time for that later...*

Jonathan and I compare notes on which sessions we each plan to attend today. While Dr. Gantt made it clear that our top priority at the conference is to present on our project, and she doesn't expect us to report back on the sessions we attend, the CERA conference is full of other scientists and students who get excited about the same nerdy stuff we do. I have a long list of presentations I want to learn from, and Jonathan does, too.

I plan to attend a session on seagrass restoration, while Jonathan decides to brush up on blue carbon offsetting, just in case he decides to take the job Dr. Perron is offering. We agree to meet for lunch and take off in separate directions.

After spending all day yesterday together, even this short morning apart feels brutal. We keep up an ongoing text conversation as we sit through the sessions.

Jonathan:

I hope our presentation won't be as boring as this one. Seriously, I'm falling asleep, and I didn't even stay up late last night

Molly:

Too bad for you. I just learned about an ecological modeling program to predict eutrophication

Molly:

So I'm happy

Jonathan:

Cough. NERD. Cough.

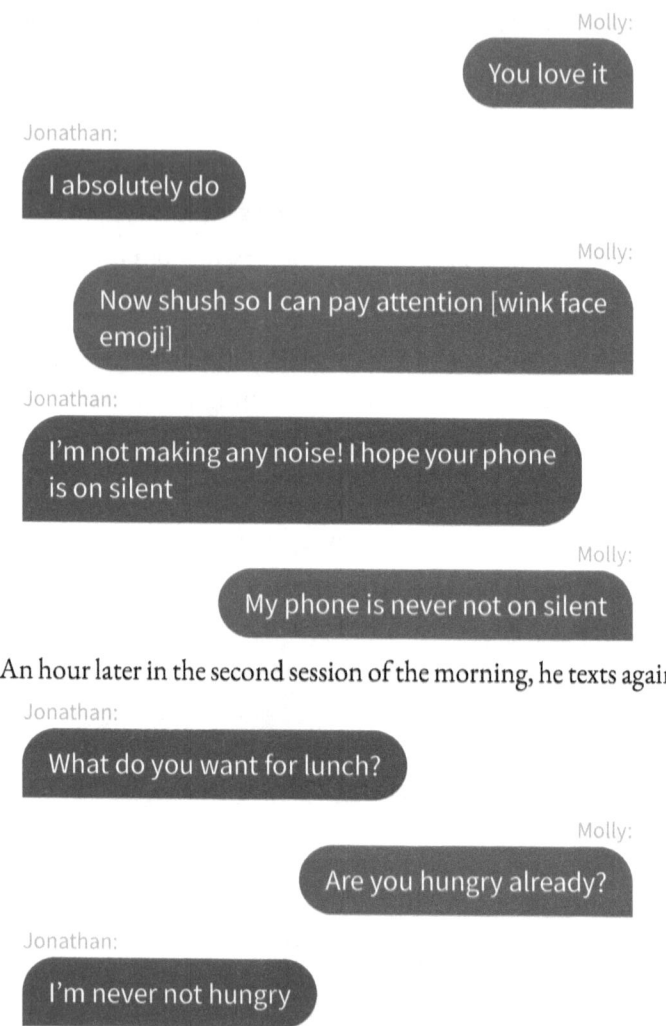

Molly:

You love it

Jonathan:

I absolutely do

Molly:

Now shush so I can pay attention [wink face emoji]

Jonathan:

I'm not making any noise! I hope your phone is on silent

Molly:

My phone is never not on silent

An hour later in the second session of the morning, he texts again.

Jonathan:

What do you want for lunch?

Molly:

Are you hungry already?

Jonathan:

I'm never not hungry

Finally, the break for "lunch on your own" arrives. I find Jonathan, and we head outside where several food trucks are waiting. We choose a truck that serves corn dogs, chicken tenders, and other comfort foods. The line's long, but it moves quickly.

Almost everyone from the conference is out here in this courtyard for lunch. I can tell by the name badges everyone is still wearing on lanyards around their necks, including me.

As we wait, a middle-aged woman with long black hair approaches me. Her dark-blue suit looks too formal for this setting—or maybe I'm underdressed? I look around and see that no, my business casual is right on par with what most everyone is wearing.

"Hi, Dr. Delaney?"

"Yes," I confirm, taking a step back.

"I saw your name badge and had to introduce myself. My name is Dr. Almay Jones. I'm the deputy director at the Hollings Marine Laboratory at the National Centers for Coastal Ocean Science in Charleston, South Carolina."

I glance quickly at Jonathan and feel his hand settle on the small of my back, calming my nerves. I take a steadying breath. "Hi, Dr. Jones. It's so nice to meet you," I manage to get out. The National Centers for Coastal Ocean Science is the arm of NOAA—the National Oceanic and Atmospheric Administration—that focuses on coastal stewardship.

"It's wonderful to meet you," she enthuses. "Harmful algal bloom monitoring and mitigation is a huge area of interest for us. I'm looking forward to your presentation on Friday."

"Thank you," I stammer. One of the heads of a major research organization stopped to talk to me? And wants to see our presentation? My brain starts reeling with what this could mean for my career and everything that's riding on a good presentation on Friday.

Jonathan presses his fingers into my back to remind me that he's here. "Oh, I'm sorry. Dr. Jones, this is Dr. Jonathan Stanch, my ... co-researcher."

Jonathan pulls his hand from my back to shake Dr. Jones's. I immediately mourn the loss of his touch, which was helping me feel more confident talking to Dr. Jones.

"Ah, the fieldwork director. Very important job," she says, smiling. "I'll let you two get back to your lunch, but I'll see you at your presentation."

"Thank you! Nice meeting you," I call as she walks away.

I turn to Jonathan, who's giving me major side-eye. "So, I'm back to being just your co-researcher, huh?" The corners of his lips quirk in a way that tells me he's trying not to smile.

I shove his shoulder. "No, of course not. But 'co-researcher' seems like a more appropriate title to use than 'boyfriend' in this setting."

"Sure. I see how it is." He sniffles showily, and when I try to take his hand, he pulls it away. "No, no. You can't just be holding hands with a co-researcher! What will the pearl-clutchers say?"

I put a hand on my hip. "Jonathan."

He echoes my posture. "Molly." When I roll my eyes, he laughs and pulls me against his chest. "Seriously, though. That was cool! I mean, the deputy director of the Hollings Lab introducing herself to you?"

"It's a big deal," I admit. "It feels like there's a lot at stake with this presentation."

He squeezes me in a hug. "It will be great. I know it."

Nicole:

Presentation day! Good luck!

Nicole:

Oh, I forgot about the time difference. Am I texting too early?

Molly:

You would think so, considering it's 6 a.m. here, but I've been up for an hour

Olivia:

Ugh, why are you both blowing up my phone so early? It's only 8

Nicole:

You'll do great, Molly!

Nicole:

Thanks for sending the picture of the program yesterday. It was so cool seeing your name!

Molly:

Yes!

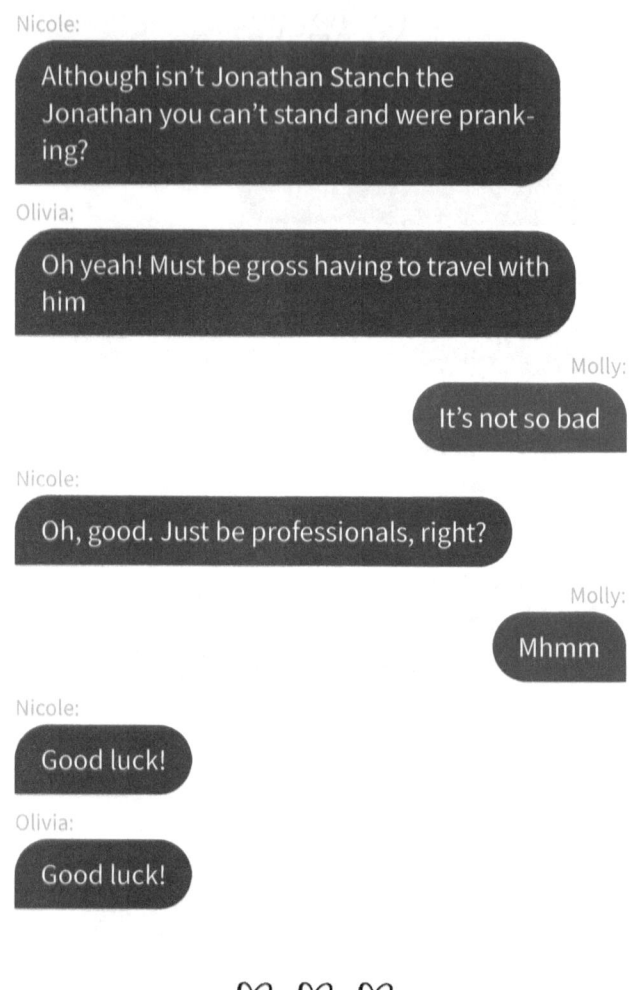

Nicole:

Although isn't Jonathan Stanch the Jonathan you can't stand and were pranking?

Olivia:

Oh yeah! Must be gross having to travel with him

Molly:

It's not so bad

Nicole:

Oh, good. Just be professionals, right?

Molly:

Mhmm

Nicole:

Good luck!

Olivia:

Good luck!

Friday morning, Jonathan and I meet Dr. Gantt for breakfast and to go over our presentation one last time. I'm all nerves, in stark contrast to Jonathan and his typical laid-back ease. I do feel ready, though. I know this research backward and forward and inside out.

I could talk about it for days, never mind forty-five minutes. Even still, our time slot is at eleven, so I'm concerned everyone will be over the presentations and ready to get to lunch.

We walk into the presentation room fifteen minutes early. Dr. Gantt meets the facilitator at the front of the room to check that the slide deck is queued up and the projector is working. Sure enough, the title slide from our deck soon looms over the room on two large screens at the front.

People start trickling in, and soon every seat is full. A few people stand at the back or sit against the walls on the side of the room. I see Almay Jones from the Hollings Lab seated in the second row. She's with a few other colleagues, all with notebooks or tablets out to take notes.

Earlier this year, I was in the audience for a presentation Nicole gave at a library conference in New Orleans. It was packed almost as much as this room. I get the feeling, though, that her audience was more supportive. We are absolutely collegial in science—don't get me wrong—but there's also a degree of competition.

One of the whole points of preprint servers is to establish early ownership of an idea so no one else can swoop in and claim it.

I'm not half as talented a public speaker as Nicole, but I'm not nearly as bad as her boyfriend and co-presenter, Adam. Plus, Jonathan's triple helping of charm can't be for nothing. We'll be okay. Right?

The presentation begins with Dr. Gantt, and then we pass back and forth between the three of us until we share our final takeaways.

The facilitator opens the floor for questions, and I breathe a sigh of relief. The presentation went smoothly. I feel good about it.

The satisfaction turns sour in my stomach though when the questions start coming. Some are supportive and similar to the questions raised in the comments for the preprint article. Two members of the audience, in particular, don't hide their derision as they try to pick apart the project.

A tall man with thinning white hair directs his questions solely to Jonathan, the only man sitting on a panel that also includes the PI and the originator of the research. To his credit, Jonathan sits with his hands in his pockets and a pleasant smile on his face while Dr. Gantt and I respond.

"Your results don't seem to be generalizable. You tracked one hurricane in one location. What makes you think that represents the effects of all hurricanes in all locations?"

"We aren't claiming to represent all hurricanes in all locations," Dr. Gantt clarifies. "We're reporting on our early findings from this particular hurricane event. We'll continue to track conditions to see if we can link the tropical system with any harmful algal bloom outbreaks in our area."

"I can't see what impact this has, then," another man on the other side of the room grumbles.

"It's a starting point," I say firmly. "A starting point for collaboration efforts across organizations to better protect against harmful algal blooms."

Several people in the audience clap at my words, including a certain tall, handsome, curly-haired scientist to my right. He's a little biased, though.

The room settles down after that. We field a few more questions, including one about the safety of the fieldwork aspect of launching the gliders ahead of the storm. Jonathan gives a good answer, highlighting modifications he would recommend for similar future voyages.

I wonder if he's thinking about that hot kiss in the rain. Definitely not something I would want to change about that trip. If Jonathan's thinking anything similar, he's better at hiding it. He's cool and calm as he talks, while I can feel myself blushing at the direction my thoughts are taking.

Finally, the facilitator announces that we're out of time, and the room starts to clear. A few of the audience members make their way to the front to ask additional questions or compliment our research. Fortunately, the two men who were looking for holes to poke exit quickly.

Dr. Almay Jones is one of the people who approaches us. Well, me, really. She shakes my hand. "Wonderful presentation, Dr. Delaney. Do you have lunch plans today? I'd love to sit with you and discuss your research further."

"Uh..." I glance at Dr. Gantt, who's deep in conversation with someone from the audience. Then I look at Jonathan. Someone is talking to him, too, asking about the type of boats we have, but I can tell Jonathan is focused on me, not on the colleague in front of him. He gives me an almost imperceptible nod, pairing it with a grin that tips up just the side of his mouth that's closest to me. "That sounds great," I finally respond.

After a three-hour lunch and conversation with Dr. Jones, I retreat to the quiet of my hotel room. I text Jonathan so he doesn't worry about where I am.

Jonathan:

Do you want me to come up?

Molly:

Not right now. I just need to decompress. Come by at 4?

He answers with a thumbs-up as I shed my shoes and collapse on top of the bed. My head's spinning. Almay gave me a lot to think about and a lot I need to talk to Jonathan about.

I'm excited about the potential big changes for me and my career, less so about what it could mean for my relationship with Jonathan. Of course, we figured things would change for our careers with this project. It thrust us into the spotlight, especially me as the originator of the idea and the first author on the paper.

I just didn't think things would change this much this quickly.

There's a knock on my hotel room door. I sit up, glancing at the clock on the nightstand. Has it been an hour already? I get to my feet and peek out the peephole once I reach the door. It's Jonathan, of course.

I take a deep breath and open the door to Jonathan's grinning face. He sweeps into the room, pulling me into his arms as he moves.

"You were so great at the presentation! You are amazing. Man, it's like four hours later, and I'm still amped up." He kisses my forehead and spins me around. "Dr. Gantt had to leave right away for the airport. She said her niece has some sort of thing this weekend? Anyway, she's heading home, but she told me to tell you what an excellent job you did."

"Jonathan."

"What did the lady from the Hollings Lab want to talk to you about? I watched her during the presentation, and she looked super impressed." He laughs. "I wanted to take you out for lunch myself to celebrate, but a celebration dinner is even better. Anywhere you want."

"She offered me a job," I blurt.

Jonathan freezes and, leaving his hands on my shoulders, backs up enough to see my face. His is pure enthusiasm. "Carrots, that's awesome! Congratulations."

"Yeah." I bite my lip, unsure.

"What kind of job?"

"It's a PI position in their harmful algal bloom mitigation division. A new team that I'd be heading up, securing funding, everything."

He cocks his head, watching me with a neutral expression. "Is that a position you'd want?"

I nod slowly. "Yes. It's an opportunity to create my own research project and bring in a team to help me with it. I could frame the lab around what I'm interested in, rather than just working toward someone else's vision."

His face relaxes into a pleased smile. "Good. I think you'd be amazing at that." He pauses, studying me. "Why are you hesitating?"

"Uhh, because it's far away! I'd have to move to South Carolina. What about us?" I wring my hands in front of me until Jonathan steps forward and takes them between his hands.

He shrugs, maintaining eye contact. "I would come with you."

"And give up your work at NOSU? What about the job Dr. Perron offered you? Your own PI opportunity."

Jonathan sits on the edge of the bed and pulls me down next to him. "I'm not even sure I want to head up a lab, to be honest. I would miss fieldwork too much. And if I stay in Louisiana, I'd miss *you* too much. If you're moving to Charleston, I want to go with you."

He sounds so sure, so certain, very unlike the uncertainty banging around in my head.

"We've only been dating a couple of months. I can't ask you to move your whole life for me."

"You're not asking. I'm offering."

"I don't know..."

"What if we were married? Would you feel better about me moving with you, then?"

"What?" I'm sure I heard him wrong, but at the same time, my heart lifts, and I feel like it's floating inside my chest. What if I heard him right?

He repeats himself in a steady, quiet voice. "You could ask me to move with you if we were married. It's totally normal for married couples to move together for a job."

"We're not married."

"But we could be." He grins, and I'm not sure how to take his statement.

"How?"

He chuckles. "As Angela pointed out earlier this week, we're in the perfect city for it."

"You want to get married? But why?"

His face turns serious, and he cups his hands around my cheeks. "Because we're in love."

"Jonathan, are you kidding right now? Is this a joke to you?"

His eyes search mine earnestly. "No joke, Mol. I'm completely serious."

"Is this a proposal, then?"

He sighs and runs a hand through his hair. "This is a suggestion. I love you, Molly. I want to marry you. I'll do it tomorrow. Hell, I'll marry you tonight. But it's up to you."

"My family doesn't even know we're dating and now, what, we're going to show up at Thanksgiving and tell them we're *married*?"

"If that's what you want."

What do I want? My immediate, strong impulse is to say yes. *Shout* yes. But I'm warring with ten years of instinct that tells me to tamp down the impulse and reject it. I'm trying not to do that anymore.

I think back to the morning after Jonathan and I first kissed, when I told him about suppressing my impulsiveness. "Even if it's something you want?" he had asked. It seemed so important then, critical even, to *not* give in, even though it broke my heart.

I had ten years of not giving in, of fighting against who I am, and suppressing myself. In the barely two months I've now spent embracing what brings me joy, I can't remember anymore why I punished myself for so long. Or why I would deny myself the unabashed and sometimes overwhelming love of the man sitting next to me.

But marriage is a big step. My thoughts are whirling, and I can't summon the calm I need to quiet my mind enough to think this through.

Jonathan tips my chin up and kisses me softly on the lips. He leans his forehead against mine. My thoughts still, and I know exactly what I want.

Chapter Thirty

Jonathan

"I'm sorry, WHAT?" Molly's youngest sister, Olivia, shouts from the other side of the couch as we sit in the Delaney home in Austin, Texas, after Molly introduces me to her family. We arrived at the house a few minutes ago so we can celebrate Thanksgiving with them tomorrow. Molly did not tell them I was coming, just that she was bringing a "friend."

Nicole, the middle sister, holds a hand up toward Olivia. "Okay, just hold on a minute," she placates. Nicole's boyfriend, Adam, places his hand on her thigh in support. Nicole turns her attention to Molly. "Mol, forgive me, but I thought you didn't even like Jonathan?" She grimaces at me in apology.

I can't help but grin. "She *thought* she didn't like me," I say. Molly elbows me in the ribs.

"So now, what?" Olivia demands. "You're dating this guy?"

Mr. and Mrs. Delaney are quiet, watching the scene unfold. Molly's dad looks curious, but Molly's mom looks smug.

"Actually..." Molly begins. I wrap my arm around her, and she leans her head back onto my shoulder. "Actually, we're not dating. We're married."

"WHAT?!" Olivia jumps up from the couch. Molly's dad stands too, his mouth agape. Nicole and Adam share a look that I can't read. Even Mrs. Delaney looks stunned.

Molly takes a deep breath. "And," she says. "I'm moving—we're moving. To South Carolina."

Everyone starts talking at once with a million questions. When did we start dating? Why didn't Molly tell them? What's in South Carolina? Why did we get married?

Nicole raises her voice over the din. "Wait. Everyone! Hold on." The room quiets. I guess librarians really are good at shushing people. "Molly, start from the beginning."

Molly regales them with the quick version of how our relationship transformed over the last couple of months, skimming over the more private or dangerous parts. I add my two cents when I feel the story might be lacking in color.

"Wait." Olivia raises her eyebrows. "Is this who you were making out with on the sidewalk when I was there for the parade?"

Molly's face turns bright red. I try to suppress my grin as I think back to that evening. Some of our finest work.

"You saw that?" Molly grimaces.

"I think everyone in New Orleans saw that," Olivia says dryly.

Molly's dad glares at me in a way that makes every "dad with a shotgun" cliché I've ever heard feel very accurate. My urge to smile disappears. Adam shoots me a sympathetic look but snaps his eyes forward again before Mr. Delaney can see. *I get it, man. Save yourself. No reason to get dragged down with me.*

Molly continues her story, ending with a description of our presentation, her job offer, and finally our sweet, elegant wedding ceremony.

As she does, my mind wanders back to Friday evening, also known as the best day of my life.

After Molly said "yes" that afternoon, the rest of the day moved quickly. We shopped for rings and a wedding dress. We changed our airline tickets so we could enjoy a short honeymoon in Las Vegas and then fly directly to Texas for Thanksgiving on Wednesday instead of going home to New Orleans first. We booked a room—just one!—at a hotel a little farther down the Strip for our extra four nights. Molly called the cat hotel back in New Orleans to extend Beaker's stay with them.

From the way movies and TV shows make it look, you'd think you can just walk into any of the numerous wedding chapels in Las Vegas, and they take care of everything. Not so.

We first had to go to the Clark County Marriage License Bureau—which is open until midnight seven days a week, by the way—fill out an application, show our IDs, and pay the fee.

Quite a few steps, requiring quite a bit of mental energy. How Ross and Rachel did all that while drunk out of their minds is something I really don't understand. I asked the clerk at the marriage license bureau about the whole pop culture, drunk Vegas wedding thing, and they said it's played up for dramatic effect. They won't even issue a marriage license if either person appears visibly intoxicated.

It's the long hours the marriage license bureau is open and the fact that there's no required waiting period between getting the license and the actual ceremony that makes Las Vegas a destination for elopements.

We weren't in any rush, though, so after getting the license, we went to dinner. After dinner, it was back to the hotel to figure out which wedding chapel to use. Molly's requirements were "not tacky and not expensive." My only requirement was Molly as the bride. We ended up asking the hotel concierge for a recommendation. He suggested a newer place up the Strip differentiating itself as elegant and reasonably priced, and open to walk-ins.

I must have asked Molly if she was sure at least twenty times that evening. Standing in front of the marriage license bureau: "Are you sure this is what you want?" At dinner as we made plans for the wedding: "Are you sure?" Getting in the rideshare to drive to the chapel: "It's not too late to change your mind."

Finally, she smoothed the back of her hand over my cheek. "Are you the one who wants to change your mind?" she asked, her eyes tender, maybe a little apprehensive.

She had to know how much I love her. "I'm 100 percent in, Molly. Forever and always. I just don't want you to regret this tomorrow."

She smiled and took my hand, blinking back tears. "In thirty years when we come back to Las Vegas to celebrate our anniversary, I *still* won't regret marrying you."

I grinned as the car pulled up outside the chapel. "In that case, let's go check another thing off the bucket list."

High-pitched coos shake me from my memories. Molly is showing her family pictures on her phone, and apparently her mom and sisters love her dress.

Mr. Delaney watches quietly as his wife and daughters squeal at the photos. Finally, his soft voice breaks through the chaos. "My first daughter to get married," he says, his eyes drooping as he focuses on Molly's face. "I wish I could have been there."

Molly instantly moves to sit next to him. "Daddy," she fusses, throwing her arms around his neck. "I'm so sorry you feel left out. Our decision to elope was just something we needed to do. Besides, you know I would have hated any kind of big wedding where I'd have to be the center of attention."

Mr. Delaney—who has *not* yet invited me to call him by his first name—sniffs as he returns his daughter's embrace. "I know. I'm sorry. I don't mean to make this about me." He pulls away and smiles at Molly. "It's just one of those things girl dads look forward to."

"Oh, Ben!" Mrs. Delaney hugs his other side and presses a kiss against his cheek. "Don't worry. We still have two more."

Molly and her dad laugh as Nicole's eyes go wide—she's doing her very best not to look at her boyfriend—and Olivia nearly chokes.

I decide to curry favor with my new sisters-in-law, while potentially further damaging my chances with my new father-in-law, by taking the pressure off them. I join the group hug, flinging my arms around Molly and her parents.

Molly's mom laughs, her cheeks turning red as she swats me away. Mr. Delaney glares at me, the arrangement of his face so familiar that I grin. I can see that Molly came by her angry stares honestly.

"Welcome to the family, Jonathan," Molly's mom says, patting my cheek.

"Thank you, Mrs. Delaney." I turn on my most charming smile. In my peripheral vision, I see Molly roll her eyes.

"It's Amy," she corrects. She turns to her husband.

"I'm still deciding," he grumbles.

"I totally understand, sir." I can win him over. I've got time. From all Molly's told me about her dad, he's a teddy bear who only wants his daughters to be happy. It won't take him long to see that she's happier than ever, though that's mostly her own doing, not mine. I probably deserve a little credit, though.

The relationship between a father and a daughter is special. I see it firsthand with my dad and Tamara all the time. But father-son relationships are also important, and I know Molly and I need to tell my family about our marriage soon, too.

Molly and I step into the gorgeous, tree-covered backyard that extends into a forest beyond and settle onto the patio love seat to call my family. Even though the holiday isn't until tomorrow, I know Tamara will be at my dad's house tonight helping with the prep.

At Molly's insistence, we do a video call. Tamara picks up and smiles. "Hi! Jonny, I'm so glad you called because if I have to devil another egg, I will go insane. Hey, Molly!"

Molly waves as I clear my throat. "Tams, are you with Dad?"

"Yeah, I'm at his house. Why?" She leans her face closer to the screen. "Where are you guys?"

"With Molly's family in Texas. Can you go get Dad? I want to talk to both of you."

Tamara's image on the screen bounces as she walks through the house to find Dad. When she does, his face appears on screen alongside hers, then the image flips to landscape view and Sharon is there, too.

I open my mouth to go full bratty kid and insist on talking to my dad and sister alone. As if she's reading my mind—or maybe has just gotten good at reading my expressions and energy—Molly puts her hand on my knee and squeezes. With just that one touch, she communicates support, love, and acceptance, making me rethink my reaction. At least 30 percent of it might also be that I'm hesitant to be at my worst in front of my new wife. Maybe save that for when we've been married for at least a week.

I take a breath and turn on my smile. "Thanks, Tams. Hi Dad, Sharon." I try to keep my expression as neutral as possible. "This is Molly. Molly, this is my dad, Pete, and his fiancée, Sharon."

Okay, that was good. I'm proud of myself so far. I can tell Tamara approves, too, because she nods at me through the screen. I can be an adult about this—a mature, married adult.

My dad grins, waving a hand clumsily at Molly. "It's good to meet you, Molly, after everything I've heard about you." Mostly from Tamara, I'm sure.

"Nice to finally meet you, Mr. Stanch," Molly says, clutching my arm a little tighter. "And you, too," she adds, looking at Sharon.

"Please, call us Pete and Sharon," Sharon says with her pinched smile.

I clear my throat. "So, anyway, Molly and I wanted to tell you that ... we eloped last week. We're married."

"I knew it!" Tamara shouts.

She must drop the phone because our view shifts to flashing colors and then black, as if the phone is face down on the floor. It means I can't see how my dad reacts. Or Sharon. Although I'd like to see them try to disapprove of my marriage while still trying to get me on board for theirs.

I realize I'm holding my breath waiting to see what my dad will say. Finally, Tamara retrieves the phone and holds it back up. My family comes back into view.

My Dad is smiling. "Congratulations to the both of you." Sharon nods her agreement next to him.

"Thank you. Wait, Tamara, what do you mean you knew it?" I narrow my eyes at my sister.

"Please. You've been obsessed since, I don't know, at least September. You told me you were going to Vegas for a *conference*," she makes air quotes with her fingers here, "and I figured you'd come back married."

I can feel Molly's body shaking next to mine. I glance at her to find her almost doubled over with laughter.

I turn my attention back to the phone screen so I can fact check my sister's little speech. "First of all, we *were* at a conference, presenting very important research because we are very important scientists—"

"Aw. Of course you are, sweetie. Now, I believe Molly is a very important scientist. She just has that, like, glow of intelligence around her. But you, Jonny?" Her eyebrows are raised, the slight furrow communicating her incredulity. Her mouth is a thin line quirked to one side, showing a hint of amusement. "Don't forget I know all about how you cheated in order to beat me in Scrabble growing up."

"That was *one* time!" I sputter. "Are you serious right now?"

Molly pats my knee. "Of course she's not serious, *Jonny*." She winks. "She's just doing her big sisterly duty and giving you a hard time."

"See, Molly gets it. Told you she was smart." Tamara smirks at me through the phone.

I risk a glance at my dad. He's chuckling, his eyes soft and bright. "In all seriousness," he cuts in, leaning into the phone camera so his forehead takes up half the screen, "We are so incredibly proud of both of you. Molly, we're so happy to have you join our family. I want to meet you, in person, soon."

"Maybe for Christmas?" Sharon asks hopefully.

I pretend I don't hear her. "Thanks all. Molly's dad is calling us inside now, so we have to go. Love you all! Bye!" I press the button to end the call and stare at the blank screen.

When I finally look up, Molly's watching me, a thoughtful expression on her face.

"What?" I ask.

She reaches up her hand and smooths my hair, moving a curl off my forehead. "Your smile," she finally says, "it's the same as your dad's."

She drops her hand to my knee, squeezing it before she stands up. She leans in, quickly kissing my lips, then disappears inside the house, leaving me alone with my thoughts.

Chapter Thirty-One

Molly

As the shock from our news wears off, my parents and sisters seem to calm down. We have a relatively normal dinner before watching a Hallmark Christmas movie and going our separate ways for bed. Nicole bunks with Olivia, while my parents assign Adam to Nicole's childhood bedroom.

My dad seems to be back in good spirits after his disappointment earlier about missing my wedding. I would have loved to have my family there, but I also love how simple and intimate our ceremony was. It was all about me and Jonathan—no stress and no one to impress. I would choose an elopement in Vegas all over again.

"Well, we did have the couch reserved for you, sir," my dad tells Jonathan. "But given the, uh, circumstances, I'm guessing you'll be more comfortable with Molly." He looks distinctly uncomfortable

with this situation but pretends to be laid back about the whole
thing.

Jonathan and I get ready for bed in the attached bathroom, falling
into the already-familiar patterns we've established in just a few days
of marriage.

I climb into the double bed next to my husband, and he playfully
rolls toward me.

"We're not going to *do anything* in my childhood bedroom at my
parents' house with my sisters in the next room," I hiss.

"But we're newlyweds," he pouts, as if we haven't spent the last
four days holed up in our Las Vegas hotel room together.

I heave an exasperated sigh. "It's been a long day. Let's just get
some sleep."

"Carrots, if you really don't want to 'do anything,' you shouldn't
get mad. That makes it so much harder for me to resist you."

I can't help but laugh. I kiss him softly on the lips. "Good night,"
I tell him pointedly.

"Good night." For all his talk, he's asleep in minutes. My brain
isn't as easy to turn off.

I creep into the kitchen once everyone's asleep, and the lights are
all off. I'm startled to see Olivia sitting at the kitchen table, the shine
from her phone screen lighting up her face as she scrolls. She has a
spoon sticking out of her mouth and an open container of chocolate
pudding in front of her.

"Hey," I say quietly.

Her head snaps up. A flash of guilt crosses her face when she sees
it's me. "Hey," she says.

We're quiet as I rummage through the pantry and pull out a Pop-Tart. When I sit down across from her to eat, Olivia looks at me with a grimace.

"I'm sorry I overreacted," she blurts. "Earlier."

I smile at her gently. "I wasn't going to bring it up, but since *you* did ... are you okay?"

She sighs. "Yes. No. I don't know. I've been feeling lost since I graduated. Probably before that, if I'm being honest."

I take another bite of Pop-Tart and wait.

"It's just another way you and Nicole have your lives together where I don't," she continues, waving the spoon to punctuate her words. "Nicole isn't engaged yet, but let's be real, she'll be walking down the aisle sooner rather than later. You turn up married without telling anyone. You both have these successful careers. And what am I doing? Living with Mom and Dad. Earning pennies as a youth soccer coach. It's not hard to feel left out, left behind."

I put my hand over my sister's. "First of all," I start. "You're a lot younger than either of us—"

"Yeah, but you both have always known what you want to do." She shrugs. "I have no idea."

"I really think that Nicole and I are in the minority on that. Most people are like you, still figuring it out after college." I break off a piece of my pastry and pop it in my mouth.

"Fine, but you walking in with Jonathan, making your big announcement, it just hit me hard that both you and Nicole are all in love while I'm sitting here playing third wheel to our parents." She makes a face, and I laugh.

"Annie's not getting married," I remind her.

"Annie has a boyfriend," she says, raising her eyebrows.

"Ah. Well, again, you're a lot younger than us. You're twenty-two. You still have so much time to find the love of your life before we have to start calling you an old maid," I tease.

Her nose wrinkles, and she shakes her head. She mumbles something that sounds like, "Or maybe I've already missed my chance."

"What was that?" I ask.

She shakes her head again. "Nothing. Anyway, I'm really sorry. And despite how I reacted earlier, I'm really happy for you, sis." Standing, she bends down to give me an awkward hug.

I squeeze her hard. "Love you, kid," I say through brimming eyes.

"Love you."

My family is apparently still getting used to the idea of Jonathan as they take turns staring at him the next morning at breakfast. We're all sitting around the table with a spread of breakfast casserole, cinnamon rolls, and fresh fruit in front of us.

"So, Molly," Nicole starts, "with all the excitement yesterday, I didn't get to ask you about your presentation. How'd it go, Dr. Delaney?" She pauses, an uncertain expression on her face. "Or now is it Dr. ..." Nicole trails off as she stares at me and then darts her eyes over to Jonathan. "I just realized, I don't know ..." Her cheeks turn pink, and she leans toward Adam sitting next to her, as if for support. "Jonathan, what's your last name?"

Jonathan has a mouthful of cinnamon roll, so I answer for him. "It's Stanch. But I'm not changing my name. I'm still Molly Delaney."

Nicole nods, while my mom gapes at me. "You're not taking your husband's last name?" she asks.

Jonathan wisely takes another large bite of his breakfast. Under the table, he lays his hand on my thigh and squeezes.

I shake my head. "It doesn't make sense to change my name. I already have so many publications under Delaney. It's easier to just keep the same name."

Plus, just thinking about all the bureaucratic processes and paperwork changing my name would entail makes my head hurt.

My mom pinches her lips together but makes no further comment.

"To answer your question, Nicole," Jonathan cuts in, his mouth finally empty, "the presentation was fantastic. Molly knocked it out of the park, hence the Charleston job offer."

I blush. "I wasn't the only one presenting. Jonathan and our boss were great, too."

"Tell us more about the Charleston job," my dad says.

Nicole claps. "You'll be so much closer to me now! Charleston's only about four hours from St. Anastasia. Adam and I will have to drive up to help you get unpacked."

"It's an exciting position—an opportunity for me to lead my own lab studying harmful algal blooms in a cooperative way with other labs around the country. They want me to start the second week of January. I've heard Charleston is a beautiful city."

"No beignets though," Jonathan teases.

I wave my hand. "I'm sure Charleston has other delicious baked goods."

"Biscuits," Olivia offers. "Charleston is known for biscuits, both sweet and savory. The team always looked forward to it when we traveled to Charleston for games."

"What about you, Jonathan?" my mom asks. "What are you going to do about a job after this move?" The question could be based in curiosity, but it sounds more like disapproval.

Jonathan glances at me, and I see a rare glint of uncertainty in his eyes. I jump in to answer. "Actually, as part of my contract, I'm going to negotiate a job for Jonathan, too."

My dad looks surprised. "You can do that?"

"Yep. It's called spousal accommodation and is more common than you'd think." I hold my chin high. "We think I'm enough of a commodity that the Hollings Lab will be pretty open to giving me what I want."

"*You* think; *I* know. They want you bad." Jonathan grins. "You might even be able to get them to pack up your stuff and move it for you."

I gasp. "Someone else can pack for me?" I'm so dreading the packing and unpacking part of moving. "But anyway, spousal accommodation is *one* reason, but certainly not the most important reason, we decided to get married."

Neither of my parents look pleased with that explanation. Jonathan must notice, too. "I know it might sound like I'm just out here riding Molly's coattails, but you need to know that I love your daughter, and there's nothing I wouldn't do to make sure we're together. I don't care where I am as long as I'm with her."

"Jonathan is actually turning down a job in New Orleans—PI at a new lab at NOSU—to move with me. He has options."

Jonathan bumps his shoulder against mine and holds my gaze. "Any option that isn't with you isn't really an option for me at all."

Nicole and Olivia simultaneously let out a reflexive "awww." Even Adam looks impressed.

We finish breakfast, and I help clear the table, taking dirty plates into the kitchen to wash. I'm bellied up to the sink with my arms half-submerged in hot, soapy water when my mom finds me.

She leans back against the kitchen counter and folds her arms. "I have some concerns about your new plans."

My mom and dad are still acclimating to our news, but they'll come around. Last night, I thought my mom was actually excited, but after she talked with my dad and heard about our less-than-traditional plans, she must have realized some fresh doubts.

Without taking my focus off washing the dishes, I say, "I'm sure you do. I'd be surprised if you didn't. But I'm happy with my decisions, and they were my decisions to make."

"But that's just the thing, honey. It's not like you to make such a big decision so suddenly."

I turn to look her full in the face now. "Actually, impulsive decisions are exactly like me, only I've been subduing that part of me, a lot of parts of me actually, for a long time now."

She frowns. "What do you mean?"

Pulling my hands from the sink and drying them off, I share with her, for the first time, what I went through that first semester I spent away from home. She knows about my grades, of course, but always chalked it up to the adjustment to college-level academics. I never corrected her.

"Ever since then, I've been trying to be as *not* ADHD as possible. But I've come to realize that while, yes, ADHD makes my life harder in a lot of ways, it's also a huge part of my strengths. It makes me who I am."

Mom rests her hand on her chest over her heart. "I had no idea you felt that way. I hate that you felt that way all those years. What made you realize that you're perfect just the way you are?"

I smile, my eyes almost overflowing. "My husband. There's nothing about me Jonathan doesn't love. Makes it kind of hard for me not to love myself, too."

Her eyes gleam with tears. "I can understand why you married him, in that case." She hesitates. "Honey, when you were growing up, I know I wasn't always the best mother for you. You were my first baby, and you were so challenging. We had to learn how to parent you, usually through trial and error. I know I made mistakes. I'm so sorry if I contributed to you feeling like you needed to change who you are."

I shake my head. "You didn't. I always felt loved and supported. I still do. How could you know what was going on inside me when *I* didn't even know most of the time?"

My mom leans closer, a smile touching her lips. "Can I admit something?"

"Of course."

"There were so many times, even after your sisters were born, when you would say something insightfully wise beyond your years or something so witty I'd laugh out loud, that I would stop and think 'this little person is my favorite person on the planet.' I love you so much, Molly. And I trust you."

I wrap my arms around her in a hug, blinking to keep the tears from falling. I sniffle, then laugh. "Don't worry. I won't tell Nicole or Olivia."

"Or Dad," she cautions.

"Or Dad," I agree.

Chapter Thirty-Two

Jonathan

I know I've made it with the Delaneys by the way Molly's father sees me off at the airport the Saturday after Thanksgiving. He pulls the car into the departures area at the Austin airport, shifts into park, and opens his door to pull our luggage from the trunk. After setting the suitcases on the sidewalk, he wraps Molly in a bear hug.

Then, he turns to me. He shakes my hand. "Take care of her, Jonathan."

"I can try to help, Mr. Delaney," I tell him with a grin, "but she's pretty good at taking care of herself."

The smallest hint of a smile creeps across his lips. "Call me Ben." He shakes my hand one more time before getting back into the car to drive away.

I meet Molly up on the sidewalk. "Did you hear that?" I hiss in a stage whisper.

She takes my hand and intertwines our fingers. "I did."

"Does your dad like me now?" I ask hopefully.

She smiles. "Maybe. How could he not, though? It was only a matter of time."

We spend the rest of the weekend combining apartments as much as makes sense when we'll be moving in a month. Even though Molly's place is teeny tiny, we decide to stay there these last few weeks. It's close to work, and her lease is up sooner than mine. We can sublet my apartment for the six months remaining.

I'm sorting my belongings into piles based on what I'll need before the move to Charleston and what can get packed into moving boxes already when my phone rings.

I wipe my dusty hands on my jeans and pull the phone from my pocket. It's my mom. I called her on Thanksgiving to let her know about my life updates, but I got her voicemail. Of course, they don't celebrate Thanksgiving in India. I left her a message to call me back.

Even though I didn't hint in the message that what I had to say was life altering, I thought she would call me back sooner.

I swipe to accept the video call and move to the couch to sit down.

"Happy Thanksgiving, darling!" my mother greets me as her face appears on the screen.

"Happy Thanksgiving, Mom." I pause awkwardly. "Listen, I have some really great, but surprising news."

"Okay. What's your news?"

"I got married last weekend. In Vegas." I realize how that sounds and rush to add, "But it was on purpose, and no one was drunk!"

She's quiet, an unreadable expression on her face. "That's … reassuring, I guess?"

I chuckle. "What I meant to say is that we decided to get married while we happened to be in Vegas, so it was sudden but not hasty."

"Okay. Just trying to wrap my head around this. I didn't know you were dating anyone." Her eyebrows pull together, emphasizing the deepening wrinkles on her forehead. How long has it been since I've seen my mother in person? Years, at least.

How long since I last talked to her, even? Not since the summer, so no, she wouldn't know about Molly. "Yeah, for a few months now."

More awkward silence. "Well, congratulations. I'm happy for you. Tell me about your wife."

My wife. Still sounds so weird but amazing at the same time. Molly Delaney is my wife.

"Her name is Molly. We work together. We've known each other for a while—had classes together in graduate school. She's amazing. The whole reason we were actually in Las Vegas was to present her research at the CERA conference. Research so impressive, one of the attendees offered her a job right after the presentation. That's my other news. Molly and I are moving to Charleston in January."

"A researcher, hmm? Sounds like she and I will get along. And Charleston is lovely. Maybe I can get away sometime next year to visit so I can meet her."

"That would be great. And yeah, I think you'll love her. Her research and career are really important to her, and they're important to *me*, too, so we can avoid the kind of problems you and Dad had."

More silence. I've never seen my mother so at a loss for words. "What do you mean? What kind of problems were there between your father and me?"

"You know," I say. "He didn't support your career. When you got the job opportunity at WHO, he didn't think it was important enough to move for."

"Is... is that what he told you?" She blinks several times in a row.

"No, he didn't have to tell me. I saw what happened. You got the job, and we stayed in Ohio without you." The familiar bitterness creeps into my voice.

She rubs a hand against her neck. "Darling, that's not what happened."

"Of course it is." I was there. I know what happened.

She grimaces. "No. I ... I asked your dad for a divorce at the same time I told him about the job. He was never ... included ... in my plans to move to Switzerland."

Meaning Tamara and I were never included in those plans either? Meaning *she* left *him*, and not the other way around like I've believed for almost twenty years? "What? That can't be true."

"Your dad was happy with his life in Ohio. I didn't want to disrupt that. Besides, our marriage hadn't been what it should have for years at that point. I thought you knew."

I shake my head slowly back and forth. "No."

"Jonathan, I love you and your sister more than anyone. I loved your dad once, too. But, all the moving around I've done, from country to country, that would have been a hard life for you kids. You had stability with your dad in Ohio that I couldn't give you."

I'm drowning in cognitive dissonance. Wrapping my brain around this kind of paradigm shift, finding out that what I *knew* to be true isn't true at all, leaves me feeling lost. I'm a sixteenth-century astronomer listening to Copernicus suggesting the sun is the center of the solar system. I'm a geologist in the early twentieth century learning about Wegener's theory of continental drift, introduced to the possibility that maybe the continents are *not*, in fact, fixed in their positions.

But I have to know. I push deeper, wanting more answers. "Would Dad have gone with you, moved all of us to Switzerland, if you had asked him to?"

"You'll have to ask him that question, but I believe he would have. It's why I couldn't ask him to. It wouldn't have been fair to him, not when I wasn't as invested in the marriage as he was. I felt that I could do more in my career without ... well, without that weight in my life."

She might as well have slapped me for the way that statement shocks and hurts. "And Tamara and me? Did we weigh you down, too?"

"You and Tamara were better off living a stable life with your dad in Ohio," she repeats firmly.

I force a smile, as if my mother hasn't just turned my world upside down. "Listen, Mom, I've got to go. Nice talking to you."

"You, too! Congratulations on your marriage and your move."

"Thanks," I mumble before ending the call.

I'm not sure how long I sit here, my head resting on the back of the couch, my eyes staring vacantly at the ceiling. I feel almost disconnected from my body, detached and aloof. I'm not sure that this time spent spinning the new information around in my mind, turning it this way and that, is helpful in solving anything, least of all the intense guilt and shame I feel for the way I've treated my dad all these years.

"Jonathan?" Molly calls, coming through the front door of my apartment. She spots me on the couch and holds up a stack of flattened moving boxes and packing tape. "I brought more supplies."

When I don't answer, she drops the boxes and tape and moves closer. "What's wrong?"

Instead of responding, I reach up a hand and pull her into my lap. She yelps as her feet come off the floor. Her head nestles against my chest, and I hold her against me. Instantly, I'm in my body again, feeling the pit in my stomach and the tension in my shoulders.

The anger I've been holding onto for almost twenty years is gone, replaced with shame. I think of my dad, left to finish raising two kids on his own—one of those kids a preteen boy mad at the world and taking it out on him. And all the while, trying to cope with his own heartbreak and grief over losing the woman he loved. For years, not having the relationship he wanted with his only son. Finally finding someone new to love and watching his grown son pout like a child over his well-deserved happiness.

Molly strokes my cheek. "What's going on, Jonathan?" she asks softly.

"I think I ... we need to go to Ohio for Christmas."

Molly doesn't bat an eye at my announcement of the new plan for our first Christmas together. She slides off my lap onto the couch cushion and motions for me to join her. I lie on my back next to her, my head in her lap.

As I tell her about my conversation on the phone with my mom, Molly combs through my hair with her fingers. It's soothing, but I'm not sure I deserve to be soothed.

"So, in summary, I've been a jerk to my dad for nearly twenty years because of an initial misunderstanding I never bothered to clarify."

Molly is quiet for a moment. "I think you're being too hard on yourself. You were just a kid."

"At first I was, but I haven't been a kid for quite some time now, and I've still been acting like a brat."

"It probably feels emotionally safer to lash out at the parent who stays than the one who doesn't."

I close my eyes and lean into the feeling of her hand in my hair. "How did I get lucky enough to have such a smart wife? You're the best." I still feel raw from my mother's revelation and my own realization that I've been a terrible son to my dad while he's been hurting in his own way. But at this moment, I feel safe and loved, like no matter how badly I've messed up, I can make it right.

She laughs. "Me? You've been doing sweet, thoughtful things for me for months now."

I open my eyes and smirk. "I've been trying to impress you."

Molly leans down and kisses my lips. "You've succeeded."

"I've also been trying to get you to see yourself like I see you: practically perfect in every way."

She laughs again, but then her face turns serious. "I'm getting there on that, too, but I feel like it's going to be a long process. I have to undo years of thinking. I hope you can be patient with me."

I sit up and pull her against my chest, kissing the top of her head. "Of course. As long as it's me you come home to at the end of the day, I can handle just about anything, wife." I pause. "You do believe I love you, though, right?"

She blushes. "Yes. You've done a pretty good job convincing me of that, even if I don't quite understand why yet."

I kiss her forehead, then each cheek, and then the tip of her nose. "Then I'll just have to keep showing you. Fortunately, it'll be a lot easier now to leave sticky notes on your refrigerator."

She smiles. "No more breaking and entering?"

I shrug. "I had a key so there really wasn't any breaking, just entering." I hesitate. "You don't think you'll ever feel like I'm weighing you down, do you? Like my mom felt about my dad?"

"Jonathan," she says gently. She puts a hand on either side of my face. "You don't weigh me down. You ground me when I need it so that when it's time to fly, we can soar together."

Chapter Thirty-Three

Molly

The next few weeks are a whirlwind of decluttering and organizing as Jonathan and I try to combine two households while simultaneously getting ready to move to another state, now with a week-long trip to Ohio in the mix. I'm proud of how Jonathan is handling the issues with his dad, though. Even before his mom's revelations, I felt like he needed to make the trip. I didn't say anything because I didn't want to interfere.

The week after Thanksgiving, I call Almay Jones and formally accept the principal investigator position at the Hollings Lab. I negotiate my contract to include moving expenses—with enough to cover packing both apartments and unpacking in our new apartment in Charleston—and a position for Jonathan on the ecological assessment team in a different lab within the National Centers for Coastal Ocean Science.

It's easier than I thought it would be. As soon as I send over his CV, Dr. Jones provides three options for open positions. The ecological assessment team conducts a lot of fieldwork, so it's a perfect fit. They even have someone who can help us find housing, since we won't be able to get to Charleston to scope out apartments before the move.

One of the most difficult tasks on our list is talking to Dr. Gantt and putting in our notice. We've kept quiet about the job offer, and our marriage, until all the details were worked out. The day after I sign the contract, which is the second week of December and about two weeks after Thanksgiving, we ask to meet with her in her office.

"What's going on, you two?" Dr. Gantt asks as we sit in the chairs across from her desk. We've all still been working with the glider data from Hernando, and Dr. Gantt is working on a grant application for additional funding to continue data collection during future tropical systems that come near New Orleans.

Jonathan and I glance at each other. "There's no easy way to say this," Jonathan begins. "We wanted to let you know about our plans to leave this lab, and NOSU altogether."

Dr. Gantt's eyes widen. "What's going on?"

"First, I want to say how grateful I am for the experience you've given me here," I say. "Watching my research ideas become reality has been amazing, and the opportunities you've given me here directly correlate with me even having an option of leaving." I take a breath. "After the CERA presentation, I was offered a PI position heading up harmful algal bloom mitigation research at the Hollings Marine

Laboratory in Charleston, South Carolina. I've decided to accept it."

Dr. Gantt clasps her hands together against her chest. "Molly! That's an amazing opportunity. Of course you have to accept. Oh, I'm thrilled for you!" Her forehead furrows. "Wait, though. You're both resigning?"

In a synchronized motion that must look like we practiced it, though we didn't, we both raise our ring-adorned left hands. Jonathan shrugs. "We got married while we were in Vegas. So, she's stuck with me. I go where she goes."

Dr. Gantt's eyebrows nearly hit her hairline. "You what?" She looks at me for confirmation, and I nod. "Well, that's wonderful news! Congratulations!"

"Thank you." Jonathan beams. "I also want to tell you how much I appreciate you, Dr. Gantt. When you recruited me to your team, I know you planned on me staying more than nine months, but life had other plans, I guess. This has been a dream job, even more so because it gave me an opportunity to finally get to know Molly. Turns out she's the woman of my dreams."

Dr. Gantt blinks rapidly, as if trying to hold back tears. "Thank you, Jonathan. What's next for you in Charleston?"

"I'll be working on the NCCOS ecological assessment team, so fortunately, my days of piloting boats are not over yet."

"Sounds like you'll both be in good situations. I won't try to pretend that losing you isn't a blow to this research team. I don't look forward to trying to replace you. I'll be hard-pressed to find two better scientists, especially who work so well together, despite the occasional prank war." She gives us a knowing look, and I drop my eyes guiltily to the floor.

I can hear the grin in Jonathan's voice as he asks, "How much did you know about?"

"Oh, I know about much more than you might think, Dr. Stanch." She smiles. "I'm thrilled you'll both have the opportunity to continue building your careers and your life together."

At this moment I know that my new career goal—well, one of them at least—is to aspire to be as kind and insightful a PI as Dr. Gantt someday.

Jonathan's family is ecstatic when we tell them we're coming to Ohio for Christmas and Pete and Sharon's wedding two days later. Jonathan's dad sounds suspiciously choked up when we talk to him on the phone. If he's getting emotional now, I can only imagine how he'll take it when Jonathan initiates their long-overdue heart-to-heart.

Tamara texts us every day with another dish she or one of the other relatives are planning to make for Christmas dinner. I guess she figures that if Jonathan's tempted to back out, having the food he'd be missing fresh in his mind might stem the tide.

The list of foods Jonathan assures me are Midwestern delicacies rolls in. HoneyBaked Ham. Green bean casserole. Homemade yeast rolls. Fruit salad. Buttery mashed potatoes with brown gravy. Not to mention Dutch crumble apple pie, homemade fudge, and an excessive assortment of cookies. Plus, something called a Kringle?

I'm looking forward to meeting everyone in person, especially Tamara. She reminds me of my sisters—or, what I imagine it might be like if I had an older sister instead of always *being* the older sister. And Jonathan's nieces. We don't have kids in my family, so I'm nervous about interacting with them. I haven't been around little kids since Olivia was a little kid.

"Oh my gosh." I don't realize I've mumbled this out loud until Jonathan looks up from the suitcase he's packing.

"What?"

"I'm an aunt now. Your nieces will call me Aunt Molly because I'm married to their uncle."

Jonathan grins. "Don't worry. The girls are the best. I just give them whatever they want and roughhouse with them, and they love me."

"What are their names again?" I'm not sure why I ask, because five minutes from now the names will have already leaked out of my brain like water through a sieve.

"Charlotte is the oldest, then Hannah, and then little Mia."

"How old are they?"

"I don't know. Charlotte and Hannah are, like, elementary school age, and Mia is not yet."

I roll my eyes. "That's not helpful at all." I gasp. "Oh my gosh, we need to buy them presents! We still need to get *everyone* presents!"

Jonathan smirks. "Do we, though? I kind of figured our presence was present enough."

I groan. "Absolutely not." I pick up a notepad from where I've left it on the bedside table. I'm trying out list-making to help me keep better track of all the tasks that need to get done. I have notepads all around the apartment, so there's always one close at hand when I need to write something down. "We only have two days before we leave. Let's see ... Tamara and her husband. The girls. Your dad and Sharon." I tap the pen against my chin. "Do we need to get them two gifts? One for Christmas and one for their wedding?"

I feel the panic and overwhelm brewing in my chest as my brain tries to keep hold of all the tasks looming over the next few weeks. Between traveling for Christmas, moving to a new state, changing jobs, and being recently married, I think I've hit most of the life-change events they tell you to watch out for on those stress tests. My old routine is so far gone at this point that it wouldn't be able to see me with binoculars.

Jonathan shrugs. "It's really not that big of a deal, Mol. Nobody's expecting anything, except probably the girls."

All of a sudden, Jonathan's laissez-faire attitude irks me in a way it hasn't for months. The annoyance flares into rapidly-igniting anger, and before I can even identify why I'm upset, I'm a raging wildfire.

"Is this my life now? Really? I have to take care of all the little details because you don't think it's a big deal and won't do anything to help?" I hear my voice shouting, but I don't feel like I'm in control of the words or volume.

While the thought *Stop, you don't want to do this*, surfaces in my brain, the words are quickly drowned out by sensations hitting me hard and fast from every direction. I can't reach the place of logic that produced the warning. Everything in my body feels all wrong all at the same time. My skin is too warm. The room is too small. The waistband on my leggings squeezes my stomach uncomfortably.

"I thought I was getting a partner, but I guess it's just more work for me to figure out alone!" I shut my eyes against Jonathan's stunned expression. Turning, I escape into the bathroom and lock the door behind me. I crumple onto the fluffy rug and release sob after sob in giant convulsions. Bit by bit, the softness of the rug and the cool fiberglass wall of the bathtub next to me lull me out of the meltdown.

I sit up and cover my face with my hands in embarrassment. A freaking ADHD meltdown. I haven't had one like that in years. On the one hand, the fact that I expressed what I was feeling instead of bottling it up is a big step. On the other hand, I know I absolutely need to find healthier ways to express those feelings. Love or not, he shouldn't have to put up with scenes like the one I just caused, especially when I know how stressed he is about this trip and talking to his dad.

A quiet tap sounds on the bathroom door. "Molly?" Jonathan calls in an equally soft voice. "I'm sorry."

I heave myself up from the bathroom floor with a sigh. I catch sight of myself in the mirror—my eyes are puffy and red, the skin on my face blotchy. I open the door, letting my hair cascade over my face to hide myself.

Jonathan's face is a study in concern. His eyes flit from my face to the rug imprints on my knees. "I'm sorry," he repeats. "Of course I should be the one to figure out gifts for my family."

I shake my head, causing my hair to swish back and forth over my cheeks. "No, *I'm* sorry."

Cautiously, he reaches out and puts his hand on my arm. "Are you okay?"

"Yeah. I just—" I suck in a wavering breath.

"Hey," Jonathan soothes. "Come here." He tugs me against his chest, wrapping his arms around me.

"I never wanted you to see me like that. You don't deserve emotional ambushes. But listen, it's rare, okay? For me to have a meltdown. It's been years. I guess with everything changing right now, I'm feeling overwhelmed. I'll keep working on healthier ways to express my emotions."

Jonathan pulls away from the embrace enough to comb the hair out of my face. "If it's a part of you, I want to see it. I want to know. Life *is* overwhelming right now. We made our choices, and they're all good changes for the most part, I think, but there's still a lot going on."

"I just don't ... don't want you to think you made a mistake, tying yourself to me. I tried to warn you; I'm a lot to deal with."

He holds my gaze, his fingers still in my hair. "Stop waiting for the other shoe to drop. I'm not going anywhere. I'm not perfect either, if you haven't noticed." His lips tip up in a tentative grin.

I sniffle. "I *haven't* noticed. You seem pretty perfect."

"I'm not." He smiles sadly. "Just ask my dad."

I squeeze him tighter. "Your dad loves you. He'll go easy on you."

He sighs. "Maybe, but he shouldn't."

I stretch onto my tiptoes, aiming my lips at his nose. At the last second, he lifts his head, smirking, and I land on his lips instead.

"Hey!" I laugh. He pulls me back to him, and everything else—the tension with his dad, the to-do lists, the upcoming move—fades away.

Chapter Thirty-Four

Jonathan

I'm dreading this trip, even as Molly and I walk down the Jetway at the airport in Cleveland. Molly's excited to meet my family, and of course I'm excited to see them, too, but despite all the delicious Christmas foods and desserts Tamara has been tempting me with for the last week, I know that number one on my menu is humble pie. Not my favorite dish.

Dad picks us up from the airport, and we greet each other awkwardly while I introduce him to Molly. I hope once he and I really talk we'll feel more at ease with each other, but now is not the time for that.

We drive forty-five minutes south to the suburb outside of Akron where I grew up. Molly marvels at the dusting of snow on the ground, barely enough to cover the brown grass. She's never lived up north, so it's a novelty for her. I have to admit that I haven't missed the snow at all in the more than ten years I've lived away from it.

I reminded Molly three times to pack her one and only winter coat—which she wears maybe a week out of the whole year in New Orleans—and still I was the one who stuffed it into her carry-on before we left for the airport this morning. She was glad to have it when we stepped outside at the airport and a cold wind blasted us. Her eyes went wide, and she nestled right up against my body like she could burrow into me for warmth.

The closer we get to my dad's house, and my childhood home, the more I recognize. I notice and catalog the differences—a park I used to visit that has replaced the old wooden playground with a colorful plastic set. A block that used to be lined with small mom-and-pop shops that now houses a big box store. A vacant lot where a gas station used to be. We turn onto a residential street, and now it's like nothing has changed since I was a kid. New coats of paint on the houses, maybe a new fence here and there, but the vibe of the small two-story houses positioned at the front of each lot, with postage-stamp backyards behind them, feels the same.

Dad pulls into the driveway, and nostalgia hits me over the head. I step out of the car. My old basketball hoop is long gone, but the foul lines I painted on the driveway are still there, though faded. From here, I can see the top branches of the tree in the backyard that I fell out of when I was ten, breaking my arm. It's a lot taller—if I fell out of it now, I'd break more than an arm.

After my dad unlocks the front door, we go inside, which also looks pretty much the same. The photos on the walls have been switched out—in addition to Tamara and me through the years, there are framed pictures of Tamara and Mike's wedding and my nieces. I'm surprised to see a photo of me from a couple of years ago, standing at the helm of a boat, my hair flying backward from the wind. It's one of my favorites; it was my profile picture on social media for a long time. And next to that, a print of Molly and me in Las Vegas, dressed up and beaming under an archway covered in white flowers. It's the one I texted Dad and Tamara only a few weeks ago when they asked for a wedding photo.

My heart swells and pricks, love and shame all wrapped together. Molly moves to stand next to me, intertwining our fingers, while her other hand comes across her body to grip me at the elbow. How does she always know when I need her most?

"I'll take care of your luggage," Dad says. "I actually have some work I need to finish up this afternoon, so Tamara and the girls are expecting you over at their house."

"Oh," I say. "Okay." I thought maybe I'd be able to sit down and talk to him this afternoon. Rip off the proverbial bandage.

My dad shifts from one foot to the other. "Is that all right?"

"Yeah, definitely."

The conviction I'm trying to convey must not come across in my words because my dad explains more. "I took vacation time starting tomorrow through the end of the year, and there are just a couple of projects I need to get to a stopping point on before I leave. The girls are eager to see you."

"I'm excited to meet them." Molly smiles at my dad, and he visibly relaxes.

"You're welcome to take my car or you can walk. It's just one block over." He motions with his thumb in the direction of Tamara's house.

"Let's walk," Molly suggests.

"Sharon and I will meet you there a little later for dinner."

It only takes Molly and me a few minutes to walk to my sister's house. We ring the doorbell, and the door flies open. Tamara greets Molly with a hug, as if they're best friends who haven't seen each other for years rather than new sisters-in-law meeting for the first time.

"Um, hello. I'm here, too." I wave to my sister.

"Oh, Jonny. Hi. I didn't see you there," she teases as she ushers us inside.

We hang up our coats on the hooks near the front door. Looks like Tamara and Mike have redecorated since the last time I was here. Most notable are three little cubbies near the front door, labeled with my nieces' names. They each have their own little coat hook, another hook where Charlotte and Hannah have their backpacks for school hanging, and a shelf low to the ground for shoes.

"Cute," I comment, pointing to the cubbies.

"Necessary," Tamara corrects. "This house is chaos."

As if on cue, three tornadoes spin into the entryway, chattering and laughing in a swirl of energy. My nieces stop in front of us, and

I can't believe how big they are. I swear it hasn't been *that* long since I saw them last, has it?

"Girls," Tamara says, "this is your Aunt Molly. She's married to Uncle Jonny." They stare at Molly curiously until Hannah tugs on my arm.

"Uncle Jonny, last time you were here, we played on the trampoline for, like, twelve hours. Do you remember?"

"I do." My legs and back were sore afterward for days.

"Can we do that again?"

I look at Tamara, who shakes her head. "Remember, we already put the trampoline away for the winter? It's too cold for the trampoline right now."

"Oh, yeah." Her little face deflates, brown eyes drooping.

"We can play something else, though," I suggest. "Maybe Aunt Molly will even play. How about Legos?" A calm and gentle activity.

"I have a better idea!" Charlotte squeals. "Let's play octopus, like in *Bluey*."

Hannah and Mia light up. "Yeah!" they both scream.

"I don't know how to play octopus," I tell them. "What about you, Aunt Molly? Do you know how to play octopus?"

"I don't," she says, her eyes twinkling. "But I'm sure if you girls explain to Uncle Jonny how to play, he'll be a great octopus."

"What about you?" Mia asks in her tiny voice.

"I actually need Aunt Molly to help me with something," Tamara says, flashing a grin in Molly's direction. "But she's right—Uncle Jonny will be a perfect octopus. Show him the episode so he knows the game."

"Really?" I say dryly. "Ganging up on me already?"

Tamara steps past me, squeezing my shoulder. "The girls missed you. Plus, I really do need Molly's help with something."

"Yeah, right."

I let the girls pull me into the living room where they queue up a show. I spend the next ten minutes watching cartoon dogs, who are apparently Australian, make up an increasingly complicated game where an octopus—which I presume will be me—tries to capture the little fishes who want to steal his treasure.

The episode ends, and three very serious little faces stare up at me. "Got it?" Hannah asks.

I nod solemnly. "I think so."

Charlotte jumps up. "We need treasure." She pulls a plastic bin of Hot Wheels cars over to the couch. "Now, Uncle Jonny, you hang on the couch, like Bluey's dad did, and try to stop us from getting the treasure."

"But you can't talk!" Mia yells.

"Right," Hannah agrees. "You can only make octopus sounds."

The octopus game keeps us occupied for almost twenty minutes before they decide to switch to "keepy uppy" instead. This involves keeping an inflated balloon from touching the ground. I leap over furniture and crash into walls in my attempts to bump the balloon back up toward the ceiling. The girls scream with laughter.

We move on to a game they call taxi driver. They each take turns being the driver, while the rest of us are passengers in the taxi, inventing characters with outlandish requests or destinations. Hannah says she's a mom, and she needs a ride to the hospital to pick up a new baby brother for her daughters.

"Hannah!" Charlotte scolds. "We aren't supposed to say anything, remember?"

"I didn't say anything!" Hannah shouts back.

I'm about to play referee when Tamara steps in. I glance toward the entrance to the living room where Molly watches me with a smirk.

I disentangle myself from the blanket I've been using as a shawl and stand. "How much of that did you see?" I ask Molly sheepishly.

"I've been standing here a while, *Rita*," Molly teases. That's the name Mia insisted on giving me. I was supposed to be an old, apparently "cheeky" woman.

"Well," Tamara says as she walks toward us. "I guess it was silly to think the girls could keep any kind of secret, never mind a big one."

I look at Tamara in bewilderment. "What secret?"

"He has no idea," Molly tells her. "Totally clueless."

"About what?" I look between my sister and my wife, clearly missing something.

"Amazing," Tamara marvels.

"See?" Hannah shouts. "I *didn't* tell anyone that we're having a baby brother."

Charlotte rolls her eyes. "Well, *now* you did."

Understanding dawns. "Wait! Tamara, you're pregnant? With a boy?" I scoop her into a hug. "Congratulations!"

Tamara beams. "Thanks. We were going to wait until after Dad's wedding to say anything, but we made the mistake of telling the girls, and now I think even our mail carrier knows."

This neighborhood has had the same mail carrier for fifteen years. "Frank knew before me?" I joke. "I'm hurt."

That night, lying on the squeaky mattress in my dad's guest bedroom—which used to be Tamara's bedroom; he turned mine into a study—Molly shifts onto her side to talk to me. "Today made me realize that in our haste to get married, we skipped over a few important talks we should have had beforehand."

I yawn. "Like what?"

"Children. Do you want to have children?"

"Considering how tired I am after playing with my nieces for just a few hours today, I vote no."

"I'm serious."

I consider it. "Honestly, I don't think I have a preference. If it's important to you, I'm open to it. But it's not something I dream about or anything."

Molly looks relieved. "I ... don't think I want children. I know now that I can be more flexible in my life than I have been, but I'm still getting used to it. Still getting used to sharing my life with you. Parenting requires so much focus and attention to do it right. I think it would take away from being the best scientist and partner I can be.

I know lots of people make it work, and that's great for them. It just doesn't feel like a priority for me."

I run my thumb across her cheek. "Okay."

"Okay?"

"Yeah, Carrots. Whatever you want."

She bites her bottom lip. "Thanks. I reserve the right to change my mind, though."

"Always." I pause. "Except about me. You're never allowed to change your mind about me." I tease.

"I would never even consider it." She smiles and yawns.

"Any other big topics we need to tackle?"

She pats my shoulder. "Not tonight."

I can't sleep, so I make my way to the kitchen for a snack. The house is dark and quiet except for a light shining through the sliding glass door to the back porch. I know without looking that my dad's out there. It's his spot for thinking, or just letting his mind wander, even when it's the dead of winter and below freezing outside, like tonight.

It was hovering just above freezing all day, but now that the sun has set, it's got to be in the low twenties out there. After more than ten years living in warmer climates, I can't handle this kind of cold anymore. I bundle up in my coat and slide my sneakers on before joining my dad on the porch.

Even then I'm not prepared. "What the h—" I glance at my dad. "—eck kind of weather is this?"

Dad chuckles. "When you were a kid, you'd be outside in worse than this for hours, building snow forts and playing with the neighbors, challenging me to snowball fights."

I sit on a chair next to him. "Yeah, yeah. That was before I moved south, and my blood thinned out, huh?"

"You said it."

We sit quietly for a few minutes while I gather the courage to say what I need to say.

"Molly's great," Dad says, breaking the silence before I can.

"She is," I agree. "She's amazing."

More awkward silence. I really need to learn to communicate with my parents better.

I take a breath. "Listen, Dad. I owe you an apology. Actually, I owe you about eighteen years' worth of apologies."

"What for?" He turns his head to study me.

I look down at my lap. "I've been mad at you for a long time—about Mom leaving, about the divorce. It felt safer, I guess, to lash out at you rather than face the grief I was feeling. I'm sorry I let that continue for so long."

"I appreciate the apology, son. What I really want, what I've always wanted, is a relationship with you."

I lift my head, staring out into the murky backyard. I blink back the tears threatening to form in my eyes. "That's what I want, too. I'm not angry anymore, but I miss the relationship we could have had, you know? I miss all the memories we could have made together. We've lost so much time."

"We still have time to make memories." My dad lays his hand gruffly on my shoulder and squeezes.

My eyes still trained on the backyard, I watch as one snowflake floats gently down from the sky and lands on the frozen ground. Soon, the sky is sparkling with wafting snowflakes. I puff out a breath and watch it freeze in front of me.

I turn to look my dad square in the face. "Like right now." I smile and jump up from the chair, racing down the steps of the back porch. I scoop a handful of snow from the ground, the new mixed with the old, and pack it into a ball.

Before I can spin and launch the snowball at my dad, something hits my shoulder and snow bursts around me. Laughing, I twist to find Dad with his arm raised, another snowball in hand. Before he can throw, I send mine flying toward him, and it explodes against his chest.

Dad shoots two more at me before I can even form my next snowball. "I guess I'm a little rusty," I call.

"You should practice against Hannah," he shouts back. "She is fierce."

I laugh. "I believe it."

We toss snowballs back and forth for another fifteen minutes before I concede. We're both out of breath as we settle into our seats on the back porch. I'm warmer now, at least.

"Jonny, there's one more thing I need you to do to make things right between us. I need you to apologize to Sharon and be more respectful of her going forward." His voice is stern, a tone I recognize from childhood that means Dad won't tolerate anything but compliance.

My eyes widen a little, but it's a fair request.

"Think about Molly," Dad says quietly. "How would you feel if I treated her the way you've been treating Sharon?"

My heart thrums in my ears just thinking about it. "I'd be furious," I admit. "I'll talk to Sharon tomorrow. I promise."

"Thank you. Come on, let's get inside before you catch your death." He stands, holding out a hand. I take it, and he pulls me to my feet. Instead of stopping once I'm up, I throw my other arm around his back in a bear hug. He returns the embrace.

As my chin comes to rest on top of his shoulder, my nose stings. I know I need to forgive myself for causing a wedge between us for so long—Dad already has—but I also know I'll never forget how many moments like this I've robbed us of.

Once we're inside and unbundled, we say good night at the bottom of the stairs. I tiptoe back to the guest room and climb into bed, careful not to wake Molly. She stirs a little anyway, reaching her hand out for me, so I scoot closer and hold her in my arms.

"Babe, you're so cold," she murmurs sleepily. "Are you okay?"

"Yeah," I whisper. "Better than I've been in years."

Chapter Thirty-Five

Molly

"Merry Christmas," I hum, sitting up in bed and jostling Jonathan awake on Christmas morning.

"Not time to wake up yet," Jonathan grumbles, pulling the covers up to his neck.

"But it's Christmas morning!"

He cracks one eye open. "I don't care if Santa Claus came already. I need more sleep."

"Oh, come on, where's your Christmas spirit?" I poke his shoulder.

"My nieces destroyed it," he mutters, "along with all my energy."

We've been in Ohio for two days now, both filled with a lot of family time, which for Jonathan means a lot of high-energy games with Charlotte, Hannah, and Mia. For me, it means time chatting with Tamara and Sharon.

I'm so glad Jonathan and his dad are on better terms now, because I couldn't dislike Sharon if I tried. She's quiet, but witty. She comes up with the perfect zingers at the perfect time in the conversation, surprising everyone. It's clear how much she loves Pete and treats his family like her own. She was married twenty years before her husband passed away from an early heart attack, but they never had children, so her relationship with Pete gives her the chance to step into the role of grandmother. She's very good at it, judging by the number of cookies she slipped the girls yesterday. Actually, all that sugar probably explains their insane energy levels.

Today, we're seeing even more family members. I'm told that Christmas dinner, which kicks off in the early afternoon at Tamara's house, is big and loud and includes Jonathan's grandparents—Pete's parents—as well as aunts, uncles, and cousins. More kids, and if they all demand Jonathan's attention the way his nieces do, some extra sleep this morning really is crucial.

Leaving my husband snoozing, I take a shower and get dressed. Christmas with my family growing up was a casual day—it was just the five of us, so we wouldn't dress up or do anything fancy for our Christmas dinner. Not so for Jonathan's family. Jonathan described the attire for the big family Christmas dinner as "business casual." I wear a pair of black slacks I bought for Vegas, along with a white cowl-neck sweater with threads of silver woven throughout it.

I quietly open the door to the guest bedroom when I go back in to put my pajamas away, but Jonathan isn't here anymore. The bed is made, and lying at the foot is a beautiful hand-knit stocking, dark green with an ivory cuff and my name spelled out in sparkling gold stitching.

I duck my head out into the hallway to see if Jonathan's loitering nearby, but I can't find him. I text him a picture of the stocking instead.

Molly:

What's this?

Jonathan:

Your Christmas stocking. For you to open at your leisure and in private

He remembered what I told him about memories of opening my Christmas stocking when I was a child. My chest fills with warmth. Of course he did. That's Jonathan. He's thoughtful and sweet and so good at taking care of me. I suppose I need to get used to these acts of service.

Molly:

How did Santa find me [wink face emoji]

Jonathan:

Christmas magic

I know I told Jonathan how much I used to relish opening my stocking while my sisters were distracted—the peace and magic I felt going at my own pace and inspecting each item—but I find that now there's something I value more than that solitude.

Molly:

Come upstairs and open it with me

Jonathan:

Are you sure?

Molly:

I want to share this moment with him, share every moment—big or small—with Jonathan for the rest of my life. I know that was the point of getting married a month ago, but it's hitting me now, being here with him and his family on my favorite day of the year, that my relationship with Jonathan, our marriage, is really real. Intensely real. I get to spend my life with this handsome, charming, attentive man, and he loves me.

By the time Jonathan cracks open the bedroom door and slips inside, my eyes are brimming with tears as I stand next to the bed.

"Hey," he says softly. He's still dressed in the flannel pajama pants and T-shirt he slept in. He steps toward me and cups my face in his hand. "Are you okay?"

"Yes." I sniffle. "I just really love you."

He grins. "I love you, too, Carrots. Merry Christmas."

"Merry Christmas," I repeat. Jonathan tips his head down and kisses me tenderly.

The warmth in my chest spreads throughout my entire body. I increase the pressure of my lips on his, and he eagerly echoes my intensity. Jonathan slides his hands off my face and down my arms, finally looping them behind my back, pulling me closer and deepening the kiss. When we break apart, we both need a minute to catch our breaths.

"Hey now," Jonathan teases. "I didn't come up here for that. Open your stocking."

I smile at him and take a step back. "It's beautiful. Where did it come from?" I sit on the edge of the bed next to the stocking.

Jonathan sits down beside me. "My grandmother made it. She makes Christmas stockings for all her children, grandchildren, and great-grandchildren. I went to her house yesterday to pick it up while you were shopping with Tamara."

My eyes go wide. "How in the world did she make it so quickly? She didn't have much advance notice that I was joining the family this Christmas."

He chuckles. "She said she already had the stocking itself made, so she just needed to stitch your name on it."

"I can't wait to meet her later today and thank her." I pick up the stocking to look at the stitching more closely.

Jonathan caresses my back, running his palm over my soft sweater. "She's looking forward to meeting you, too."

I poise my hand over the stocking's opening. "Ready?" I ask.

He shrugs. "I'm ready whenever you're ready. This is your show."

I pull the first item out of the stocking and laugh. It's a scented candle in a pretty glass jar. The label on the front reads, "Having me as a husband is really the only gift you need."

"Oh, really?" I give Jonathan some side-eye and shake my head.

"I'm just saying." He shoots me the smirk I've grown to love. "You kind of hit the jackpot in Vegas. We both did."

"No arguments here."

I reach back into the stocking and find a bag of my favorite chocolates. "Yum," I say. "You put all the essentials in here, huh?"

He nods toward the stocking in my hands. "Maybe. Keep looking."

"Uh-uh. My show," I remind him. I open the bag and peel the foil wrapper from one of the chocolates. I pop it in my mouth while unwrapping a second piece. This one I give to Jonathan.

"Thank you," he mumbles around a mouthful of chocolate.

I put my hand back in the stocking. This time I come back with a large bag of Cafe Beignet beignet mix. I laugh.

"So you can still have beignets when we move to Charleston," Jonathan explains.

I give him a skeptical look. "You think I'm going to make beignets?"

"Of course not," he scoffs. "I'm going to make them for you."

"Ah, good." I smirk. "That works for me."

The next item that emerges is a large rosette ribbon, blue with gold lettering that says, "Prank Queen of Louisiana."

"Does this mean I won the prank war?" I ask between gasps of laughter, thinking back to Jonathan teasing me about his high school title of "Prank King of Ohio."

"Um, obviously." Jonathan rolls his eyes like a preteen. "I knew I couldn't beat the frozen-specimens-on-the-day-the-big-boss-visits prank, so I didn't even try."

"Okay, Dr. Perron's visit was *not* supposed to be part of the prank," I protest.

"That's why it was so genius! Truly, I'm in the presence of a master."

I shake my head indulgently and go back to the stocking. The next thing I find is a package of hair ties, the kind I like that are gentle on my hair. "Can never have too many of these."

"Agreed."

I'm getting toward the bottom of the stocking. I can tell by the weight that there are only a few items left.

Reaching my arm down, I pull out a booklet of sticky notes. I flip through it to find messages scrawled on each page. Some are sweet. Some are encouraging. Some compliment the more—ahem—*intimate* aspects of our married relationship.

I blush. "I'll read these later."

Jonathan smiles at me smugly. "Not right now? You can take your time. I'm not in a rush."

I glare at him. "Later is fine."

He chuckles. "Suit yourself." He nods toward the stocking. "There's one more thing in there."

I stretch my fingers all the way to the toe of the stocking and wrap them around a box. Slowly, I guide it around the bend at the heel of the stocking and lift it all the way out. Not just any box—a jewelry box. A ... ring box?

I pop it open and gasp. A gorgeous diamond engagement ring sparkles back at me. It's gold with a single ideal-cut diamond at the center. The sides of the band are twisted in an intricate, interwoven pattern that reminds me of a knot.

I look at Jonathan. He's watching me with an unsure, self-conscious expression. He pulls the ring from the box. "I figured since you didn't get an engagement ring or even a proper proposal..." he trails off as he slides it onto my left ring finger, fitting it gently against my wedding band. "If it sits too high or is too tight, or bothers you in any way, we can return it."

"Don't you dare," I breathe out. "It's perfect."

Jonathan perks up. "You like it?"

"I love it. It's gorgeous." I hold out my hand, admiring the ring on my finger. "Rings don't tend to bother me unless they come up too high and bang on things. I don't think this one will do that."

Jonathan smiles slowly. "Good. That's one of the things I looked for. What do you think of the sides?"

"The knots? They're beautiful. It makes me think of..." I twist up my lips, trying to place the errant thought.

"Ropes?" Jonathan suggests. "Like on a boat?"

I snap my fingers. "Yes! That's it exactly."

He grins. "Good. You know, as much as our love story took place in the lab, it really started on a boat."

"It did," I agree. "That first trip we took together on the *Pulse*, I knew I was falling for you." I snort. "I hated that it was happening, but I couldn't deny it. At least not while being honest with myself."

Jonathan holds my gaze, and just like when we were out on the water that day, I'm spellbound by his hazel eyes. "That first day on the boat? Carrots, I was already gone."

My lips part in surprise, and my husband takes the opportunity to cover them with his own.

Today, we'll call my family to wish them a merry Christmas. Then, we'll celebrate with the whole Stanch clan. In two days, Jonathan will stand by his dad's side as best man when Pete marries Sharon, the love of his life he worried he'd never find. We'll fly to New Orleans, finish packing the last of our belongings, and make the long drive to our new home in Charleston together.

Come January, we'll both start our new jobs. We'll navigate finances and communication and intimacy and our families together as we learn to balance our individual needs with our time for each other. We'll argue and make up. We'll wake up each day and choose to love each other.

But for now, for these next few minutes on our first Christmas together, I don't think about the future or plan my next move. I just enjoy the moment, basking in the overwhelming, intoxicating love I never thought would be mine. For now, I'm focused on how much I love Jonathan Stanch's stupidly handsome face.

Epilogue

Four Months Later

When Jonathan suggested taking a belated honeymoon that could double as a celebration of my thirtieth birthday, I thought it was a great idea.

My new lab is at a stage where it can afford to do without me for a week or two. We're waiting for confirmation of funding after I spent most of January and February creating the budget requests. Until that confirmation, I can't hire staff or start any research, so I'm in a bit of a holding pattern.

Jonathan has quickly become a fieldwork star in his new job, so much so that they want to send him to Alaska for three weeks for an ecological assessment of Kachemak Bay. He agreed with the caveat that he could take this time off with me first.

So, we packed our bags and drove to Florida—a week and a half relaxing in St. Petersburg before we need to be in St. Anastasia for Nicole and Adam's wedding at the end of April.

The problem is, I'm not sure I've ever actually tried relaxing before, and I find that I'm not particularly good at it. We've spent the last three days driving all over the city visiting amazing museums and restaurants, and Jonathan showed off the beautiful campus where he went for undergrad.

Today, the plan is to take advantage of our beachside hotel and park ourselves in the sand and water for the day.

Thirty minutes in, Jonathan is dozing contentedly in his lounger under our rented beach cabana, and I'm... well, I'm totally bored and scrolling aimlessly on my phone. I tried reading a book, but even a light beach read couldn't hold my attention.

I end up on a new social media site where scientists have started their own community to share research and chatter. I'm browsing the posts tagged with the "coastal science" hashtag, glad Jonathan is asleep so he can't scold me for doing something work-adjacent while we're on vacation.

On the site, a former colleague from NOSU has posted an article link, so I click it to learn more. I skim the headline and first sentence. Gasping loudly, I sit up and flail my arm toward Jonathan, smacking him square across his bare chest.

He bolts upright, simultaneously groggy and on high alert. "What happened? What's wrong?" He darts his eyes around for any threats.

"Babe! You'll never guess what just happened at NOSU!" I practically shout.

Jonathan stills, blinking toward me. "What happened to who where? Are *you* okay?"

"Me? Oh yeah, I'm fine, but you have to hear this!" I hold my phone up and wave it in front of him.

He rubs his eyes. "Wait. Are you on your phone looking at coastal science news?"

I purse my lips. "Maybe."

He levels me with a stern expression. "We're supposed to be relaxing."

"I hate relaxing!" I whine. "I'm so bored!"

Jonathan checks the time on his phone. "We haven't even been out here a whole hour yet!"

I toss my hair. "Regardless, the important thing is this news from NOSU."

"Fine," he sighs. "What is it?"

"Dr. Perron has been fired!" I announce dramatically.

"Wait, really?" Jonathan turns so he's sitting upright with his bare feet on the sand in the space between our two chairs.

I hold back a smirk. "Yes! Apparently that new lab he was forming to study blue carbon offsetting—"

"The one he wanted me to run?" he interrupts.

"Uh-huh. It was funded by a huge fossil fuel company." I name one of the most prominent big oil companies in the country. "*But* ... Dr. Perron didn't accurately disclose that fact to the university."

"Uh-oh."

"Yep." I'm skimming the article on my phone now and paraphrasing the information out loud. "When the administration found out, there was a big investigation. They didn't want to be associated with the study because they were concerned about potential bias—"

"As they should be," Jonathan cuts in.

"Turns out, Dr. Perron *lied* on the paperwork for the university about the funding organization for the project because he didn't want them to find out who was paying for it."

Jonathan leans forward, his elbows balanced on his thighs. "So, what happened?"

"The university completely shut down the project. They also fired Dr. Perron. Turns out that in addition to lying on the forms, apparently he was getting personal kickbacks from the fossil fuel company. He bought his own boat!"

Jonathan's mouth drops open. "No way!"

"But here's the best part. Guess who's taking Dr. Perron's place as the dean of the College of Coast and Environment?"

Jonathan's eyes glimmer. "Is it—?"

"Yes!" I shout. Catching myself, I lower my voice as I read directly from the article. "'Dr. Phyllis Gantt, a longtime faculty member, has been permanently promoted to the position.'"

"Good for her. Well deserved." Jonathan nods thoughtfully. "Can you imagine if I had taken the position in that lab, though?"

"You wouldn't have taken it," I argue. "Not without knowing the funder, and once you found that out, you definitely wouldn't have been involved."

"No, I know. But if I *had*. My career would be over. Who would hire me after a blot like that?" His eyes grow comically large as he teases me. "You saved me when you married me!" He feigns a prostrate bow, both arms out.

I hold up a finger. "Not necessarily. You could totally pull off the whole slick-and-charming-evil-scientist thing if you had to. Even your name sounds like a corrupt oil baron."

Jonathan squints at me in confusion. "The name Jonathan sounds like an oil baron?"

"J.P. Stanch," I reply, enunciating each syllable.

He leans back in his chair, considering. "Huh."

"Right?"

"Total villain vibes," he admits.

I tsk. "With your charisma and pretty face, they'd be eating out of your hand. You could get away with murder."

Jonathan sits up again, facing me. "I'm pretty sure that you're teasing me, but you know I wouldn't actually do something like that, right?"

His expression is so earnest I can't keep up the farce. I take his hand between both of mine and squeeze. "Of course I know that," I tell him softly. I lift his hand and press a kiss onto his palm.

He exhales. "Okay, good."

"But *I* might murder someone if I have to keep lying on this beach 'relaxing' for much longer."

He laughs. "What do you want to do?"

"Go for a swim, build a sandcastle, pack up the beach things and go kayaking. *Anything* else. Please."

He stands and pulls me to my feet, tugging me toward the water.

"Wait!" I stop to remove my cover up, leaving me in a black one-piece swimsuit with a scalloped deep V-neck.

Jonathan looks me up and down, a ravenous glint in his eyes. "A swim is definitely a good idea," he says huskily.

"This is a family beach," I scold him.

Jonathan looks around. The beach isn't crowded by any means, but we're within sight of several other couples and some families with young kids. "Okay, new plan. A quick swim and then back to the hotel room."

I tap a finger against my chin. "How about a long swim, then sandcastles, then back to the hotel room to shower and change for lunch, and *then* kayaking?" I remove my glasses and drop them into my beach bag.

He pulls me against his chest. "You drive a hard bargain, Dr. Delaney, but I'm in." I can't see his face, but I feel his muscles tense just before he drops his arms and takes off running. "But you have to catch me first!"

I try to chase him, but my feet slide in the sand, and I can't stop laughing. I finally make it to the shoreline where Jonathan waits for me, hands on his hips.

"What took you so long?"

I take in the sight of him as he comes more into focus the closer I get. My husband. His skin is tan and gleaming, accentuating the strength in his arms and legs. His torso is chiseled above his board shorts, leading up to muscular shoulders. His lips are open in that heart-stopping smile I love so much, the one that makes me weak in the knees. His eyes are mischievous, the swirls of green and brown electrified against the water behind him. His dark curls are devastatingly handsome as they fall across his forehead.

More importantly: his fun-loving spirit, his sense of humor, his thoughtfulness, his magnetic personality. The way he loves me as I am.

I shake my head. Why *did* it take me so long to see this man clearly?

I walk up to him, my feet skimming through the shallow water where it meets the sand. Standing on my tiptoes, I kiss his chin, then his cheek. Finally, I brush his lips with mine.

I pull back enough to meet his eyes. "I'm here now, and I'm not going anywhere."

Bonus Epilogue

For a peek at Molly and Jonathan ten years in the future, download the bonus epilogue!

https://BookHip.co
m/FWNVQRQ

Or visit **www.juliemilo.com** and sign up for my newsletter!

Acknowledgements

Love in the Lab is about a scientist with ADHD who lives in New Orleans. Seeing as how I am not a scientist with ADHD who lives in New Orleans—I am a librarian with anxiety who lives in Florida, like Nicole in *Love in the Stacks*, the first book of the *Delaneys in Love* series—this book required more research than my previous work. But writing it was so much fun!

It was important to me to get Molly's ADHD right, not only because there are people I love who have ADHD, but also because the value of representation in books is in accuracy and authenticity. To prepare, I read and took copious notes on two wonderful books: *ADHD is Awesome: A Guide to (Mostly) Thriving with ADHD* by Penn and Kim Holderness and *How to ADHD: An Insider's Guide to Working with Your Brain (Not Against It)* by Jessica McCabe. These are books by adults with ADHD, written for other adults with ADHD and they gave me wonderful insight into how someone with ADHD might experience the world.

I'd also like to acknowledge Denis Phillips, the popular Tampa Bay meteorologist known for his helpful, no hype information, who inspired Dennis Jackson in this book.

Thank you to Katie Johnson, Maddie Grosu, and Cindy Felker for being willing to be critique partners for this book. Their comments and suggestions strengthened the story and writing.

Thank you to beta readers DeAnn Grady and Hannah McGillis (especially for her science expertise). They provided thoughtful and helpful feedback on my early manuscript.

Thank you to Sharon Crosby, Patrick Hopkins, and Andrea Hac for help writing the blurb for this story. I really, really hate writing blurbs, and additional sets of eyes help make the process easier.

Another round of thanks to Sydney Christensen for the amazing cover design and character art for this book. She is so fun to work with and always manages to catch my vision and translate it so beautifully.

Thank you to my awesome book coach and editor, Ruth Shilling (www.rseditorial.co). Her feedback and encouragement throughout the writing process kept me on track and helped me produce a better book.

Thank you to Alicia Whitaker (@aliciasalwaysreading on Instagram), who provided proofreading services and did not shame me for being so bad with commas in compound sentences.

Above all, thank you to my family. My son, Gabriel, was my go-to for prank inspiration (I hate pranks, and he loves them, so he was delighted when I asked him for ideas). My daughter, Ana, is my biggest cheerleader and supporter. I read her some passages out loud while I was writing and she gave me good suggestions! The biggest thank you to the love of my life and inspiration for all things romantic: my husband, Andy. I love you bunches and bunches and lots and lots. For real.

Finally, thank you to my readers. The support you've given me for my previous books, and your excitement for this one, makes this whole endeavor worthwhile. If you've loved this, or any of my other books, consider leaving a review on Amazon, Goodreads, or another bookish platform. Reviews truly make a huge difference for authors, especially indie authors like me!

Also by Julie Milo

Delaneys in Love series

Love in the Stacks

Love in the Lab

Second Chance in Asheville

ABOUT THE AUTHOR

Julie Milo spends most of her time reading and writing. When she's not reading and writing scholarly stuff for her day job, she's reading romance, nonfiction, and literary fiction for fun. She writes closed door/kisses only (also called "sweet") romantic comedies.

Julie was raised, but not born, in Florida where she started dictating stories to her parents before she even knew how to write. By kindergarten she was writing and illustrating picture books and subjecting her classmates to read alouds at school. While the illustrating did not stick (her drawing skills never evolved past about third grade), the writing did, and for most of her childhood, her answer to "What do you want to be when you grow up?" was "an author." Returning to writing decades later is a dream come true, and Julie is proud to finally be able to call herself an author.

Julie currently lives on the Gulf coast of Florida with her thoughtful husband, two amazing children, and two dogs (one delightful pit bull and one very energetic black lab). She loves dessert and hates cold weather.

You can learn more about Julie and her books at www.juliemilo .com.